CARVING SPACE

The Indigenous Voices Awards Anthology

SELECTED BY

JORDAN ABEL, CARLEIGH BAKER, AND
MADELEINE REDDON

McClelland & Stewart

Library and Archives Canada Cataloguing in Publication data
is available upon request.

ISBN: 978-0-7710-0485-8
ebook ISBN: 978-0-7710-0486-5

All acknowledgements to reprint previously published material appear on pages 375-378.

Book design by Talia Abramson
Cover art: Lisa Boivin
Typeset in Janson by M&S, Toronto
Printed in Canada

McClelland & Stewart,
a division of Penguin Random House Canada Limited,
a Penguin Random House Company
www.penguinrandomhouse.ca

1 2 3 4 5 27 26 25 24 23

Penguin
Random House
McCLELLAND & STEWART

Alongside the many successes came the findings of the Canadian Truth and Reconciliation Commission that in 2015 released its final report and 94 Calls to Action, outlining the work needed to educate Canadians about our history and break the multiple barriers that Indigenous peoples continue to face. Seemingly unaware or unconcerned about this history, in 2017 the editor of the Writers' Union of Canada magazine stated in an editorial for an issue dedicated to Indigenous writers that he didn't believe in cultural appropriation, and declared that there "should even be an award for doing so"; in support of his comments, an editor of a leading Canadian magazine called for the establishment of a literal "Appropriation Prize." A wave of people from across the country rose up in opposition to these remarks and expressed the need for continued support of emerging Indigenous writers, with over a thousand people and multiple organizations contributing to a crowd-funded prize. Both individual and corporate patrons stepped up, determined to support the next generation. With the help of Cherokee writer Daniel Heath Justice, the newly established Indigenous Literary Studies Association (ILSA)—with members including Cree-Métis scholar Deanna Reder and settler scholars Sophie McCall, Sam McKegney, and Sarah Henzi—was asked to envision a structure for the administration of the awards. The Indigenous Voices Awards (IVAs) came into existence in this heated moment of controversy, resistance, and alliance-building.

The IVAs (pronounced eye-vahz) honour the sovereignty of Indigenous creative voices, and support and nurture the work of emerging writers in lands claimed by Canada. The awards celebrate the work in all its diversity and complexity; they reject cultural appropriation, respect the integrity of Indigenous voices, and affirm the ongoing significance of Indigenous Peoplehood. To date the IVAs have dispersed a total of $143,000 (CAD) in literary awards for published and unpublished writing in English, French, and Indigenous languages. The range of rotating categories, including poetry, prose, and graphic novels, helps transcend the individualism of prize culture and encourages community-building. The IVAs have always fostered community among Indigenous writers at all phases of their career by facilitating mentorship and professionalization opportunities, and creating networks of support among established and emerging literary artists. At least seven IVAs finalists in unpublished categories have gone on to publish their work—a manifestation of the tangible impact of the awards. Until 2021, the IVAs was the only literary prize for Indigenous writing in French in Canada, and indeed the world. Supporting writing in Indigenous languages and in French are key priorities of the IVAs and areas for growth in the future.

As Co-Chairs of the Indigenous Voices Awards, we'd like to profusely thank all those who have supported emerging Indigenous writers in the initial crowdfunding campaign and over the past five years. We'd like to especially mention the ongoing patronage by author Pamela Dillon, Penguin Random House Canada (especially Kristin Cochrane), the Giller Foundation, Scholastic Books Canada, and Douglas & McIntyre, the latter of which pledged portions of the earnings from a new collection of writing by the late Anishinaabe writer Richard Wagamese. We thank the jurors who over the years have dedicated themselves to the work of witnessing a new generation of Indigenous writers and who are themselves award-winning, critically acclaimed authors and scholars. We'd also like to express our heartfelt thanks to the entire IVAs team, including past co-chairs Sam McKegney and Sarah Henzi, our newest co-chair Marie-Eve Bradette, our publicist Katie Saunoris, PR specialist Michael Jenkins, and the many amazing Research Assistants who have helped with running the prize and preparing this manuscript: Maisaloon Al-Ashkar, Hannah Big Canoe, Treena Chambers, Kimberly John, Jaron Judkins, Yaser Nozari, Elise Couture-Grondin, Isabella Huberman, and Alison Wick. A special shout-out to Maisaloon for securing the permissions and keeping the manuscript on track. Thank you to the team at PRHC for generously supporting this project, and for making such a beautiful book. To the co-editors of this volume, Jordan Abel (Nisga'a), Carleigh Baker (nêhiyaw âpihtawikosisân / Icelandic), and Madeleine Reddon (Métis), we are deeply moved by your vision, hard work, and care.

Above all, we thank the contributors themselves for their fierce brilliance and uncompromising vision of pasts, presents, and futures. The words of Métis writer Warren Cariou, a juror for the inaugural year of the IVAs and a long-time supporter of the awards, capture the scope and dazzling variation of form in the work that you will find in the pages that follow:

> It is difficult to encapsulate the broad range of work on these shortlists, and this difficulty is itself a sign of the vitality of Indigenous literatures today. We see experimental writing that pushes the boundaries of form and subverts colonial categories of genre and authorship, we see writing that is deeply based in the traditions and languages of particular Indigenous nations, and we see writing that engages in powerful critiques of colonial ideologies and practices. In all of this remarkable work,

I am particularly struck by the artists' refusal to accept the standard western literary categories, a willingness to remake the rules of literary writing in order to tell our stories in the ways they need to be told. Many of these works also approach gender and sexuality in a similarly innovative way, drawing upon Indigenous teachings to critique colonial definitions and to show us the way toward more flexible, grounded and ethically engaged—and specifically Indigenous—understandings of identity and desire. Many of them also explore powerful, embodied modes of land-relations and environmental sensibilities, based upon the vast lived experience of our nations and our kin (human and beyond). To me, the work on these shortlists represents the continued flourishing of Indigenous presence in our territories, and I come away from the reading experience with a sense of deep gratitude for the gifts that these artists have shared with us. I know that these gifts will be well received by the next generations of Indigenous writers, some of whom are no doubt beginning to form their stories now.

DEANNA REDER & SOPHIE McCALL
Co-Chairs of the Indigenous Voices Awards

TABLE OF CONTENTS

SELECTED FINALISTS AND AWARD RECIPIENTS 2018, 2019, 2020, 2021, AND 2022:

Part III Intimacy

Part IV Memory

Introduction

The prose categories of the Indigenous Voices Awards include fiction and non-fiction, the latter encompassing creative non-fiction, personal essays, and memoir. The process of comparing these substantially different genres may seem daunting, until we remember that their most core element is the same: storytelling. There are many ways to tell a story. Writers may choose to write from lived experience and record things just as they remember, or they may bend and shape memory into something new. They may imagine completely new worlds, or articulate complex futurisms. The process varies, but the desire to share a story with readers is what unites us.

All our stories, regardless of how they are told, reflect the brilliance of our hearts and minds. They sow seeds for future generations. Reading through the IVA's English prose selections for the past five years has been a humbling experience. The only thing more exciting than experiencing this stunning collection of writing from the last five years is imagining what the next five, ten, fifty years will look like for Indigenous literatures. Like our stories, we are dynamic.

While the voices in these narratives are varied, the immense strength of the writers is a constant. Strength in family and community. Strength in vulnerability. In this collection, authors like

Francine Cunningham and Helen Knott face dilemmas of the body and spirit. Amanda Peters explores the relationship between intergenerational suffering and the suffering of the land. In his memoir *Half-Bads in White Regalia*, Cody Caetano shares complex family histories that had me laughing and weeping in equal measure. Writers like Troy Sebastian and Aviaq Johnston display a deep attention to literary craft, which means different things to different cultures. Indigenous writers will not be dictated to by a canon of long-dead white men. Like our stories, we are more sophisticated than that.

I'm struck not only by the power of our stories, but by the growth of our creative communities over the last five years. Writers "emerge" at all ages, and the breadth of wisdom and experience in this collection is a wonderful thing. Many of the unpublished prose works have gone on to publication. Many have been recognized with awards, and there will be many more to come. I know you'll enjoy reading through these selections as much as I did. And I encourage you to seek out more stories and essays by these writers. Follow them on their journeys, read their books, and share their stories with everyone you know.

—CARLEIGH BAKER

⁂

"Que serons-nous / Par-delà ce tumulte? . . . . Immanent festins"
PIERROT ROSS-TREMBLAY, *CONFLUENCES I*

"What will we be, beyond this turmoil?" asks Pierrot Ross-Tremblay in his devotional ode to Indigenous life. As writers, readers, and community members, we may not know what we are "becoming" but, in spite of this, Ross-Tremblay assures us that we have much to celebrate. The "immanent feasts" of Indigenous life are already here! As the editor for the French selections for the Indigenous Voices Awards, I had the great pleasure and honour of reading a broad array of texts in multiple genres including poetry, theatre, and prose. Rigorous, provocative, stylish: the selections in this anthology represent some of the veritable "feast" of Indigenous writing in French that I encountered.

As you will see, the French-language authors in this anthology demonstrate a high calibre of craft and offer a distinct set of aesthetic and political sensibilities. For instance, Émilie Monnet's neo-surrealist play *Okinum* is a story about illness and grief that examines the intersections between land and body through nested images of dreams, beaver, and tumours. Jocelyn Sioui has written the first substantive biography of his uncle, Jules Sioui, a complicated and controversial political activist for Indigenous rights in Canada. Sioui's humour and sensitivity allows him to speak in compelling ways about important and difficult histories for our communities. Édouard Itual Germain offers a poetic meditation on residential schooling. Posthumously released by his daughters, Germain's poetry is an evocative and subtle exploration of memory and grief from a poet who was taken from us too soon. This collection also includes new and emerging poets including Shayne Michael, Félix Perkins, Marie-Andrée Gill, and Maya Cousineau Mollen. Using a range of electric and dissident styles, these poets are part of a new generation of Indigenous authors grappling with identity and intimacy.

Too infrequently circulated outside of Québec (either in French or in translation), these writers represent the vitality and dynamism of an incredibly rich body of Indigenous writing in Canada. My hope is that the Indigenous Voices Awards will continue to bring much-needed national exposure to Indigenous writing in French and that readers will continue to read and support these authors after getting a taste of their exciting work. Please enjoy and maarsii/kinanâskomitin to the authors for their incredible work!

—MADELEINE REDDON

❋

When I met my dad for the first time in my early twenties, one of the things I asked him about was his artistic practice as a Nisga'a carver and painter. I remember spending hours and hours of my youth thinking about how he carved the small totem pole that I had in my possession. As we walked around Stanley Park together that day, I asked him how he approached carving. I asked him what he did when he picked up the piece of wood he was going to work with. I remember he told me quite plainly that the shape is already in the wood to begin with and that sometimes you just have to wait to see it.

When I think about my work as an editor for this anthology, I'm also thinking about this small moment with my dad. I'm thinking about all the writing that I've read for the IVAs and about the many possible shapes that might form out of those writings. My work in *Carving Space* was often about finding moments where pieces spoke to each other, overlapped, or converged. I loved, for example, reading the overlapping intimacies in the work of Tyler Pennock and Billy-Ray Belcourt, the concrete and numerical layers that are shared between jaye simpson and Joshua Whitehead, and the entwining sense of humour of Smokii Sumac and Tenille Campbell. My hope is that you will find your own moments of interconnection, and that this gathering of emerging Indigenous writers will be a springboard into the world of Indigenous Literatures.

Carving Space is also a moment of celebration—a moment that reminds me of the astounding number of Indigenous writers that have emerged in the last five years. Many of the writers here in *Carving Space* have already shaped the contours of the field of Indigenous Literatures, and I'm hopeful that they will continue to do so for years to come. We need to read Indigenous writers. We need to teach Indigenous writers. We need to listen to Indigenous writers. I hope that *Carving Space* is a moment where all of that is possible.

—JORDAN ABEL

PART I

INTERIORITY

FRANCINE MERASTY

From *Iskotew Iskwew: Poetry of a Northern Rez Girl*

Nohkom

Nohkom, my Grandmother
was born in a wigwam
close to Burntwood River
up in northern Manitoba

She remembers the day
her one eye opened
to see the sunlight
through the opening at the top

She spent her childhood with Ohkohma
remembers the time they killed a moose
along with her Mushoom
while on a morning canoe ride
telling me she was the one who spotted the moose

One time Ohkohma tied her to a bedpost
went to look for firewood
Nohkom untangled the knot
walked to the lake, a child of five
hearing Ohkohma approaching

she went back to the bedpost
and tied herself back up

The next day she heard Ohkohma
tell a friend she had seen her tracks
down by the lake, there was snow on the ground yet
Nohkom had to follow Ohkohma around after that

Nohkom was a convert to Catholicism
after going to the United Church
with Ohkohma and Ohmohsoma
in a horse and buggy way up in northern Manitoba

Ohtawiya, her father called her nisto-mitanaw, thirty,
never satisfied with one piece of candy
holding out her hand to say kotak, one more

Nohkom is ninety
she still has her amazing memory
her sharp wit and intelligent humour
Nohkom

Since Time Immemorial

I've heard these words
Spoken repeatedly
As a child
The story of my
Indigenous history shared
With audience after audience
Burnt into my memory
We've been here since time immemorial

It means—a time, so long ago
That people have no memory
Or knowledge of it

Filling out my law school application
How long has your family lived in Saskatchewan?
I pause for a moment
Then write
Since time immemorial

What would have been other options?
Before Saskatchewan was, we were
I got in; nobody questioned my answer

Fierce

I have overcome

residential school
the reserve system
lateral violence
inadequately funded education
no plumbing
the language barrier
moving for education
depression
anxiety
racism day by day
discrimination little by little
sexism ongoing

and you want me to believe
I'm a savage, a squaw, stupid,
a drunk, a liar, a thief

I don't think so
motha anima yako nitha,
that is not me

Reclaim

I walk
I talk
I live
Can you see my past?
It leaves a dark trail where I pass

We lived free
Before the settlements
Long before residential schools
Beading, storytelling, praying

I was invaded
My land then my body
My territory so beautiful
Innocent and pure
The water
The trees
The barren lands
A sliver of light in December
The cold wind passing through
Day after day

We were civilized, you know
More than some

Colonialism crept slowly under me
Through me

Without consent
Touching, grabbing, hurting me

I will reclaim my body
I will reclaim my territory
I will reclaim my land
Beading, praying
And telling my stories

RENE MESHAKE, WITH KIM ANDERSON

From *Injichaag: My Soul in Story*

Quest for Words

Sometimes I think my whole life is a vision quest, and it moves around with me. Like when Joan and I went to Ireland. My introduction to this crazy world of the quest was a big key chain at the hotel when we arrived.

It had a big heavy metal ball on the end—it looked like a weapon. You could have knocked somebody out with it! I put it in the keyhole and the door wouldn't open—it was just stuck, and I was all jet-lagged with no patience at all. So I was starting to curse and felt like giving up, but then I just pushed the doorknob straight ahead without even turning the key and it opened! I was trying to figure out *what's going on here?* Maybe you only have to nudge the Irish people very gently to open the door of stories? Then they'll give you a story, just like every cab driver did as we travelled around Dublin.

So the stories are part of the quest. That's what Nagweidisowin means: vision quest. Nagwe is things appear, and you appear with them. Nagwe is to take care of, to nourish, even yourself. Idiso is yourself—the self begins with you. Sowin is the action and the state. You pull these three together and you get this vision quest. You're seeking, and when you seek, that vision takes care of you.

That first day I arrived in Ireland, while I was resting in a semi-sleep, I heard these voices saying, "Don't ever be afraid of your words."

Your words.

So, when I came back to Canada, I started writing poetry again. I feel freer now than I ever was when I was writing.

When we first met, Joan didn't know I was fluent in my language because I hardly ever talked to her in Ojibwe. Now I speak to her in Ojibwe, and I speak to anyone in Ojibwe. When I'm performing I use it. But when you are in Indian residential school you are told so much about the inferiority of your language you think that it's irrelevant. Even within the Anishinaabe community at day school I was made fun of by other students because I spoke the Aroland dialect, and of course the nuns didn't want me to speak that language. So then you start to disrespect your own mother—that's your mom, the language—or your grandmother.

That internal suppression of the language even affected how I used English, and I could never write the way I wanted to. Words were so hidden, packed away somewhere in my soul. The only words I felt very comfortable with were the swear words, you know, "Fuck you." Every sentence was "Fuck you, fuck this, fuck that." I was afraid of using something that was meaningful, beautiful, encouraging, or nourishing. I couldn't even compliment someone.

Fear of words.

So you never know what the Irish and their land did to me. And when the spirits of their ancestors told me, "Don't be afraid of your words,"—man, now I'm not.

Grandmother Pipe

There is a spiritual world of women with lots of room for mystery; even Anishinaabeg had mermaids. But what I've seen is Grandmother Pipe.

She came one morning when my grandmother and I were visiting a relation along the CNR tracks. CNR had these sections and each section had a foreman with a house. These CNR foremen often married Indian women, some of whom were our aunts. So my grandmother and I went visiting our relative who lived at this beautiful big log house out in the bush.

One morning I woke to hear them saying, "Wegonesh indawendamon? Angodjiishan oma . . . angodjiishan oma!" They had been busy washing dishes, and suddenly were standing by the doorway. I saw them looking out, calling, "Angodjiishan." To paraphrase, that means go away from here, and what do you want?

I got curious. I thought, *Who are they talking to anyways? Is there a big bull moose out there by the door?* I ran to them and then I saw this apparition in the treetop of a big spruce; a woman, just glowing and flowing. It felt natural, just like another grandmother, so I wasn't scared. But my grandmother said, "Bego ginwensh gana wahamaken. Gamadjiinig." She was telling me, "Don't look at her for too long. She will take you away." Gamadjiinig—that means she's going to take you away if you look too long. But only if you stare at her.

I ran outside, but I listened to my grandmother's words. I went to the bedrock at the foot of the tree and started piling little rocks in circles, pretending this was a fort and I was battling enemies outside the circle. Inside the circle was my family and I was protecting them. As the enemies came at us, I piled my little rocks higher and higher.

Every now and then I'd peek up at this tree and I would see her there. She was like a light but dressed in these robes—a regalia that was translucent, the colour of blue ice. Her regalia sparkled in the sun and the fabric sounded like crystals. That's quite a fabric, to ring like that; to chime as she moves and breathes. It's like icicles in the springtime smashing against each other; a really natural sound, this beautiful soft music. I hear it sometimes if I go near the lake. When I hear the ice moving, I think she's there somewhere.

I think that was godjiewisiwin for me. I was being tested about obedience; whether I was going to obey my grandmother or the Grandmother Pipe. I kept on playing, looking down, and when I eventually looked up again she was gone.

The grandmothers knew something about it, but they never told me. I guess these things happened in the past—kids go missing and never come back. Giwanishin means they must have been lost or taken away by spirits. Whether these spirits are good or bad, we don't know.

For the longest time that troubled me because I didn't know what it was all about. But when I started sobering up in Pedahbun Lodge I described it to an Elder. After listening carefully, she told me, "That's Grandmother Pipe; the tree is the stem and that little fort you built was the bowl. It's made of rock." Then I saw it immediately, and now every tree I see reminds me of that image.

I've heard other stories about Buffalo Calf Woman, who walked out of the mist and gave the sacred bundle when the people were starving and had started to disrespect the earth. That sounds like

Grandmother Pipe too, and maybe that's the message. And we can still find Grandmother Pipe at the places we build for her.

PIERROT ROSS-TREMBLAY

de *Nipimanitu / L'esprit de l'eau*

LES CONFLUENCES I –IMMANENTS FESTINS

(À nimushum Paun Rus Sr)

De ce territoire
Où nul n'a franchi la rivière
Les parois rocheuses
Élevées en murs inouïs
Gardent une vallée claire

Vivifiante lueur

Et si nous étions
Héros du jour
Face à la lumière
Qui nous inonde
Jusqu'à nous faire adorer
La fraicheur de nos ombres

La grande chute
Fait entendre ses fracas
Et nos corps qui voguent paisibles
Ne savent plus oublier leur route

Que serons-nous
Par-delà ce tumulte ?

Des chants de joie
Ruissèlent des fosses
Unité tragique
En fleurs promises aux monarques
Fécondant de passion
D'amour en amour

Des fruits exquis

Quel cœur entier qui s'offre
Pour générer la confluence
Pour que ce ridant devienne la mer
Et que nous soyons sevrés de nos deuils

Ascendance
Fortune inédite
De lire les signes
Savoir que rien ne nous éloigne

Que tout nous unit

*

Que la douleur résonne intégrale
Et que ses poussières
Blessent nos yeux naissants

En vain l'oubli
Feindre de ne pas avoir vu
Simulacre de rupture
Avec les sons et leurs sens

À en perdre les horizons

Opaque absence
Amnésie du besoin
Avalé par l'exil

*

Nutshimit

Guérisseur de la honte
Eau limpide du devenir
Capable d'abreuver
Le fœtus

Sacre du monde
Denses liens
La mère porte nos pas sur son cœur

Frères esseulés sur l'ile
Du destin de l'un

Où mènerons-nous notre canot ?
Portons ces voyageurs passagers

Aux bras du grand souhait

Immanents festins

5 mai 2011

PRINTEMPS DU DON

Au-delà des vastes horizons
La vue seule accablée de mystère
Parois reluisantes
Reflets brulants
Fantasques paysages

Aux habitants légendaires
Le terreau a fait foi
Racine abreuvée d'absence
Plaines arides
Fécondes de mirage

Au brasier succombèrent
De peines inconsolables
Gloires et vues
Exil de l'humaine voix

Printemps du don
Nos mains mères d'espoir
Se déploient

28 mars 2016

DIANA HOPE TEGENKAMP

From *Girl running*

If the measure of love is loss, why not live in it, this light?

Spindle of light turns in the corner of the room.

Window frames blue
where clouds read the sky awake.

          This I know:
the dead are not gone. They are present.
Their ephemeral absoluteness made from
refraction, bone, sight.
Curve of her head, sea-shadows.

Motherfield

Breaking blue, let it in.
Louvered edge of the rise is for me,
        peripheral bloom of passage.
So close, I could ask its name.

Night's uncoveredness
        beyond the building; it knows
        how to lift the line.

Slight waver of tree branches.
I turn and follow the concrete ledge
        along the grooved wall that holds the stairwell
        out back.

Curious corners trace pale dome.
        Sky loosening, white clouded.

Call it cicatrice, and it's rhythm.

Keep silent, it's a star.

Thumbprint moon erases itself from east,
        flock of balconies, pale undersides
against the not-yet-there sky.

I can't see it, only apprehend its gesture—
derelict wingspan,
descent through shadow.

Rise, I think, like pine trees in a boreal forest.
Back to the river, I think, like the lab frogs in *E.T.*

I'm in the day as I wait.
Elm tree has no regret.
Small light inside reflects.

I can't hear it, only sense its reach,
telluric and tender.

KATŁĮÀ

From *Land-Water-Sky / Ndè-Tı-Yat'a*

Flying over the North, Deèyeh didn't expect to see that half the landscape was sheathed in rock. In between the rock, shades of light and dark turquoise pools of glacial water dotted the Earth like giant raindrops welling up from deep groundwater crevices.

Deèyeh admired the strong rock shield that was jaggedly dispersed throughout the landscape. The water-filled basins reached as far as the eye could see. Noticeable only from air, she could see the different coloured lines in the Earth around the shorelines where water levels had significantly dropped.

When she flew over the great lake, she could see a jumbled heap of broken ice where the wind had pushed it to the corners of the lake, trapping it in one place.

When the wheels of the plane touched down on the small narrow runway of Coppertown, Deèyeh was eager to start her adventure.

Instead of going into town, she decided to drive her rental car straight from the airport and check into the house on the reserve that the Háyorîla Nation had made ready for her.

When she was handed the keys to her rusty rental car, she asked, "Do you have any maps?"

The rental agency clerk laughed at her. "You're not gonna need one, my dear, there's only one road outta here." And nodded in the direction that Deèyeh needed to go.

"Are you sure?" Deèyeh continued, but the lady behind the small counter just rolled her eyes.

Noticing that the tank was half empty, Deèyeh stopped at the local gas station to fill up and ask for directions.

"Twenty, please."

The attendant wasted no time asking, "You ain't from round here, eh?"

He bent over to get a better look at her. Deèyeh just nodded her head, trying not to engage with him.

"Where yah off to?" he continued as he filled up her car.

"I'm headed farther north."

She wasn't one to make small talk with strangers and didn't want him knowing where she was going. She wondered how he could tell that she was from out of town until she remembered the rental plates.

"You know you ought to be careful out there, 'specially at night. That highway's haunted," he warned.

That got Deèyeh's attention. "Oh? How so?" she asked, looking at him in her side mirror as he finished filling up the tank.

"I hear stories all the time from tourists comin' and goin', saying they seen strange animals on the side of the road or a woman hitchhikin' in old-fashioned clothes. Lots of accidents on that road too, people dyin'."

"Okay, well thanks. I'll be sure to keep my eye out for anything out of the ordinary."

Deèyeh tried to forget about what the man said, but on the lonely drive out of town she started to wonder if there was any truth to it. As she travelled farther down the winding highway, she was glad it wouldn't be getting dark any time soon. After all, she was now in "the land of the midnight sun," where it never got dark in the summer months—or so she was told—and this set her mind at ease.

Still, the thought of seeing a woman hitchhiking in old clothes on the side of the road sent a shiver down her back, and Deèyeh shuddered. She turned up the radio and tried to get her mind off the thought of seeing anything unusual.

But halfway to her destination, the radio became fuzzy and she turned the volume down only to hear a large banging sound on the top of her vehicle. Deèyeh slammed on the breaks and a wave of her coffee broke through its cheap plastic lid, splashing onto the console.

She looked up to see a deep dent in the middle of the roof. She shook in fear, not knowing whether she should step out of the vehicle or lock the car doors. She did the latter, quickly reaching over and behind, pressing down on all the locks and frantically cranking up her window.

Deèyeh paused and looked around at her surroundings to see if there was anything that could have caused the dent, but the highway was quiet. There was not a sound or a movement on either side of the road; even the trees seemed to keep still in the blustery wind.

Deèyeh fumbled through the bottom of her purse for her inhaler. She tended to rely on it when she felt afraid; it gave her a sense of calm. Thankful that she remembered to pack it, she shook the small blue container and sucked in two deep puffs to catch her breath.

She wondered if whatever caused the large dent could still be on top of the vehicle, but she didn't want to get out of the car to find out. Instead, she put the gearshift in reverse and drove backwards as fast as she could for a few seconds, stopping abruptly. Whatever it was, if it had still been on the car, it would have fallen onto the hood, but nothing happened.

Still, Deèyeh didn't dare get out. She pressed on the gas and sped down the highway, this time breaking the speed limit and dodging large potholes in the road. She loosened her grip on the steering wheel when she finally saw a sign that read, "You are now entering Háyorîla Nation."

Deèyeh drove slowly through the streets of the community. It was far removed from the city and was nothing like she had ever seen before. Forgetting about what happened on the isolated highway, she was pleasantly surprised by how bright and colourful the houses were.

When she did her research, she learned that the houses had been painted when the government gave free paint to everyone to brighten their homes for when the royal family visited one summer, but now, years later, the paint was noticeably peeling and crumbled.

There were young children with long black hair chasing dogs down the middle of the gravel roads. Rows of mismatched running shoes dangled from crooked power lines. There were teepees in the front yards of every other house, and fish fillets draped over sturdy tree branches, smoking over crackling fires.

Boarded-up homes stood next to empty lots full of vehicles. On a small hill in the middle of town, a large statue of Mother Mary dressed in blue cloth was surrounded by a low picket fence haphazardly strung with unplugged Christmas lights.

Women were outside their houses in their bare feet, busy

beating hides stretched out on wooden frames. They stopped what they were doing to give Deèyeh a disapproving look, wondering if she was just another outsider coming into the community trying to tell them how to raise their children.

Deèyeh made her way to the house Bertha had booked for her. "Look for the blue and white church. It's the old brick house right beside it. The door should be unlocked. Make yourself at home," she had said when she phoned Deèyeh with her itinerary.

The church was a quaint blue and white chapel with a European-style steeple. A group of elderly men sat in a row on the steps of the church; some stood with one foot propped up on the stoop. Most of the men puffed on cigarettes. One had an old pipe hanging from the corner of his frowning mouth. Unbothered by the swarms of mosquitoes that buzzed around them, the Elders moved their eyes collectively, following her as she pulled into the driveway where the large square redbrick house stood.

The barred windows that were meant to prevent teenagers from breaking in made the house look uninviting. The Elders watched her curiously from across the street as she got her bag from the back of the rental. They were so stoic and surreal that Deèyeh thought they could have been sculptures, but the smoke rising above their heads gave them away.

The first thing Deèyeh did was inspect the damage to her rental car. The dent wasn't a perfect circle; it was more of a twisted depression. The only thing she could think that could have caused it was a large bird of some sort, possibly an owl or an eagle, but she was certain she would have at least seen it struggle to fly away. Whatever it was, she hoped that it wasn't suffering somewhere on the side of the road.

Deèyeh walked up to the front door and carefully opened it, looking into the empty foyer. Before she stepped inside, a woman's voice called out from the kitchen.

"Finally, you've arrived. Come in. Make yourself at home." Favouring her right foot, the woman walked up to Deèyeh to greet her.

"Uh, hi. Thank you." Deèyeh hadn't recalled the receptionist mentioning that she would be a guest in someone's house. She thought for sure the house was empty, at least that was how it looked from the outside. The furniture was sparse and dusty, the shelves bare. In a way she was relieved that someone would be there with her in the large foreboding house.

"I'm Àma," the woman said without offering a handshake. Deèyeh could have sworn she recognized the woman, but she couldn't place where from.

"You look . . . so familiar," Deèyeh blurted out, forgetting to formally introduce herself.

"Oh, do I? So do you, dear. Maybe we were old friends in a past life," the woman said, looking straight into Deèyeh's eyes for any sign of premonition, but saw none.

Àma showed Deèyeh to her room, which had an unobstructed view of the large grey lake that she would soon be travelling on. Near the dock was a dark blue flag that waved gently in the wind with a picture of a single raindrop, the distinct Háyorîla Nation symbol.

Deèyeh wanted nothing more than to take a hot bath to warm up and relax, but it would have to wait. She would be disappointed in herself if she missed the opportunity to be surrounded in the culture of the Háyorîla Nation before heading to the island.

It was the weekend the community was hosting their annual hand games tournament. The community was full of people from the surrounding communities who were participating in the games. Hand games, she had learned, were one of the most popular traditional games amongst the Indigenous Peoples in the North, and she was excited to be a part of the action.

Deèyeh didn't know what to wear, so she played it safe, dressing casually. But when she pulled up to the parking lot of the rec centre, she could see that most of the men were wearing fantastic handmade caribou hide vests adorned with fine beadwork. The women were wearing ankle-high crow boots decorated in beautiful beaded flowers and had white rabbit fur and colourful embroidered barrettes in their long, straight brown hair. Deèyeh was underdressed and wished she knew someone who could make her a pair of special moccasins or some traditional jewellery.

She walked into the rec centre, where the hand games were taking place, and took a seat amongst the locals on the bleachers. She tried to blend in, but she quickly got the sense that she was on display. She looked around, realizing how out of place she must have seemed. She had the same colour skin and auburn eyes as most of the people in the room, but she was different. She didn't know the culture or traditions and she didn't speak their language—she felt like she didn't belong, but once the drums were warmed up and the games began, she was able to ignore the curious looks and focus on the game to try and learn the strategy.

There were teams of five men kneeling across the floor from each other. Each team took turns trying to hide a rock or an object of some sort from the other team while the opponents guessed where the object was hidden. The opposing team then made different hand signals to the beat of the drum as a form of distraction.

The entire event was loud and energetic. The room smelled of sweat and moosehide. Free bottles of water were passed around to the players to keep them hydrated. In the corner of the gym Red Rose tea and watered-down coffee with powdered milk sat in large metal cylinders on a plastic fold-up table covered in a red-and-white checkered cloth.

Even though Deèyeh knew nothing of how a team won or lost, she was in awe. The loud sound of the drums and the cries of the drummers singing songs in their language spoke to Deèyeh's heart, hypnotizing her, and time escaped her.

"Mbogǫǫ̀." One of the locals interrupted her gaze when he walked up to her and handed her a small piece of drymeat from a brown paper bag.

"Mbogǫǫ̀," he repeated.

"Sorry, I don't speak . . ."

"It's drymeat, try some." He laughed, his English perfect.

"Oh . . . um . . . thank you," she said, smiling. She fought off the feeling of being generally uncomfortable with nice gestures from strangers. She wasn't about to say no, so she folded the drymeat up in a napkin to save for later.

Over the course of the evening, Deèyeh became accustomed to the weak coffee, but the caffeine wasn't enough to keep her from yawning. In fact, it had the opposite effect and made her tired. It was late in the evening by the time the games were over. To her amazement, the sun hadn't completely set and gave off just enough natural light along the horizon that she didn't need a flashlight.

Exhausted from her long day of travelling, Deèyeh walked to her car, glad to be out in the fresh summer night air. She couldn't wait to get back to her room and have a good night's sleep, but her thoughts of rest were interrupted when she heard heavy breathing behind her. When she turned to see what it was, she saw a large stray dog with similar colouring to that of a half-breed husky.

"Easy," Deèyeh said quietly. She didn't want the animal to pick up on her fear, but the dog growled in her direction.

Deèyeh wanted to run but thought better of it. She had always been a bit cautious around larger dogs even though she had never been bitten by one. She tried to ignore the dog as she walked a bit faster, hoping it wouldn't follow her. But when she turned back, she saw that its front legs were bent down and its tail was sticking straight up on guard.

"Hey there, pup, it's okay." Deèyeh tried to let the dog know she was not going to hurt it, but it let out a loud bark and leaped in the air.

Deèyeh let out a sharp scream and ran for her car. She didn't have time to grab for the keys and unlock it, so she braced herself for the attack as she closed her eyes and pressed her body to the driver's side door.

Deèyeh waited for the pain, but it never came. She opened her eyes after a few seconds and, to her surprise, the dog ran past her and crouched down low a few feet in front of the car. Jumping from side to side, it played with a large raven that was perched on a patch of grass next to her parking spot.

With deep relief, Deèyeh laughed at herself, feeling foolish. She wasn't a target after all. The raven and the dog played together innocently in the small field between her car and the rec

HELEN KNOTT

From *In My Own Moccasins*

On my three-year sobriety mark, I packed my bags and tossed them to the back of my car. I was on a continual journey forward and I was excited. I could feel the anticipation in my stomach as I readied myself to embark on a bold new adventure.

I'd already worked toward and received my bachelor's degree in social work. It's the reason my uncle gave me a car. A silver pony with a missing hubcap.

I'd awoken early on that morning of my graduation ceremony. I held my sleeping son, and I reflected on how far we had come and how well we have been since my last time in treatment. And even through all that turmoil—of struggling through school, of close encounters with relapse—I somehow knew we'd make it.

I promised him when he was born that we were going to make it. I told myself this as I scrubbed urinals and desks, years ago. Mathias was barely one year old when I knew we were going to have a good life. When he was born, nine pounds and five ounces, we had no money but his mama had hope.

We were finally on the road to a hopeful future filled with opportunity.

As for my next step, I'd be on the road soon too, to Edmonton. A city I have learned to see in a different light since the darkness has left me.

I have had some really amazing things happen in my life, things that continue to put me in a space of awe and humility. As these events take place I silently acknowledge that, with everything I have been through, I'm not even supposed to be alive. But I am, so I tell myself to be grateful, be humble, be real, and do good things.

So, I was headed back to Edmonton. The city where I almost lost myself in blurred lines of cocaine while I was spinning in circles. I had been given the chance to create my own space of healing—for others. I had found my voice.

I had applied for and received an arts grant to make two poetry videos that focused on ending violence against Indigenous women. They were to be filmed in Edmonton. I wasn't spinning in circles anymore, but coming full circle.

Small things had to happen for bigger things to follow suit. It started from a blog that I wrote while in my third year of the social work program in Merritt, British Columbia. That's how I met Cheyenne, a Métis filmmaker who followed my writing. The blog was called *Reclaim the Warrior.* It was dedicated to processing and sharing my decolonization journey. Cheyenne emailed me and asked to use one of my older poems for a small video. I said yes, and who knew I was opening the door to larger projects and ultimately to a woman I would eventually think of as a sister.

The main focus of the project was the poem "The Things We Taught Our Daughters." It was a culmination of my healing journey, countless conversations, and reflection on violence in Indigenous communities in both urban and rural settings. I realized more and more as I held space for other women over the years how pervasive silence is. The more I shared stories with

Indigenous women across the country, the more I realized how common some of my experiences were. There are women out there holding onto these stories without ever letting them see the light. I wanted to be brave, not only for me, but to help create some change for them.

The Things We Taught Our Daughters

Sometimes we taught them silence
to let the secrets stay on their lips

Sometimes we taught them to look away
to forget and not bear witness

We showed them how
to play hide and seek
with historical afflictions
to pretend that the monsters from the closet
didn't escape. Don't exist. Are not real.
Sometimes to protect our own wounds
we forced our daughters not to feel

Maybe we were taught this ourselves
If you focus hard enough on forgetting
You can live through any kind of hell
Hush. Quiet Now. That's enough, my girl.
Silence.

Fat lips and bruised eyes
Say more than the mouth will tell you
Show less than what the eyes have seen
It didn't happen. Forget about it. He didn't mean it.
We don't call the police on our own.
Just learn to stay away . . . Stay Away. Stay
Away

Somewhere we learned how to create an asylum
for the very things
that plague our dreams
Somewhere we learned blind eyes
          and buried skeletons
provide just enough relief
to live just enough
without ever really living

We stuck sexual abuse up on the mantelpiece
Picture-framed the portrait of rape
and named the old rez dog Domestic Dispute

We gave all of this shit a home
the aggressive interloper intrudes
and we accepted its right to exist
Love just isn't really love
if he doesn't say it with his fists
Enough now. Quiet. He didn't mean to.
They would never hurt you like that.
Your uncle, he loves you.

Our inaction translating to
another generation
accepting the presence of violations
When we were little girls
We should have slept safely in our beds
Mothers should have said

My girl, you are worth a thousand horses
and any man
would give a thousand more

We would know the phrases
Speak up. It is never your fault. No means no.
You have the birthright to be free from harm,
and any man who would violate these
        treaties between bodies
would be dealt with by the women.
Because we protect our own,
even if this means calling the police on our own.

Because my girl,
You are sacred, valuable, indispensable,
        and irreplaceable
This is what needs to be said, needs to
        be shown, needs to be told.

Because our daughters . . .
Will one day grow old
and maybe they'll be women

with short-term memories
practising daily burial ceremonies
focused on forgetting.

It is time to remember.
Time to summon our voices from
the belly of the earth.
Time to feel, cry, rage, heal, and to
truly live life instead.
It is time to tell ourselves and our daughters,
the things that should have been said

The words I had written spoke to Cheyenne, and the poem immediately became the main focus of our collaboration.

But, just before I left for Edmonton, there was an unforeseen twist to the project that gave me pause. Cheyenne no longer wanted just to use my words and voice to narrate it. She asked me to be present in the video and not just the voice of it. I hesitated. I called my mama, who had become an anchor for me in my sobriety and healing.

"Do you know what this means?" I said to my mom on the phone later that night.

"What?" she asked.

'"I'll be the face of sexual abuse and violence experienced by Indigenous women."

"And?"

"Mama, if I do this, I'm going to be single for the rest of my life," I said before I started laughing at the real possibility of it.

"No, you won't!" my mama said. She was supportive, the way a mom is supposed to be. We laughed together, and she added, "Oh well, the things you know need to be said."

And it was decided. Or rather, Creator decided a path for me and I paid attention for the signs and moved when I was supposed to. I trusted that I would be taken care of.

I am taken care of.

Still, the thought of reading my poem in front of a camera and to a room full of strangers made my stomach tighten. It wasn't a new sensation. Reading my poetry in public has always frightened me. I remember the first time.

It was years ago, after returning from my first trip to Nicaragua. A community event was being held at a local coffee shop. My boss at the time had asked me to read poetry with her at this event as part of an International Women's Day celebration.

"I'm not doing it," I told my best friend Kyla.

"Why not?" she asked.

"Poetry is different. What if nobody likes it?"

"Who cares if they don't? But you know as well as I that you're a damn good writer. Just do it."

"But . . ." I hesitated.

"But what?" She was still trying to convince me.

"I'm scared shitless," I had to admit.

"Don't you always tell me that if there is fear there is room for growth? So if you're scared that's a good thing. You'll grow from it. You have to do it."

I grimaced. All that self-help-book talk came back to bite me in the ass and was forcing me to display my innards to a crowd of strangers. Poetry, and reading poetry to strangers, has always been different for me because my words are a part of me. Sharing words that I've written with people has another level of vulnerability that I still sometimes struggle with. It is me baring my soul with each stanza to a room full of people I will never know on a first-name basis.

But Kyla talked me into it. And so I stood there, on International Women's Day, about to recite my own words to the public for the first time.

When they called my name, I asked my boss to stand beside me in support. Women have always been there to support me, to help me on my journey. She placed her hand on my back as if to absorb some of the nervous energy that coursed through my being.

I used to have a bad lip quiver anytime I was nervous presenting to a crowd. Back then, the lip quiver was in full effect and I heard the girl in the front row comment to her friend, "Why is her lip shaking?"

That. Damned. Quivering. Lip.

I'd gone to Toastmasters a few years before, hoping to develop the confidence to get rid of it. It didn't help, and I struggled through that first reading.

I survived it.

It scared me.

And I did it again. I read in public again. And again.

Sometimes my knees still quake, even today. But I left that lip quiver behind me.

But each time on stage is different. And each poem opens up a different kind of vulnerability. Each time I have to tell myself to be brave.

I hoped that my legs wouldn't quake and I would remember my lines for this film project.

Indeed, during my long drive to Edmonton I tried to sort through the anxieties and fears that surrounded my performing in front of a camera and film crew. I practised my lines for most of the eight hours of the drive. My mind still ran a little rampant but I tried to let the fears go.

What if they expect me to be some epic spoken-word artist and have all my stuff memorized?

What if they are disappointed?

What if my lip quiver comes back?

I knew I'd be required to stand in front of a room full of strangers and declare that I have been sexually abused and raped.

I almost turned my car around several times before finally arriving at the film set.

What did I get myself into?

That's it . . . I'm fucking crazy.

Okay. Okay. I got this. Pray. Trust. Breathe.

The grandmothers must have been travelling with me. I found the courage to do this project.

There were seven people in that film crew. They set up the lighting and backdrop while I stood outside and rehearsed with Faye. She was a production assistant and part of her job was to make sure I felt comfortable. Faye was a long-haired and beautiful Haida woman with a gentle spirit. She cued me when I needed it and gave me encouragement when I faltered. "One more time," she'd say, as we sat outside on a wooden bench, the sun overhead and a breeze fluttering my papers. When rehearsal was finished, I excused myself. I found an empty room and called my mama.

Over the years of our sobriety, and a few really solid talks, my mom and I had healed our relationship. It didn't happen without a lot of work, a lot of forgiveness, and a lot of love. Mom became Mama again. She represents the roots that keep me grounded and the person who breathes life into me when I need it the most.

"Mama, we are about to start," I said.

"That's good, my girl," she replied.

"Mama?"

"Yes?"

"Will you pray with me?"

Pray. Trust. Breathe.

FRANCINE CUNNINGHAM

From *On/Me*

On How to Keep on Living / *Passing*

i move through the world passing—

as mentally well
as a white woman
as over my grief
as successful

i am none of these things,
at least not fully

On Identity /
Origin of a Designation

i hadn't heard the term *white passing* until recently
it wasn't something i grew up with—*white passing,*
said like bad words, strung together to hurt, to designate, to
demarcate

like i should be something other than white
like i should have skin other than what i have
like i was called *white buffalo* growing up, a difference in the
lineup of cousins

marked but not known why

mixed blood
métis
half-breed
hybrid
off reserve
scottish
indian
steinhauer
a part of the land
aboriginal
cunningham
quantifiable
belgian
a bill c

indigenous
cree
calahasian
urban
non-speaker
prairie dweller
native
status card holder

the buck stops with me,
my mom always said that to my sisters and me growing up
the buck stops with me,
as if to say
you are not indian in the government's eyes
you are not indian in the people's eyes
you are not
indian

but then why do i hear cree in my dreams?

On Mental Illness
/ Lists

Francine:

general anxiety disorder
possible borderline personality disorder
bipolar ii disorder
depression
ptsd

family (a combination or singular):

general anxiety disorder
borderline personality disorder
bipolar disorder
multiple personality disorder
schizophrenia
paranoid schizophrenia
ptsd
attempted suicide
suicide
addiction (alcoholism, drug abuse, gambling)

On Family
/ Mother

met my father in a horse stall
kept dating him even after
their first date
when he took her to a restaurant
and dined and dashed

i never understood why
she chose him
when they were so unalike

married twenty years
still don't know if either of them was happy

locked herself in her room for
almost a year when he finally left
sitting in the living room with my sisters
listening to the sound of her rocking chair
thump against the floor of her bedroom

learned to take care of myself
when i learned my parents
wouldn't
or couldn't
or maybe they were just human
and going through
the complicated motions of life

On Teasing
/ Aunties

head thrown back in laughter,
hands out whacking shoulders

On Identity
/ Descriptions of Self from Outside of Self

indianhalfbreednativefirstnationsaboriginalindigenousmetiscreendn
treaty6urbancityoffreserveeducatedyoungpersonbeaderwriterartist
whiteskinbrownhairgreeneyesoneofthegoodonesseperatedstatusmooch
prairieheaddresswearingspiritualwarriorrecoveredsavageteepeeliving
freeloaderluckysurivorredskinanimaltotemlovingculturetraditional
pancakebuttbannockmakingwomanofthekitchenrenegadeforward
movinghorseridernobellovinglonghairedsquawdreamcatchingearth
lovingteacherlisteningtothewindonthebackofhistoryconquered
vanquishedkilledthrivingalivestillbloodnationhooddancingtraitors
identityoutsideofselfinsideofself

On TV
/ Pocahontas

going to my granny and grandpa's
so proud to show them
other natives on tv
they were sad

FRANCINE CUNNINGHAM

From "Teenage Asylums"

My dad's face turned from white to red to white again. He stood staring at my mom, his lips moving but no words forming. This is when he would usually burst into some form of anger but instead, on that night, he turned and left the room in silence. I looked over at Dahlia who had her book up in front of her face but she wasn't reading anymore. Her shoulders were tense, her knuckles white. I strained listening. I heard my dad upstairs, he stomped around and slammed a door. And then there was silence. But not like normal silence. This silence seemed important. It felt filled with something I didn't have knowledge of yet. This silence lasted so long that I finally got up and walked into the living room. My dad was standing by the front door, his hand clutching the fake gold knob. His body rigid and unmoving. There was a large beige duffle bag slung over his shoulder. Glancing backwards I followed the sliver of light reflected on the carpet coming from the kitchen to where my mom and Dahlia were locked motionless. Afraid to move, I watched Dahlia as she lifted her hand from the table, and in a smooth motion, gripped my mom's. My mom didn't look up, instead her eyes stayed focused on the plate of grocery store chicken in front of her. The only sound in the house was the rough inhalation of breath. The only thing I could feel—my chest going up and down. I looked over at the wall beside me. The only picture my mom had managed to hang since our move looked so sad on the large white wall. It was a picture from our last vacation to the cabin. My mom was so much smaller than the rest of us; her black hair was spinning in the wind, a timid smile on her lips. My dad had his arms stretched around Dahlia and me. Dahlia was laughing at something my dad had just said, looking effortlessly beautiful in the process. I looked more like my mom than Dahlia. I had dark hair that looked almost black, brown skin and green eyes while Dahlia just looked like our dad, dirty blond hair, hazel eyes and white skin. We were all happy in that moment. At least I think we were.

And then I took a step forward and everything changed. One second the stillness held us together as a family, and the next we were floating islands separated by a deep murky darkness. My dad turned the knob and walked out of the house. My mom's fork clanged on the plate as Dahlia stood up and pushed her chair back from the table. I followed my dad outside into the night. His car lights turned on and I blinked into the sudden brightness. I think I saw a shadow of a wave but I'm not sure. Then he was gone.

At night when this memory clings to me, I wail into my pillow even though I try not to because I know. It's just the beginning. For the rest of the night the last few months of my life will play over and over again. Each moment surfacing, inflicting its knife wound before retreating, leaving space for the next one. I will be shown every moment where I was wrong. Where I made the wrong choice. Where because of me, people were hurt. Destroyed. And when the light finally does peek into my room and I can move again, I'll breathe deep and the shaking will stop, but then I'll remember. Again. And again. And again.

MIKA LAFOND

From *nipê wânîn: my way back*

têpiya pîkiskwêwina

macîhtwâwin
nicîpotônêyin
tâpiskohc sîwinikan mîna wîsakosâwas ispakwan

kîmohc pîkiskwê
namôya kipêhtawâw ê-itwêt
ayisiniskêyiw
nititwahok
namôya mîwacisiw
pasci mamitonêyita kîkway takî îki mêkwahc
namôya kwayaskopayiw
kamiyito

tâpiskohc kimôwanâyâw
pîkiskwêwin kâpahkitêk
nitônihk
pâpahkawin
yîkwaskwan pîhkwêyitamômakan
namôya awiyak mîwêyitam kimôwan
niya piko

just words

cantankerous
I purse my lips
the taste both sugar and lemon

whisper
inaudible slurs
met with gestures
pointing at me
bitter
overthought moments
of indiscretion
shared

precipitation
the word that pops
on my lips
the drip-drip serenade
grey clouds are depressing
nobody likes rain
except me

namôya kwamwahc ayâmakan
tâpiskohc niya
âspîs niwâpamikawin âspîs nipêhtakawin
âspîs ninisitohtâkawin
kâkêkâhc nipômân
mâka nisôkêyitên

mâmitonêyita
kocista
pîkiskwê
masinahikê
têpiya pîkiskwêwina

teetering
like me
rarely seen, heard, understood
nearly toppling
but holding ground

think
taste
speak
write
just words

LESLIE BUTT

From "Tanked"

Adam took me to parties on the weekends. When we were both off work, we often stayed out into the early hours of the morning. There was no one waiting for me at home, no one to reprimand me on staying out too late, or how my breath reeked of alcohol and grass.

Even Adam, at twenty years old, answered his cell phone at midnight when his mother wondered when he would be home, or wanted to make sure he was okay. When he got too drunk to drive, she would pick him up, no matter where he was, no matter the time.

Adam always paid for everything. I got to try some pretty good food, and new kinds of alcohol I had never even thought of. I learned I liked Porn Stars, Singapore Slings, anything fruity made in a blender. The drinks came with little paper umbrellas and sweet orange slices on the side of the glass.

I became a drinker of dry red wine. My favourite was Zinfandel. I ate spicy tuna roll and I loved fruit, especially mangoes. I'd never had the luxury of saying what I loved or hated. I hadn't even known. I had to eat what I could afford, drink whatever someone gave me. Now, I was someone who deserved to love or hate things. I deserved to have dreams, I even started believing that one day I could sing in a musical, sell a painting, and make an award-winning film.

Adam rubbed my back when I drank too much and got sick, and bought me greasy fast food that we ate in his car. We'd throw the garbage in the bucket outside the window. I wasn't used to attention, someone always asking if I was too hot or cold, bringing me hot green tea on the cool mornings before school, picking me up and dropping me off with a kiss and wishes for a nice day.

I always made it easy for him when he asked me how my day was; he was so sweet I didn't want to trouble him. If I got in a fight, if I got called a name or saw my own name slandered on the bathroom walls, I left out the details. For Adam, I was always happy, no matter what.

It was Friday and I left the doors of school to see him sitting outside in his car waiting to pick me up. As I got in, I hoped the popular girls looked at me with envy.

"Hey babe, how was your day?"

"Good," I responded, fluttering inside at his smile. "I had a science test. Pretty sure I nailed it."

"Oh yes, yes, yes. You are brilliant."

He put his hand on the wheel and backed up. As his head was turned, I could see the veins pumping in his neck. He started driving and laid his left hand on my thigh, giving me goosebumps.

"My parents and brother are out of town for the weekend, so I invited a few people over. I am going to head up to the liquor store now, if you want to come by and help me get ready."

"Yeah, that would be awesome."

"I figured you would be good at like, picking out some snacks to have, or something."

At the fry shop I would often browse my manager's magazines, the ones for adults who had money to spend on renovations, who needed recipe ideas. I got excited at the thought of being an adult who could one day buy ingredients for a recipe, or a couch cushion that matched a painting on the wall. He exited the liquor store with his arms full.

"I've got you some Zinfandel, and some of the sour shots for the guys, and some of these fancy beers, and this chardonnay for Melissa." He laid everything on the back seat, one by one, as if it were show and tell.

"Thank you so much. I'm looking forward to it."

"Anything for you, babe. Now, off to the grocery store!"

Usually when I went to the grocery store, I looked for things that were cheap—marked down stuff about to expire, produce that had a couple of mold spots. It was the first time I really considered that some people just put things in their cart without thinking twice. We had chips, crackers, different types of cheeses and deli meats, and pre-made hors d'oeuvres that just had to be baked for ten minutes.

I watch the rain on these window panes
The me and you
The molecular structure of time
The velocity of change

We brought our bags into Adam's house, and as we started unloading them, I felt like this could be my future. Preparing for a party, unloading groceries, cutting up cheese to place neatly onto platters, putting chips into bowls.

"A glass of wine for you, darling," he said, passing me the glass, "thank you so much for all your help. Hopefully the guys don't get too wild tonight. They can be jerks when they are drinking."

"I am used to them now." I took a sip of the delicious wine. A bottle would have cost me a day's work.

We sat down on the couch, facing the living room window. The darkness crept in, and the rain started to gently fall.

"Cheers."

He held out his glass and I obliged. He took my face in his hands and gently kissed me, looking into my eyes with a smile on his face.

"Well, we have an hour before the party starts," he winked, as he placed his hand on my leg. I closed my eyes, wishing I could stay here forever.

A few hours into the party, it was complete chaos—shot glasses were being passed to me, Adam occasionally giving me another glass of wine or a beer, everyone yelling, loud music. I'd had such a good day and felt briefly guilty that I was unintentionally tanked, but I tried my best to keep myself present and not overthink.

The voices of Adam's friends circled in and out, my drunken mind not comprehending the topics of their discussion. I watched his face from the corner of my eye, taking a full-on glance every few moments. He looked so amazing, holding a beer, talking, smiling. The dimples on the left side of his face deep enough to hold my fears forever. He saw me, with my red hair, old jeans, wine glass in hand. He smiled at me, giving me a quick wink, a wink that would melt a heart made of ice. The corners of my mouth upturned slightly, shyness keeping me from breaking into a massive grin. He gave me a deep look into my eyes, as if he could read my thoughts, his eyes like X-rays.

The house shook with the music, a beating bass from a subwoofer settled itself inside of me and vibrated my frontal lobes. People I would ignore at school now all sat around, mellow and drunk. Different groups all melded together, the alcohol letting everyone put their guard down.

I never had my own group, I just floated among the plankton in the fish bowl, making my own set of rules, inhabiting my own coral reef. For the first time, they were talking to me. I looked around at the smiling girls and their sparkling earrings and teased hair, the jocks with their hockey jackets, names scripted into the sleeves.

I stumbled outside and fell into the side of the house, bumping my knee. The alcohol made my body ignore the pain. I smoked cigarettes with people I supposedly hated, who hated me.

"Li-i-ly!" yelled Jordan, one of Adam's friends, exaggerating my name into more than two syllables. "What's up!"

"Jor-da-an!" I matched his exaggeration, as he gave me a high five and playfully put his arm around my shoulder.

"You better be ready for some fireworks, baby!!!"

"Yeah, and you better not hit anyone this time! Hey, I am Melissa." Someone reached their hand out for me to shake. She was gorgeous, with long dark hair. I knew who she was but she never had a reason to speak to me before.

"Girl, it was an accident! You do some crazier shit on that cheerleading squad for the games!"

"Seriously Jordan, don't fucking start."

"Jeremy!" Jordan called out to the blond-haired guy I'd first met with Adam. He got into our little unintended circle and took out a baggie of some sort of drug.

"I've got the good stuff, and brought my techno CDs, so this night is going to be on wheels guys!" He popped a pill of E in his mouth and passed one to Jordan, but didn't offer one to me or Melissa.

"Seriously Jeremy, you're such a loser sometimes," Melissa said, rolling her eyes. "Seriously Lily, do NOT mind them at all. Later on, we will totally ditch the guys and go upstairs to eat. They all just end up in the garage anyway. I'll introduce you to Katie. She will think you are just the coolest."

Adam surprised me from behind by wrapping his arms around my upper body. I turned around to kiss him, the smell of beer on his breath, cigarettes on mine. I cherished everything about that moment—the stars, his face illuminated by the light of the moon, the eyes I could drown in.

The night was soft, I felt light as a cloud, as if I could be reshaped. I was malleable as kneaded dough. Adam would feed me. Oh, did I have big dreams for us. He could drive me to school and to work, we could get our own place, make our own world, our own family. He was not picky, I could hang my art on the walls with no protest. I'd learn how to cook great food and we would eat supper every night together, candles blazing in the middle of our table. We'd make love under the stars, our bedroom window open to the moon. We'd fall asleep in an innocent embrace.

"We got some fireworks!" Jeremy yelled through the open door of the house. Everyone streamed out to watch the show, a few couples staying inside to continue their kissing. He walked to the middle of the lawn, fireworks in hand, and threw down his cigarette like the period at the end of a sentence.

"Sweet!" Adam turned to his friend and looked at me one last time.

I continued sipping on my fruity drink. I went from person to person, continuing conversations, sharing smokes and smiles. I observed the tree root veins in Adam's sleeveless forearms pulse in and out as he set up a firework in the grass. He lit the fuse, and it sparkled before shooting up into the sky in an array of colour, making a loud bang as it went off.

The sky lit up Adam's smile. This was my life, and tonight I could actually feel it going somewhere. I was that firework, dark and dusty, sitting on the shelf until Adam came along and lit me with his fire. Then, I exploded, making my way to the stars, suddenly full of a colour and wonder I never knew I possessed.

It became chilly after all the fireworks had been set off. I thoroughly enjoyed the scene that had unfolded in front of me. I had been scared of fireworks from a young age. Tonight, I didn't care. I stepped into the garage. A crowd of people had also made their way in there, and it was hot-boxed with marijuana smoke. I lit up another cigarette.

"Lil-Ayeeee!" Jeremy walked over to me, taking a drag of his own cigarette, his pupils the size of dinner plates. "If your gold-diggin' ass ever gets sick of Adam, let me know. I bet you'd be a good bit." He winked and grabbed me by the privates. He squeezed, and then walked away wordlessly. Jordan laughed.

The noise in the garage became deafening, the marijuana in the air sickened me. I needed more than anything to get out of there, I needed to run.

BILLY-RAY BELCOURT

From *This Wound is a World*

Notes from a Public Washroom

i never dream about myself anymore.
i chose a favourite memory
and named it after every boy
i have broken up with.
grief is easier that way.
i need to cut a hole in the sky
to world inside.
is the earth round,
or is it in the shape of a broken heart?
i drove through a town called freedom
and it looked like an accident
pretending to be a better accident.
there is a city in colorado
called loveland
and it is where alone meets lonely.
i have been there exactly two times.
i saw a lot of indians
and cried for three days afterwards.
i bought a pin that says LOVE
and i wear it on my jean jacket as a cry for help.
i asked all 908 of my facebook friends

to tell me they loved me
and they did
and i believed them.
my cousin's boyfriend punched
a hole in the wall
so i hid inside it
and for a few seconds i thought
maybe this is what heaven looks like.
i ran off the edge of the world
into another world
and there everyone
was at least a little gay.

Colonialism: A Love Story

1. colonialism broke us, and we're still figuring out how to love and be broken at the same time.
2. the first time he told me i was beautiful, i thought he was lying. i thought beauty was a plot in a story i had been written out of a long time ago.
3. what happens when "i love you, too" becomes a substitute for "i can't," when his hand finds your body and it feels like he's taking pieces of it? perhaps this is what they meant by "love requires sacrifice."
4. sometimes bodies don't always feel like bodies but like wounds.
5. he told me he'd take a needle and stitch our bodies together with the thickest thread.
6. colonialism. definition: turning bodies into cages that no one has the keys for.
7. when i invite him into the abandoned house of me, he tiptoes inside. he notices the way the walls ache to be touched again even though they know time won't let them survive it.
8. we need not pretend that love was to be found in wastelands like these.

The Oxford Journal

I.

you notice the regularity with which others avoid confrontation vis-à-vis racial oppression. this is how they think themselves outside of the world. you don't know what it is like to be in a body without it feeling like a death trap. at your desk you watch a news clip of a truck running over native protestors in reno, nevada. no one dies this time. the west is nothing if not a string of murders incriminated by a series of attempted murders.

II.

how does it feel to be an object? you wear your favourite pair of ripped jeans exposing your brown flesh to the world. this exposure is interpreted as an invitation, compelling a stranger in a centuries-old building to walk up to you, rub your skin, laugh, and walk away. you laugh too, but only because your body needs to escape itself, to identify something of an ontological rupture. this is what it feels like to almost not exist. you keep surviving anyway.

III.

you attend a mandatory session on intellectual disagreement where you are encouraged to open yourself up to speech. claudia rankine: "language that feels hurtful is intended to exploit all the ways that you are present." you decide that the history of the colonial world is a history of natives being too present. with each word, you thicken and thicken until you burst. these are moments in which other worlds seem impossible.

IV.

you are midway through an article on ideology critique when the author makes a reference to primitives who pray for rain. This, he argues, is an example of an ideological defect whereby patterns of behaviour serve ends that are cheaply related to those forces (here, social solidarity). you are troubled by the invocation of primitives as if it were prior to ideology, as if it were an anthropological given. more immediately, you pause because this is the first native you encounter in england. you are both empty signifiers.

V.

"oxford university embroiled in race row as students told to be 'vigilant' after black man seen in grounds." christina sharpe insists that anti-blackness is a "total climate," that anti-blackness is "pervasive as climate." it is the weather. in oxford the weather allows university staff to speak of blackness as that which begets "vigilance," as that which is an "unauthorized persons," as that which catches some "unaware." those of us who study and live in oxford know that the weather is always grey. but, it is also anti-black.

VI.

you are called "wonderfully exotic." a man looks at you, tilts his head, and presses that you are "too mixed" for him to pinpoint any sort of ethnic belonging. this is a world-threatening feeling: to be so other that you barely exist in a place whose imperial conquests sought the destruction of your people. when you tell him you are native he doesn't say anything. he lets the silence do the talking, as if he were lamenting the violence that went into producing someone like you. i can tell he has heard a thing or two about us. "i have never met a native american before," he adds, quieter this time. perhaps speaking in a hushed voice makes you less real. what does one do with the sense of loss that tailgates their body?

VII.

your body is a catch-22. how does one survive losing one's bearings without an exit strategy? for philosopher jill stauffer, one can feel resistant to existence when their sense of autonomy disappears from the realm of everyday life. it can also occur when one cannot escape what cornel west called "the normative gaze of the white man." the normative gaze of the white man is the air you breathe. it makes a jail out of your lungs. this is what it is to live an existential limbo.

VIII.

you and a friend are going for coffee after a lecture on marxist feminist theory and a white british man nudges you with his shoulder. your friend goes to grab a table, a table that he was also intending to grab. he gets visibly upset and, willfully and passionately, says *i'm just trying to get away from you people.* your friend is stunned and in the meantime he returns to say something else under his breath. at this point, you confront him and tell him that he is out of line even though you know that the world is his to claim. he walks away, but throws more words at you. the violence of *you people* is that it is a classic interpellative call, one that pulls you outside yourself, that seeks to trap you in a flattened form of subjectivity. for him, we were nothing. this is the ebb and flow of everyday life in oxford.

IX.

you want to capture the sense of a present that is not quite *the* present, a present that thickens in the underbelly of social reality. you stalk the prefix un-, hoping that it will let you see glitches, that it will unearth a hole in the ground, something of a gateway to a world you are spotting any- and everywhere, a world you are spotting nowhere. you are sad, so at first you believe that an un- can be found in the body of men. you begin looking for doors, not enclosures. doors without locks. doors that swing open. soon, you decide that doors are a transference of cacophonous feeling; they are ecological, unseen. leanne simpson: "she is the only doorway to this world." the un- is a woman like your kookum who rips open time.

PART II

QUICKENINGS

ARIELLE TWIST

From *Disintegrate/Dissociate*

Reckless

I've always been reckless

with the way I let men crash
into me
strangers tasting a chest
that I grew with care
sliding his
hands into my body

~~why are his nails so sharp?~~

I think I've been reckless

be gentle
I've told him
grab my hair, flip me over
they never listen
fuck me drunk, tear me open

~~I bled into my sheets that night~~

I know I've been reckless

this body I never asked for
touched

~~they never asked either~~

I've been reckless

because men

are reckless with me.

The Girls

I can flirt ferociously with lust
spit fire of cautious songs
pulsing with hormones and rage
that I acquired over time
I am intimidating to you, of course
I should be, as I am visions of a woman
you are told not to have
/canthave/
I am the kind of girl you jerk off to
under the covers in your dorm room
while your cute cis white blond skinny girlfriend is away
I am the kind of girl you match with on tinder
/againandagain/
left, left, right, left, right, repeat
swiping so you can ask these questions and validate
/dirtyfuckingdesiresdaddyhadtoo/
these girls you crave, pumping out cum
like lotion to moisturize the dryness of
a yearning pushed onto you
/soboringsobland/
I am the kind of girl you pick up in your car at three in the morning
looking for a quick fuck, a goddess without a name
/trannyslutsaresoeasyright?/
when in reality it's boys like you who make us hard
boys like you who make us feel unlovable, a biological mistake
a game, an experiment, an experience, alive, afraid
I am the kind of girl you take on dates in dark rooms

back of bars where only rats will see her beauty
and in these dark caves you are kind
/Imissthisboyinthedark/
here I learned darkness is safer than light
because light makes boys like you
/leavethegirlslikeme/
I am the kind of girl you found love with in those dark holes
love that you abandoned for being too much
too trans? too brown? too fat? too femme? too tall?
I am the kind of girl who knows I am too much
the kind of girl you left so she can find you in someone else
someone who can handle the women oozing from this body you loved
/toomuch/
I am the kind of girl that you continue to fuck behind curtains
in a bed where you are gentle and caring
/whatareyouthinkingrightnow?/
because I can't stop thinking about when you left me
for strawberries and cream, even though caramel is sweeter
for that woman who's easier to control, easier to love
/butintheendyoufuckedusboththesame/
I am the kind of girl who learned my boundaries by dating you
because you crossed them and built them up like a wall
/funnyisntit?/
that your white bodies are so used to building and tearing down at will
funny that your sex feels like colonization in this body I called home
/andisthiswhattruelovefeelslike?/
because I became this girl who stopped showing up at three in the
morning
The girl who knows I am not a secret

The girl who finds pleasure through open windows
The girl who is more desirable than fuckable
The girl you won't have
The girl you can't have
The girl who was intimidating
The girl in dark rooms
The girl with many names
The girl full of estrogen and rage
The girl who loved you even behind those curtains
And the girl who loved herself more than men
but that scares you
—*it should.*

Silent

Freedom is safety in its truest form, a luxury not ours.
I think I've found something
in the creases in your lips
the relaxation of your jaw.

Hold me, squeeze my chest
to yours and let
fear evaporate from my body.

Let me hear your breath
through every pore,
let me feel your heart pulse
through your neck
as I lie on your warm chest

finding safety in silence
safety in sleep.

MAYA COUSINEAU MOLLEN

De *Bréviaire du matricule 082*

SEPT FOIS

Au premier jour de mon premier souffle
On me baptisa avec un numéro

Au deuxième, on me donna une terre de réserve
Pour y ensevelir mes premiers rêves

Au troisième, on extirpa dans la douleur
La sauvagesse de mon âme

À l'aube du quatrième jour
Je laissai espérance, amour-propre et fierté

Étrangère en mes terres, au cinquième acte d'existence
Ma chevelure fut sacrifiée, offrande chrétienne

Au sixième, purgée de mes ancêtres
On m'avorta des enseignements de la survivance

Je laissai les mains assoiffées de ma vie
S'approprier cette septième fois

Je suis Marie Maya Mollen
« Marie Maya Mollen matricule 082, est un Indien au
sens de la *Loi sur les Indiens*, chapitre 27 des
Lois du Kanada »

ISHKUESS DU NORD

Sur le sentier glacé de ma hargne
Marchent mille femmes pâles

En moi brûle l'acidité des fluides
Point d'amour pour les filles des glaciers

Enfants des ours blancs, des froids lunaires
Héritières du Nord, déesses bafouées

Au parfum éthylique, piégées comme nymphes
Dans ces étreintes de violence que d'aucuns
appellent tendresse

Tu oses m'honorer de ton mépris
Me croire vendue pour une bière

M'envoûter par tes berceuses eugéniques
Posséder mon corps, m'avilir

Tellement plus que ton racisme
Serti de neige, mon peuple brille

Les vents nordiques ont ciselé mes traits
Je suis beauté et amante des aurores boréales

Crains ma colère, crains mes prières
Je suis le Nord et rien ne te sauvera

TROY SEBASTIAN

"The Mission"

After seven years spent at the Mission, away from my family, away from our language of land and culture, away from ka papa's horses and ka titi's ceremony, placed with pedophile priests, whip claw nuns, desperate cousins, stowaway brothers, and too many rats to remember or to forget, my only thought, the only desire I could recognize in myself, in the deep grooves of my palms, in the reckless horror of my dreams, the only present thought in my mind was to find Brother Francis and choke him to death with my own hands.

Murder provides powerful resolve.

The same hands that were taught to pray to the lord were created to hold this resolve. Such resolve has a power that cannot be lost in reckless acts. It keeps your hand steady when nerves of lesser intent would take hold and shudder the mind to bedlam. I had given this act much thought. Every morning when we were told to pray, I prayed my hands would be strong enough for the task.

My hands gripped the wheel of the '65 Impala as we made it over Rogers Pass. The last of the Golden gas station whisky passed between us. "Bah, that's not bad, huh." Raymond clapped. His mouth slipped at words with a hollow smile. He lost his front teeth steer wrestling earlier that spring, and his speech was slithery and filled with saliva. "It's alright," I said, my mind lost upon the road behind me. My knuckles holding the road ahead steady.

The drive had been slower than expected. We had set out early that morning. Though the traffic was light and there wasn't too much snow to worry about as it was still early yet, the Impala was dragging. The drag got gradually worse the higher up the pass we got. Raymond had talked around the drag enough to boil my blood, as he knew not to talk shit about my Impala. But the point was clear. The Impala *did* drag.

I bought the Impala the week before from Raymond's uncle Wes. Wes assured me that there was nothing really wrong with it.

"Tires?" I asked.

"I got them last summer," Wes said.

"The engine?"

"Sure. Fire it up and see for yourself," he replied.

"No drag," I said.

"No, not really," he replied, counting the cash.

The Mission was a red-brick building where I had lived for most of the year. A series of smaller, ancillary buildings reinforced the Mission as broken and fallow farmlands flanked either side of the building from north to south. The St. Mary's River coldly wrought the edge of the Mission from expanding further east towards the reserve's hoodoos while to the west the rail line and road to town led to bedlam and Christian civilization. God and Jesus aside, the Mission was dedicated to the training and production of farmer workers. Such dedication required much faith in Ktunaxa ʔamakis where winter is present or promising at least half of the year, the other cut between seasons of heat, sun, rain, thunder, and the restless cold of late spring and early autumn. A symmetry of passing lovers, not a land of monotheistic agrarians. Yet we were the soil that the Mission ground down day after day, month after month, and beyond.

Though the Impala was pushing empty, the ride down from the summit gave us reason to believe we would make it to Revelstoke to gas up. To really know your car, you have to know the tank. It tells you things that aren't measured on the dashboard. What gas it likes, how close to empty looks like hope and how empty looks like a lost horizon. Somewhere before Revelstoke I pulled over to take a piss and to let Raymond drive for a bit. Once back on the road I rummaged round the car looking for a map and somehow got caught up in the various items from Wes's glovebox. Inside the glovebox were a few shells for a thirty ought six, some fishing line, two empty packages of smokes, a 1970 Eaton's catalogue dog-eared to ladies' fashions and a Department of Indians Affairs pamphlet titled *An Indian's Guide to Farming.* The pamphlet was more of a fragment than cohesive work as the text was stained and marred from oil and coffee. One page was legible which read, "An inventory of farm tools and their purpose:

- field auger used for divination and fence posts
- small hammer for fence repair and shed construction
- handsaw for small woodworks
- scythe for field harvesting."

Looking through the glove box my mind became a plate of leftover dreams and memories. Mostly of the old farm at the Mission. Farms teach a lot about pain, how much trauma a body can take before it succumbs, and the futility of a drawn-out death. We slaughtered animals at the Mission. And for each task we used specific tools. Each act posed limitations as the reliance on an instrument makes the item too important; an invitation for fallibility. A rusted saw is no good. A hammer with a snatched handle, a fracture deep in the wood but oblivious to the eye, was trouble. Too many variables. It wasn't until I saw an eagle clutch a rabbit's neck with its talons that I knew my own hands offered the solution.

Brother Francis's body was in perpetual flinch. He was lean, sullen and had a confused, homesick look in his eyes that really came to the fore whenever he smiled. That is when he looked particularly lost. When his face stopped smiling, it found that small space of emptiness that it recognized as home. His shoulders had a strength commonly found in hay bale cowboys. And though he was not a small person, he was nearly silent, appearing without warning with a persistent and foreboding calm like a storm that never fully crested. His fingers were dark, dry and cracked with bursts and breaches in the skin. I knew his knuckles well enough. Most of the boys did too. They were the first I met at the Mission.

"Do you remember what he looks like?" Raymond said as the headlights from an oncoming car framed his bandit eyes.

"Gupsin?" I said, jumping out of a dream with fists and terror.

"What if he had a beard now," Raymond said, picking at the dash for his pack of Exports, his eyes on the road. "Would we even recognize him, huh?"

"I know him to see him," I replied, my hands aching from their slumber of fists.

Raymond found the pack and one-handed a smoke to his lips, flicked the dashboard lighter, waited for the click and then put the hot cherry to the tobacco, drawing in the smoke with collapsing cheeks. I took a smoke from the pack and followed suit, as my ache of knuckles and drink woke up too. We smoked for a moment in silence.

"Ya, but it's been a few years," Raymond said. "And we was just kids when he . . ."

"Jesus, Raymond, I know him to see him alright," my words slapping at the Impala's dash.

The road was quiet. The only sounds were the grinding hum of the Impala's V8 and the slow, slurping breath Raymond took and released in syncopation. We took turns thinking on and forgetting the road in front of us. The road was downhill, the summit lost somewhere a few miles back. One smoke turned to another as the highway kept running beneath us. We carried on that way as I wound down the passenger window and flicked another smoke out of the Impala, the cherry sparking on the highway behind us.

"Jezzus," Raymond said slowly. "Ya, that's it, huh. Think about Jesus, huh. Would you know 'em to see 'em if he had shaved?"

I looked back to the glovebox to check on the bullets. They were still there. Rattling around.

"What the hell are you talking about? Jesus? Raymond! Christ!"

"Exactly, Christ, Christ Jesus. Our lord father," Raymond smiled. "Without a beard. You might not recognize him."

Raymond was a crazy Indian. Everyone knew this. Back at the Mission he was always in a good mood, didn't complain about the chow, and was always being praised by Brother Francis for his folded clothes. He read everything at the Mission from the bible to the pantry's cookbooks, and it was Raymond who knew when bears were near well before the musk.

"If Jezzuz shaved, and maybe got fat like Uncle Wes, he might not be easy to spot," he said smiling in a knowing grin of contentment with a hint of what-the-fuck-you-gonna-say-about-that in his eyes.

"Uncle Wes," I sighed.

"He might have a beard. Nowadays everyone's got one. Not just hippies," Raymond said, pointing with his right hand for emphasis.

"Hippies," I said.

"Ya," Raymond replied, his fingers fiddling with radio static.

"Hippies do have beards," I said.

"Ya, and hairy women too," said Raymond, laughing me into a good and necessary cry.

"Not that you'd complain," I said, shaking my head and my smile.

"Hell no! I like hairy women," he said. Raymond's eyes looked in the rear-view mirror as the lights of an oncoming semi overtook the Impala and flanked the car in a flash of gravity and jam-packed consumer goods. The wake of the load shook his grip.

"Jeez, frigging semi-trucks," Raymond said as he kept looking for a signal through the static.

I fought my way into the Mission. Like everyone before me, my first day of school was a shit-kicking. Brother Francis got the older boys to beat up Raymond and me right after we got to our dormitory. We didn't see it coming. A door closed and the room became punches, kicks, and laughter. I worried that my pressed white collared shirt would get stained. Ka titi told me to keep my collar clean and dry at the Mission and I should be okay. After the first stain I fought back. Raymond was turtled while I dragged my nails across ankles, faces, and the shine of the hardwood floor.

Every day after morning prayers, Brother Francis would organize the punch-up. This carried on for the first week at the Mission until they made Raymond and me fight each other. I knocked out Raymond cold with one punch. Raymond never held that against me.

After that, I graduated to fight older boys. Some were cousins, from our tribe, others came from elsewhere. I got a reputation for being a tough kid. Tough enough to keep fighting, even when there was no hope. There were these three brothers from Penticton who took turns beating me up. As I got older and grew into my body they had to double-team me to beat me until one day I brought the fight to them. They were swimming in the St. Mary's when I found them. I waited until the oldest came to shore. While he towelled off, I popped up and knocked him out quick. He was the toughest of the brothers but he didn't know what hit him. The two others swam in to try to get me. I had a few good stones set aside and I took to pelting them hard, in the face and in the chest. By the time they came to shore, they were bloodied and hoarse from shouting. I took a makeshift reed bullwhip and bloodied their backs up until they were all at my feet crying, blubbering, and knocked out. They never fucked with me again.

Francis was from somewhere around Enderby. As we drove closer to Enderby we didn't speak of him any longer. We spoke about horses, rodeos, and a woman out in Wardner who held a special place in her heart and trailer for young bucks like us. We never spoke of our purpose either. The mandate was more than skin deep. It was in the blood. Blood that carried our purpose even across country we did not know.

From what we knew, Francis wasn't in jail. Not anymore. When you have someone in, you know who is out. And he was out. Jail stories arrive in letters and didja-knows told between passing family. There was some chance he got killed shortly after he got loose. That happens just as much as going back inside. But Francis was a survivor. He adapted, no matter the circumstances.

At the Mission, when everyone else was asleep, Francis would talk to me. He'd tell me stories that held me in the dark long after he was gone. He was the youngest of ten. Most of his brothers were dead or nearly gone. He didn't know all their names or their faces. But he was going to go find them after the Mission. That's what he told me, anyhow. He had one brother who went up to 100 Mile to break horses. That made me admire him, as I had always heard the horses up in 100 Mile were too tough to break. As I got older, I realized that northern horses away are just as tough to break as they are to fathom.

In time Francis confessed he never had a younger brother. But if he did, he would want a brother tough and greasy like me. That was the first night he called me Greasy. Maybe it was because of my hair. I never knew why. But he called me that. And soon enough he only called me Greasy. Others started using that name too. I gave enough shit-kickings so that no one called me that to my face. But that was what they called me in the Mission. I hated it. And I hated him for naming me so. For taking my name and my body and returning it to me as something that was his.

We searched for him. For days. In a country I had only imagined. In a country I could only feel in dying moments of summer, as towels dry riverside. A country he had told me of past midnight when locations dream into spaces where horses live beyond the paddock. We hunted for him around Armstrong motels and Vernon campgrounds. Bales of hay, broke-down Fords, Lazy Susan diners, all were scuff marks for our quest to find Brother Francis. We got as far west as Falkland a week after rodeo ended and found nothing but every reason to leave. The most dangerous place to be a Skin is in a nothing town a week after a rodeo. With no reason to stick around there is every reason to go missing. Our search found rattlesnake needles, out of sync and restless. But no Brother Francis. Each dream was yesterday's hangover like a wall-mounted calendar falling to a previous month.

At first, we took turns sleeping in the back of the Impala. The steering wheel commanded the front seat like a roundabout steer who gave no quarter to slumbering knees. Raymond slept deeper than I so he inherited the front, I reigned the back. Crammed in the front seat like a half-wit bandit, his slurping snores came quick. As much as I loved him, I hated him for his ease of sleep. I watched his stupid face, asleep, pressed into the nook of the front seat, a foal with a slipped lip. How easy it would be to place my hands over his mouth, hold him there, to witness his awakening to the moment, to feel his shudder towards a permanent darkness, to inhabit his empty body afterwards. His night farts were deadly to any dreams of murder I had. Naturally, I always slept with the window open. Only when the night was coolest could I find the space to allow my body to fully wake to its weariness. And once there, dreams of the Mission would welcome me in fits and fidgets. No matter how dusted my denim was, I'd be wet by morning. Not every day. But each night where dreams would find me close to whole, I'd need a creek bath to wash the scent from my skin.

After missing the rodeo, we checked out every bar we could find. We found where Skins were gathered and where they weren't. The King Eddy. The National and The Branding Iron. They were all bars where we were welcome. Well, mostly. It didn't take much to feel unwelcome in them places. A woman would like the wrong way I'd look at her and her old man would get pissed, or Raymond would tell a joke too bad to be funny and we'd have a fight on our hands. Sometimes we had to run, but mostly we'd stay, fight it out, and someone would buy a round after the bust-up. Those beers were always best. Those laughs were always true. That's how it went after the Mission. It still goes that way.

One night we found Raymond's Auntie Lyla singing with a pickup band. She had taken up with a faller from Head of the Lake a few years back and looked good. We were down to our last few dollars and she could smell the road on us. So she brought us back to a lakeside spread for a few nights. Lyla's cabin had an old, grey shack next to it that had been used for canning and smoking years back. We found a half-stunk mattress in there and a good view of down the lake in that beautiful country. For a while there we didn't search for anything. We'd swim first thing in the morning, have some of Lyla's coffee, and found ourselves helping round the farm with fencepost promises and barbed wire postcards. It was good living, if fleeting and borrowed.

Lyla was the only family Raymond had who didn't ask him for money or try to stab him. That's what it was like then. Just nuts. Lyla knew Raymond when he was a baby and saw something good in him and though she never said that, she was always smiling at Raymond's stories and never asked him to explain himself. Lyla didn't say much to me and I thought that had something to do with her knowing my old man or that she was simply happy to see Raymond and paid me no mind. She did ask to trade me her Chrysler for my Impala. Naturally, I said no. But she kept on about it with a purpose and sincerity I could not deny.

Our third day Raymond had left with Lyla's old man to deliver hay to a ranch out past Lavington. I was replacing a spark plug in the Impala when Lyla came by with a cup of coffee and offered me a smoke. The car's radio was on in a mix of static and memory.

"Nice car," she said with her smoke seesawing on her lips as she searched for a back-pocket lighter. I offered no reply.

My hands were smudged and my throat was dry. It was the perfect moment for a coffee and a cigarette. Even if it was Benson & Hedges.

"Does it drag," she asked looking at me over her Marilyn Monroe sunglasses, as a willow of smoke carried her smile north.

"Does it—" I started, getting ready to boil my blood. Shooting a look south down the lake I said, "Only uphill."

Lyla laughed at me and when she laughed her right elbow kicked out from her body like a pitcher getting ready to strike. Lyla had a red bandana wrapped around her head, a floral halter top, and funny lime-green shorts that led to bright pink flip-flops. She was brown, relaxed and looked at the engine like a hawk over a field of mice. She leaned over and took a good look at the engine. For a while, nothing was said. The song on the radio took my mind to someplace else as I grabbed a splash of coffee and enjoyed the smoke. Seeing the hillsides as though for the first time, I ran my mind across the hilltop horizon as far south as I could look and came back again to the north. When my mind came back to me Lyla was leaning against the car and was looking at me. Her smoke was mostly ashes but that didn't stop her from using all of it.

"Did you find it," she said.

"Find what," I said looking back to the hilltops looking for some obvious formation or animal that I had overlooked.

"Whatever you are looking for," she replied.

"I know what I am looking for," I said turning to put my face inside the engine once more.

"You do?" She laughed. "Well, let me tell you something. What you are looking for is older than you. And older than them hills or that car."

"Jesus," I said. She really was Raymond's Auntie.

"Jesus got nothing to do with it," she replied sipping on her coffee. She turned towards the hills as the drone from an aeroplane far above crawled across the afternoon. Lyla looked into those hills for a moment and began to walk away but stopped and said—

"What you are looking for is not something that can be found. It is only something that can be lost. And when you lose it, let it go. Only then will it come back to you."

That night, I and Raymond started the drive home. The Impala was right low on gas and only got us as far as Enderby. We siphoned gas from a Ford pickup parked outside of a diner after closing. The town had an empty presence like a familiar graveyard that told us to leave soon or to stay a long, long while. We had just got back in the Impala, set on making our way north to Sicamous, when a hitchhiker called out asking for a ride. The voice, though distant and rough, was unmistakable.

It was him.

Brother Francis called out to us again. He was moving slow, walking down the highway, backwards with his left thumb out to the wind.

"Jesus," I said.

"And Mary and Joseph," Raymond added.

We crawled up the road until the high beams caught up to Francis's frame. He had turned his back and was walking up the road with a sluggish gait that suggested drink. But it could have been from a fall from a horse. It was tough to say. He wore a green flannel coat too warm for the season, and brown corduroy slacks. His head was low as though he was laughing, coughing or saying a Hail Mary. I stopped the car for a moment until he turned a look over his shoulder and gave me that empty smile from the Mission.

I drove ahead of him, pulled the Impala over and Raymond hopped out, opened back passenger door. Francis got in without hesitation, and said, "Thanks Moses," and took the back seat like a stowaway pew. Moses was the name of some other kid he took to at the Mission—Moses Mitchell. Moses went missing the summer before but Brother Francis must not have known that. Raymond closed the back seat door and came back in the Impala as I turned on to the highway and headed into the night towards Sicamous.

Nothing was said. The lines on the highway were the only ones spoken. Soon Brother Francis passed out in the back seat. He must have been drinking though he didn't smell at all. Not that I could notice. My knuckles held the road as Raymond kept a steady diet of Exports burning away while Francis snored, sleeping soundly in the back of the Impala.

We drove this way for a time. I couldn't tell how long it was. Usually Raymond would start on with some story I had heard about one too many times, or we'd find some space on the radio to tell us stories we could hardly imagine. "Long Tall Sally," "American Woman," "A Horse With No Name." But on this night, on that road, with Brother Francis in the back seat of the Impala, I and Raymond were quiet, attentive and nearly invisible.

A rattle from the back of the Impala took my mind off of Brother Francis. My first thought went to Uncle Wes and some sleight of hand he may have played on my Impala.

Raymond took to my shift in focus and turned his head to listen. The rattle continued as Raymond gave a "huh." That was enough for me to pull the car over. I sent Raymond to get out and take a look. Raymond said something but all I could hear was Brother Francis' breath. It sounded old, like exhale from glaciers between ice ages.

To the west, darkness held Three Valley Gap like a cup of day-old coffee. To the east, only hints of dawn's truth could be seen. The sound of the roadside creek kept the night with us. In the back seat the limp drunk body of Brother Francis remained. He looked a lot shorter since I saw him last. Maybe it was his drunk slouch. Maybe it was the weight of the glacier upon his flinched shoulders.

Silently, Brother Francis turned his head and said, "Raymond, check the gas cap." Raymond was bent over looking at the back tire. Hearing Brother Francis' voice, he popped his head up and looked into the back seat, looking like a worried boy. I turned the car off, got out of the driver's seat, and went to the back to see what was going on. Sure enough, the siphon hose ran off the side of the car like a floppy arrow. Somehow this blinded drunk knew what the story was. Raymond stood up, dusted off his pants, and looked at me and said, "Well?"

I watched Francis in the back seat. He didn't move. He hardly breathed. He was content, lost and unaware. In a fluid motion, one learned by bailing hay at the Mission, I flung open the Impala's back door and grabbed Brother Francis by the collar and threw him into the creek to sober up. His body hit the water with a clap that rung round Three Valley. For a moment, he floated on his back like the Nazarene. Then, Francis slowly turned and sunk into the shallow water of the roadside creek, his body finding a home among the reeds and muck.

"Fuck," Raymond gasped as we looked into the creek for an awakening. None was forthcoming.

"Ah hell," I said as I hopped from the road into the shallow water below. My hands dug into the water for Brother Francis. I found his shoulders and grasped at his soaked flannel jacket and pulled his head above water. I slipped my arm under his chin as I dragged him to the water's edge, gasping for my own breath in the cold, mucky water of Three Valley Gap.

Raymond leaned over the embankment, his hand on his knees. He looked into the darkness of the ditch to see if I was okay, for any sign of life. I looked up to Raymond as I had my arms around Brother Francis. In that moment Raymond started to laugh. It was slow at first but quickly turned into a real belly laugh as he pointed at me from the embankment.

"Shit, you look like a damn steer wrestler," he said, his whole body shaking.

I looked up the embankment as the crazy Indian laughed at me, his face a flurry of lips and shaking cheeks, and then looked at myself, my forearm under Brother Francis' chin, his body underneath me. And then I started to laugh too.

"Well, Raymond, at least I still have my goddamn teeth!" I said as I released Francis and turned my body to lie flat on the embankment in a laughter of tears, cries, and deep sweats. Somewhere in that sound I found I was the only one who laughed. Raymond had stopped and was watching again. Francis's knuckles had gripped the earth of the embankment beside me, his shoulders slowly rising and falling from his exchange of breath.

I climbed up the embankment. Raymond gave me a once-over as I walked past him and got into the Impala. My boots sloshed into car. The muck and guck of the ditch had begun to cake to my legs. Raymond took one more look towards the water and then joined me in the Impala. We left Brother Francis there. Soaked but alive.

When we got home we told everyone that we kicked the shit out of Brother Francis. The truth was that he had nothing left in him. Francis was empty and long gone before we got there. Everyone said, "Oh ya," "That's good," and "Mmm hmmm," when we told the story the first time. Later, some said they had forgotten Brother Francis. Some found the tale an excuse to ask how much I gave Wes for that '65 Impala, then to say I'd overpaid for such an old and broken down machine. A few tried to trade me for rusted pickups. Nearly everyone asked how Lyla was doing. Later that summer, Raymond got killed by a semi on a walk back from town, and come winter I sold that '65 Impala to my cousin, who said the best cars are the ones you leave behind.

ÉMILIE MONNET

d'*Okinum*

UN BARRAGE DANS LA GORGE

Sur les écrans, le générique bien connu de National Geographic, *puis des captations de castors en action. Émilie descend de la plateforme et expose les faits qui suivent.*

Le 17 juillet 1990, l'été de la résistance d'Oka, un gigantesque barrage de castors a été photographié depuis un satellite de la NASA. Personne n'était au courant de son existence, jusqu'à ce que Google Earth apparaisse . . .

Il se trouve en plein cœur du parc national Wood Buffalo, dans le nord de l'Alberta. Il mesure huit cent cinquante mètres, ce qui est vraiment exceptionnel parce qu'en général, un barrage de castors mesure environ dix mètres.

Plusieurs générations de castors ont travaillé à la construction de ce barrage, et il continue de grossir encore aujourd'hui.

En construisant des barrages, les castors font apparaître de nouvelles étendues d'eau comme des piscines, stagnantes et profondes, où ils peuvent établir leurs loges.

C'est comme s'ils repeuplaient leurs anciens territoires après avoir été chassés sans relâche pendant des siècles.

Temps.

Le castor est la seule espèce
avec l'être humain
qui puisse laisser une trace sur Terre visible depuis l'espace.

Une trace laissée sur la Terre.
Un barrage pour se protéger.
Mais seulement visible depuis le monde des étoiles.

Émilie remonte sur la plateforme, comme si elle était aspirée par ce qui y est projeté. Conversation enregistrée avec sa professeure.

— Ça veut dire quoi, « okinum » ?
— Okinum ? C'est un barrage. Tu vois, c'est comme des squelettes que le castor a été chercher. « Okin », ce sont des os. En fait, c'est comme si c'était tout un empilement de squelettes d'arbres que le castor a fait.
— OK.
— Micha Amik okinum.
— Okinum : barrage de castors.

Temps.

— Comment est-ce qu'on dit « cancer » ?
— Menjesh chapeney.
— Menjesh chapeney ?
— Hmm hmm.
— Ça veut dire quoi ?

— « Cancer. »

— C'est quoi la traduction exacte ?

— « Menjesh », c'est des bibittes ; « chapeney », ça, ça veut dire « maladie », ou « absence de la santé », mais rongée par les bibittes.

— Menjesh chapeney.

Sur les écrans, des images de l'échographie de la gorge d'Émilie se superposent à celles du barrage vu du ciel. Suivent des sons de castors et de raclements de gorge.

TREENA CHAMBERS

From "Hair Raizing"

Mom digs through my belongings looking for a hat of some sort. She finds one in the presents people have been sending me. She hands it over to me, her newly energized daughter. There is nothing that brings me to life like breaking rules.

I adjust the baseball cap on my head trying to cover up the newly showing scalp. "Has Linda told you my plan?" I ask as Dr. D enters my room. I go with the direct approach. He'll see it my way if he believes I'm serious.

"Your counts aren't very high, Treena. Going out isn't a good idea. You need to stay germ free for a while longer. Give your body a few more days," David says. He can see the chances of keeping me from doing this are slim. This is his first year on the wards. He loves his job. But I've seen him try to rationalize what he has to do to my body in the hope of giving me a future.

"I'm going. Are you going to call the guards to keep me from leaving?" Defensive. Shit. That's too much. I should be charming him. Instead, I'm sitting here in my pajamas with a stupid baseball cap on, making demands. I know better.

During our first lumbar puncture and bone marrow aspiration he managed to give me three needle sticks and not draw any fluid. He panicked and wanted to quit and try another day. I had a date with a box of popcorn and a matinee the next day, so I half charmed and half bullied him into one last attempt. That's how

I discovered his secret. If I can make him laugh he will let me do almost anything. "Wrestling with them will be entertaining for the folks at the nurses' station, but you know, with my blood counts it's not such a good idea," I say cheekily. "Please. I need to do this."

"Okay. But, you need to wear a mask. Let's limit the germs as much as possible," Dr. David says. When Treena wouldn't let him in the room this morning all sorts of scenarios were parading through his mind. This is a complication he can help her with. He can give her back a bit of dignity.

I know I've won. The demand for the mask is a farce; he knows that as soon as I leave the building it will be in my pocket. We both know our roles. He sets boundaries. I test them.

"Right. Everyone out. I need to get dressed." I stand up. Whoa. Maybe this isn't such a good idea. Dizziness threatens to bring the floor up to meet me. My knees find their strength. This is a good thing. I can't remember the last time I was outside. Judging by the way my legs are acting they can't remember the last time they were used either. I miss the breeze on my face. "I'll put some clothes on and meet you at the nurses' station, Mom."

Walking out of the elevator on the lobby floor is scary. The walls and elevator keep the Normals out. Now, right now, I pass between the worlds. I walk down the street and eyes slide off me. My exile doesn't show. Not yet.

Glances will linger a moment too long to be comfortable when the hair is gone. Then the guessing games will begin. "What does she have? How sick is she?" These questions will be in their eyes as they turn away, praying I don't notice. We all compare ourselves to others. "I'm fatter than her. Skinnier than her. I'm not totally happy. At least I'm not sick like that girl I saw on the street." I used to play that game. Now, things are too complicated for that game. I reach in my pocket and rub the mask Dr. D wanted me to wear.

"Good morning, ladies," the barber says as we enter the shop. "What can I do for you?"

"I need to shave my head."

"You don't want to do that. Mom, tell her. You have beautiful hair."

I take my cap off. His eyes widen.

"Oh." How inadequate, he thinks. Kids from the hospital walk past his shop. They have been an abstraction. They walk by his shop. He makes up stories to entertain himself on slow days. What they have. Where they came from. Then this one comes in and tears the game apart.

"Well, um, first we need to trim it with scissors. Um. Do you want to keep some? Um, as a souvenir maybe?" He can't believe he used those words. Shit. A souvenir. He doesn't know what to say. "I mean as a reminder." Small talk here is about hockey, politics, or people's aches and pains. None of that seems appropriate with this young girl. Today, he thinks, I will remember how lucky I am. A lesson in gratitude.

"Okay, start trimming then," I say, "and no keepsakes." Poor guy doesn't know what to say, and I am too tired to smooth things over. The sicker I get the more people around me expect me to help them feel comfortable. People look at me. They see sickness, bad luck, and bad karma. They see what they want to see.

I watch as the barber reaches down to run his fingers through my hair. It feels like a reflex. Something he does at the start of every cut. When he draws his hand back long blond strands are woven through his fingers and cover his palms. He brushes the strands from his hands, and I can feel tendons clench his stomach. It is as if he pulled on a thread that was knotted inside him. He starts to trim the hair and watches my reflection in the mirror. I started bravely, but the front is crumbling. With each snip of the scissors a layer of my protective shell is cut away. Tears start down my face, slowly, then unchecked as more hair disappears. By the time he has trimmed enough to use the clippers he can't stop his tears. He tries to smile, wavers, and looks away. He feels as if he is the one making me sick. He reaches for his clippers and flicks them on. They hum so loud the sound dominates the shop. He flinches. The clippers vibrate so strongly he can't hold on. They slip from his hand.

I can see Mom watching the barber. He can't finish the job. This is what she was trying to protect me from. She doesn't want me to feel responsible for the fear I see in people's eyes. She didn't want me to see the moment when awareness changes to pity. People act omnipotent. I force them to confront mortality. With this new war for my life, those emotions are not ones Mom wants me exposed to.

Mom catches the falling clippers and steps between the barber and me. She raises the clippers and buzzes the remaining hair on my head. When she's done, she puts the clippers back on the barber's counter and runs her hands over my scalp. Smooth as a baby's. She had started to treat me as her equal. I'm not.

ELAINE McARTHUR

From "Queen Bee"

I closed my eyes and thought about the last time she told me a story in her room. It was late summer and she was sitting in her wheelchair with the golden afternoon streaming in. We sat quietly for a while, enjoying our afternoon tea and snacks I had brought and the sound of the crickets and the steady hum of the bees that gathered around the blooming apple tree just outside her window. After a few moments in the comfortable silence, she began to speak, her voice soft and comforting as she began another story about her time at a residential school.

"There were these big girls in school," she began softly. "We had to call the biggest one the Queen or they'd beat us up. We were all afraid of her, me and my friends. We had to hand wash their socks and underwear at night before bed." Mom took another slow sip of tea. "The nuns knew but they didn't say anything. This one time the Queen was after us to pick berries for her and her friends. We had no choice but to go."

She fell silent then. Her hand shook and spilled her tea as she took another sip. I lay on her bed on my side hugging her pillow, settling in for a good story.

"Well, one day I finally got fed up with the Queen and her gang always picking on us and pushing us around. They even picked on the little ones. The Queen and her gang made them clean off their shoes and tidy up their lockers."

"Which school was this?" I asked.

"Crooked Lake." She swallowed hard and looked out her window at the majestic crab apple tree blooming outside in plain view. Every winter she worried about her tree when the rabbits came to eat the bark. In the summer, she worried about the bees that gathered and buzzed at her screen when she would leave her window open for summer air. Her first autumn at the home, she had the staff out there picking the apples so she could do some cooking. I arrived for my usual visit when a nurse inside told me she was out back with some of the staff. I walked around the corner to see three homecare nurses standing near Mom reaching for crab apples. Mom was in her wheelchair pointing at apples.

"Anyways, I was out there picking berries," Mom brought me back to the present, "and I put them in my apron because we had no pail or anything to carry them back in. Me and the other girls were picking and talking about how much we hated the big girls and trying to figure out what we could do to make them leave us alone."

She took another sip of tea, and, in her soft voice, barely above a whisper, said: "There were lots of bees last year, they kept me awake in the afternoons. And once there was a spider. He was big and ugly. I threw a shoe at him over there." She pointed to the floor just below her now open window. "I guess he must have got in 'cause I left the window open overnight. The nurses don't like us doing that. Now I know why." She was silent for a moment staring at the tree. "I threw a shoe at him and yelled. He stopped moving and stared at me."

"Ew, he stared at you?" I asked incredulously.

She gave a little laugh and fell silent again, getting lost in her thoughts.

"So you went picking berries?" I asked.

"I found a beehive and had an idea. I dumped my berries and took off my apron. I wrapped it around the hive and carried it back like a bag. I don't remember if I got stung, probably did, but I hated the Queen so much I didn't care." She stopped here and gave a little chuckle. Her fingers, crooked and stiff from Parkinson's, grabbed a handful of her favourite snack, soft cheese chips.

"When we got back, no one was in the locker room, so I dumped the hive in the Queen's locker. I shut the door fast so none got out. My friends and I were scared, but I wanted to get back at the phony Queen so bad. Their humming was loud and echoed in the tin locker. I was afraid that the noise would alert someone to the trap, but was relieved after a while when the humming settled down and was so low one could barely hear it.

"When the Queen came down after she told me, 'There better be berries for me, Hazel, or you're going to get it.' I watched her open her locker with a yank, while she continued glaring, but suddenly all the bees came pouring out."

Mom stopped and smiled remembering that glorious moment.

"Bahhhhh!" She screamed. "Bees were everywhere, flying straight at us, bouncing off the windows and our clothes, buzzing and humming. Then everyone started screaming. We ran outside, even the nuns were running and screaming while swatting at bees. I didn't think of what I was going to do after the bees came out, I only thought of seeing the Queen with all her bees." Mom giggled.

"Her arms were flailing like this." She waved her skinny arms like she was swatting at bees. I imagined everyone running for cover.

"The Queen was shaking her head trying to chase them off her. Wherever she ran, her bees followed. We were running away from her and her bees. Even her gang ran away from her."

"Of course I got a good beating after from the nuns, but I didn't care. I kept thinking of the bees in the Queen's mean face. We didn't have to pick berries for the big girls after that."

The smile still on her face, Mom went quiet again after a moment, and then her smile faded to something like sadness. A nurse came in to check on her and left the door ajar when she left. Outside noises in the hallway—the sounds of a TV and the voices of the nurses—invaded our space, not unkindly but rather reassuringly.

I knew Mom was getting tired because she began moving her hands as if she was eating something with a spoon then chewing on food, her eyes clenched tight. She took another spoonful of her dream chewing. I sat up.

"Let's change places. You nap. I'll sit."

"No, I'm okay." She shook her head and took another spoonful of her dream.

"Yes, you nap. I'll watch TV until you wake up. I won't go anywhere, I promise," I said firmly.

"Okay." she gave up and lay down and slept. I sat and watched TV until one of the nurses came in to wake her for dinner.

I stood up, stretched, and walked over to her. "I'll come see you next weekend, and meanwhile I'll call you. Next time I'll bring us a small pizza to share." I kissed her on the cheek. "I love you. Eat lots and get some rest."

"Okay, my girl."

As her door closed behind me, I heard her pipe up: "Pepperoni!"

J.D. KURTNESS

de *De vengeance*

Ma liste de noms réfère à quelques anecdotes. C'est tout ce que j'ai trouvé à racler de ces années-là.

RÉAL et Carolanne

Je n'ai jamais su qui était RÉAL, outre que son nom fut gravé à l'Exacto à l'intérieur de l'avant-bras de la fille assise à ma droite en classe. Je la vis faire. Elle s'appelait Carolanne, je m'en souviens parce que ça me faisait penser au film *Poltergeist*. « Ne t'approche pas de la lumière, Carolanne! » Outre son nom, elle n'avait rien en commun avec cette petite fille blonde si mignonne. Notre Caro avait des traits ronds, le nez couvert de comédons et une épaisse chevelure noire. Elle dégageait cette odeur que j'ai toujours associée à la pauvreté, un mélange de cigarette et d'assouplisseur à linge. Elle faisait partie d'un groupe auquel je ne parlais jamais, assez mystérieux, dont la plupart des membres avaient doublé une année. Ceux-ci passaient leur récréation dans un coin de la cour qu'on appelait le fumoir, une surface d'environ cent pieds carrés où il était permis de fumer. C'était l'époque où n'importe qui pouvait s'acheter des cigarettes, même les enfants. Ça ne fait pas si longtemps.

Le règlement stipulait que quiconque désirait fumer pouvait le faire dans cette zone-là, mais évidemment seuls certains élèves pouvaient espérer le faire, puisque ce territoire était chèrement disputé. Les autres fumeurs devaient attendre d'être à l'extérieur des terrains de l'école, sinon ils s'exposaient à des représailles.

Quand Carolanne passait à côté de vous dans l'allée de la classe, c'est comme si on avait secoué un cendrier et une feuille de Bounce simultanément. Elle était asthmatique. Son doux râle m'accompagna durant tout mon secondaire 1. Congestionnée en permanence, elle garda la bouche ouverte durant tout son processus de gravure. Je pouvais juger de l'intensité de la douleur qu'elle s'infligeait selon la cadence de son râlement. Il s'accélérait lorsqu'elle grattait sa peau plus profondément avec la lame.

Avec un prénom pareil, RÉAL provoquait la risée générale. Il était l'objet de toutes les spéculations. Toute la classe était consciente du petit manège de Carolanne, même la prof. Pourquoi ne réagissait-elle pas? Une pudeur, le malaise de regarder les gens laids, le refus de les fixer assez longtemps pour que le regard focalise? Carolanne était tellement repoussante, avec sa peau grasse, son nez luisant, sa bouche ouverte, son odeur, son râle. Le dégoût qu'elle provoquait déviait l'attention. Elle avait son propre champ magnétique qui courbait tous vos sens. Elle aurait pu construire une bombe sur son petit bureau d'écolière, on l'aurait laissé faire.

Cette fille est devenue pharmacienne. Je le sais parce qu'elle m'a fait une demande d'amitié Facebook il y a quelques années. Demande acceptée. Elle y publie sans distinction les spéciaux d'Halloween de son Pharmaprix, des images de sa nouvelle maison et des phrases qui conjuguent sa tristesse de faire des fausses couches à répétition.

La petite sœur de Marie-Lilou est devenue un ange aujourd'hui, voilà je l'écris ici pour ne pas avoir à répondre à toutes vos questions en personne pour le moment, merci de respecter notre deuil, blablabla. Il m'a fallu toute ma volonté pour ne pas répondre qu'il fallait voir le bon côté des choses puisque pendant encore cinq jours, on pouvait faire imprimer ses photos pour 0,10 $ chacune à sa pharmacie.

J'aimerais tant lui demander si elle a fait zigouiller ses cicatrices au laser, mais je n'ose pas. Il n'y a pas de Réal dans ses contacts, et elle en a beaucoup. Partir en affaires provoque souvent ce genre de comportements sur les réseaux sociaux: les gens amassent les contacts pour la visibilité, pour faire mousser les ventes. Il y en a qui le font sans raison.

NATHAN NIIGAN NOODIN ADLER

From *Ghost Lake*

Coyote

He is lost.

Lost. Lost. Lost.

How did it happen?

Fanon knows the land like the back of his hand—hell, he knows it as well as his own dick. Or at least thought he did. Maybe it is the sin of pride? The sin of over-confidence? The sin of taking for granted his ability to navigate and find his way out in the bush. But Fanon doesn't think he is overconfident, doesn't think he places more trust in his own abilities than they warrant—he is good—it isn't bravado to acknowledge this, is it?

Besides, Nshoomis says there is no such thing as sin, or damnation, or hell. "Those are all foreign concepts, they don't exist in Ojibwe."

But still, somehow. It has happened. Sin or no sin, he is lost.

It is late October. They're out hunting, fishing, checking the traplines. The trip is planned as a two-week expedition, camping at various sites, to share traditional skills and knowledge. The party consists of Owen and Oogie Neyananoosic, Charlie Mushkeg, Valene, some of the Zeds; Zoe and her brother Zeamus, their old uncle Zeno. Fanon—and his Mshoomis, who leads the party, Giizis Dibikiziwinan. Giizis is getting on in years, though he's still in hardy condition.

"This trip isn't only about learning from your Elders." Zeno raises his arms at the start of their excursion, expounding like the Ancient Greek philosopher after whom he's presumably been named. "It is also about learning from the land, and learning about survival."

"Some of these Elders are long-winded." Fanon elbows Zeamus in the ribs.

As one of the oshkaabeywis, a *helper*, at twenty-six years old, Fanon is older than the other youth, who are still kids really. He's probably closest in age to Zoe and Zeamus, who are still years younger. Teenagers.

Owen, Oogie, Zeno, and Giizis are the knowledge keepers.

"We encourage you all to show independence." Giizis eyeballs the assembled youths, burdened under the weight of backpacks, pup tents, and other camping gear. "This is to build confidence and gain a sense of your own abilities."

Fanon takes the message to heart, and plans a solo trip at the end of their first week out.

"I think I'll go on a little day-trip," he tells Giizis and Zeno at the morning campfire. "Check on our trapline." Brews himself a cup of strong black coffee. It's still early, the others are still sleeping. Sunlight filters through evergreens, and it's actually clear for once.

"Try and be back before dark." Giizis stirs sweetener into his coffee. "And stop wearing cologne! You smell like bear-bait."

"Might as well marinate yourself." The corners of Zeno's eyes crinkle, and he yawns.

Fanon sniffs an arm pit, smelling himself.

He decides to set out on foot, rather than taking the dogsled. He leaves a trail of footprints in the fresh snow behind him. It crunches satisfyingly under his boots as he walks. Heading north and west towards the high-ground where the trees give way to more open terrain, rock and hills, and scattered tree-stands, the edges of which they've been skirting on their trek. He'll check on the traps they've left along the way, and return later in the day, burdened with the weight of their catch.

A few light flakes drift down. Nothing to worry about. The sky has been leaden for the past few days, and nothing has come of it.

He is wrong though.

By mid-afternoon, he reaches the highland, and the few flakes that were coming down have become a blizzard—and he didn't bring snowshoes. The few inches that came down in the morning are now up to his knees—and getting deeper. He trudges through it like molasses. The pantlegs of his jeans are wet. His body heat melts the snow and it drips into his boots. His feet are wet. Not good. The muscles in his legs burn with exertion. It is getting harder and harder to walk. Every step is more troublesome than the last. He considers turning back. But he's come so far. Maybe he's better off finding somewhere to make camp for the night?

Darkness comes so early now; it will be getting dark by 6:30 p.m., and it will be full dark by 7 p.m. Fanon wishes he brought more food. He only brought a sandwich, and the tough slog through the snow is sapping his energy—he can already feel his stomach grumbling in complaint. Every trap he checks is empty, otherwise he'd have a ready-made meal.

Fanon decides to keep trudging until he finds a trap with something he can cook, then he'll stop for the night and make camp. Light a fire. Head back in the morning after the storm. It won't be hard for his Mshoomis to guess what happened. His grandfather won't worry—Giizis knows Fanon has the skills he needs to survive on his own for more than a night or two.

He'll be fine.

The blizzard continues to get worse though, until Fanon can't see anything more than a foot or two in any direction. Sleet lashes at his eyes so he has to squint against the gale. He can feel his beard and eyelashes become encrusted with ice crystals. Old man winter glitter beard. He won't be able to find any traps in this weather. And he certainly can't find his way back in this weather either. He'll have to hunker down somewhere and wait for the storm to pass.

The grey light of day is beginning to bleed from the sky. He needs to find somewhere promising as a shelter. The sooner the better. When he sees the shapes of boulders rising in the distance through a break in the sleet, and a small stand of trees, Fanon makes his way towards the darker shapes against the white-on-white. Ground and sky are almost inseparable, one from the other. It's disorienting, not being able to tell which way is which.

When he reaches the boulders, he finds some shelter between the hollow of two rocks. It'll do. He collects enough branches to light a small fire in the protection afforded by the windbreak. The temperature drops. He passes a long, cold night, not being able to get much sleep, lest his fire gutter and go out, leaving him in the cold and dark without any light or warmth. The wind still finds its way to the flames, feeds the fuel too much oxygen, making the wood burn too quick. The fire needs to be constantly fed. In the morning, there is a slight lightening to the sky, which slowly gives way to the greyness of dawn, and then to the greyness of day, but the storm doesn't let up. The blizzard howls strong as ever, the sleet whips every stand of trees and outcropping of rock with equal violence.

If he can make his way back to the tree-line, there will be more protection from the driving snow. It's best to head back. Fanon pees on the small fire—not that it's likely to spread. Trudges through the blizzard again, in the direction—he's almost certain—is the way he came the day before, but his tracks in the snow are long gone. Even moments after they're made, his steps fill in with new snowfall and are quickly smoothed out by the gale. When he looks back, he can't see where he's been, almost as if he dropped out of the sky, or as if he's a ghost. No footprints. He can't use the tracks like breadcrumbs.

The sky is white. The ground is white. The only thing that lets Fanon know he's still walking on the earth is the solidity of the ground beneath his feet. And even that isn't very solid; he sinks up to his knees with every step. He passes the occasional stand of trees, and small outcroppings of rock, which are nothing more than indistinct shadows. By mid-day he is already exhausted from his efforts and—even worse—he is lost.

Even with the deep snow that makes every step a battle, he should have made it to the tree-line by now. Even with the hail that pelts him, he should have made it to the tree-line by now. Vicious beads of ice blast any bits of exposed flesh—it will look as if he's got a sunburn, but the burn won't be from the sun, it will be from the wind. Somehow, he got turned around in the seamless white, sky and land and land and sky. White on white on white. He can't be hard on himself. Not even Owen, or Zeno or his old grandpa Giizis predicted this snowstorm—they would have warned him if they'd known.

And isn't that peculiar? With their combined experience, shouldn't they have predicted the coming storm? It's hard to believe they didn't know the snow was coming. They knew, and they didn't warn him. Maybe they thought he could handle it? Maybe they thought he had the necessary survival skills, so they weren't worried—they knew where he was if he truly got into trouble. They could come find him. A test of his mettle. Or maybe he was overthinking things? Maybe the storm had simply caught them all off guard—no matter how much experience you have—nature doesn't always cooperate, sometimes she throws a blizzard or two out of left field. No one can predict the future accurately 100% of the time—not even Elders.

Fanon trudges through the snow, *pushing* his legs through the snow like a plow. It's now so deep he can't lift his feet out of the deep snow in order to plunge them back in. It makes the going even slower. And the snow is heavy, his thigh muscles and calves ache, his toes are numb icicles. He hopes he doesn't have frostbite. And he is hungry, and he is tired, and he is weak. His brain is beginning to fog. He can feel it happening. It's becoming increasingly difficult to formulate a plan, to make a decision. Should he keep walking? Is he even walking in the right direction? Should he give up and rest for a while? Or make camp for another night?

No, Fanon decides. He is running low on energy, so he needs to keep walking while he still has the ability, and sitting still will simply sap the strength from his limbs, even with a fire burning. He needs to reach the tree-line.

Fanon prays to his manitous; Grandfather Sun, and Grandmother Moon, Mother Earth, the wind and the snow even—and Kitchi Manitou, the creator—he prays that he is walking in the right direction. The longer he walks the more energy he expends, and still the snowstorm doesn't let up. The light bleeds from the sky and he knows darkness is approaching again for a second night, and that he will soon have to find shelter, and build a fire, and keep the fire going or he will freeze to death.

So that's what he does. He finds a stand of trees, a depression in the earth, and hunkers down for another night, in the protection afforded by the roots of a fallen tree. He throws a few branches over top in a quick lean-to, and soon has a cozy shelter constructed, with a small fire burning merrily in a pit. And though the snow still falls, and the wind still howls, he is relatively safe and warm though exhausted, and hungry, and weak. There is nothing he can do until morning. So he prepares a large pile of wood to fuel the fire, so he won't have to get up multiple times during the night, and tries to get some rest. This time he actually manages to get some sleep; he is so exhausted, he can't stave it off. Though he has to relight the fire twice during the night, waking up from the cold to find the fire has burned down to ash.

In the morning—a thin, grey lightening to the sky—his fire has burned down again to a few blackened sticks. He is cold and his limbs are stiff, though he knows he mustn't stay in place. He has to keep moving. He has to keep moving while he still has the energy. He has to keep moving.

Fanon trudges through the white on white. The howling wind and the pelting sleet lashing at his eyes, blinding him. And still he walks. And walks. And walks. And knows he is lost. He must have become disoriented, and walked in a wrong direction, or else he's been walking in circles, for he should have retraced his steps, four times over by now, or been back at his starting point, for the number of steps he's taken, working twice as hard, pushing his legs through the weight of the snow.

Towards mid-day, Fanon knows he's in trouble. He can barely put one foot in front of the other anymore. He feels weakness in his muscles, in his veins, in his wrists, at his throat, at his ankles and in his heart. He is so screwed. He might as well give up. And he is tired. So tired. The snow now seems soft and fluffy. Inviting. Like a down-filled comforter. King bed. White goose-feathers. And in the distance.

He hears Coyotes.

Awooooooh. Awoooonnnh. Woooh.

Howling.

They have a higher register than the howl of wolves. Long mournful notes like a train, and short sharp caws less drawn out. Whirring. Crying. Crowing. Bird barks. A spooky whistling concerto. How far away? He wonders. How many miles? How many kilometres? Fanon knows they are probably farther away than they sound. Much farther. Though they sound close. Like they are just over the next ridge. But it's so quiet. Sound can travel far out here on the highlands. But it's difficult to judge, the way the little valleys and bowls direct and redirect echoes. And the snow acts like a blanket, muffling. They could be quite near, or they could be quite far. Fanon's guess is that they are still several kilometres away, at least.

He continues walking. Trudging. Plowing through the sleet and snow. With the sound of coyotes. Yipping and calling to each other. Like they are talking to each other. And that's exactly what it sounds like. Like they are talking to each other. Calling back and forth. They sound like voices. Human voices. Maybe the valleys and rock walls are playing tricks? Maybe they aren't coyotes? Maybe they are human after all? Voices distorted and stretched out to sound like coyotes? Those aren't coyotes! Or if there were coyotes earlier, what he hears now is definitely the sound of people, laughing and talking, though their voices are stretched and distorted by distance—they are human. He is certain of it now. But what are they doing out here? Has he stumbled so far off course? Are they hikers? Or campers? Or has he come across some sort of field party?

Fanon changes course, heading towards the sound of distant revelry. He hopes he isn't making a mistake by deviating from the route he chose, but it hasn't panned out so far. So what the hell. He knows based on his position, and the layout of the land, where their camp *should* be, so he heads in that direction. But he could be wrong. He's definitely lost his way once already. And it sure sounds like people. He can almost make out the occasional word. It sounds like a good party. Whoever it is, they sound like they're having a gay old time. The closer he gets, the more distinct the voices become.

He ascends a small rise. Ahead he can see the glow of a fire burning, obscured by a thick cluster of trees, branches, and the shapes of people sitting around a fire are thrown into silhouette. Talking, laughing, drinking, and eating. They don't seem to be troubled by the cold weather. They seem to be enjoying themselves.

He's saved!

Fanon makes his way through the tangle of trees, and into a small clearing where a group of mostly young people hang about. Drinking. Talking. Laughing.

"You're welcome to join the party." An older man stands upon seeing him. He'd been sitting on a rock near the fire. His face is flushed with drink, or the heat of the flames. The man gestures welcomingly to the circle of jovial, rosy faces, and the light of their fire.

"Oh, thank the manitous." Fanon falls to his knees. "I've been walking for so damn long. I thought my ass was going to freeze off."

"And well it might have." The older man comes forward, hands clasped before him. "You're lucky to have found our get-together. Nobody disturbs us out here." And the man throws his head back and laughs. Cackles really. Odd little dude. Kind of scrawny. His dark grizzled beard is streaked with white. Fanon doesn't know why this is so funny, but he is grateful for the warmth cast by the fire. He wonders if they are nudists or swingers or into some other kind of kink that they need to come all the way out here just to get their kicks.

Someone thrusts a bottle into his hands. Firewater. And before long, he's warm, and he has a satisfying buzz going on after only a few swigs. He hasn't eaten much in the last couple days. He is introduced all around, and is introduced to each in turn, though he is so light-headed and delirious with relief, he has trouble keeping track of everyone's name. If they are telling him, it seems to be going in one ear and out the other. Maybe too many to remember. Everyone is in such high spirits, laughing and joking and teasing each other.

Fanon isn't immune to their taunts.

"So got lost did you?"

"I think I almost died." And for some reason, this is suddenly utterly hilarious, they are all howling with laughter, the whole circle of faces crack open to show their teeth, and Fanon is howling right along with them. He is laughing so hard his stomach muscles hurt, he is laughing so hard tears form at the corner of his eyes, and he is laughing so hard he is gasping to draw in breath between bouts of hilarity.

They pull at his goatee and laugh at the streak of white at his temple. "Kind of young to be *going grey* already aren't you?" More laughter. More cackling. Fanon is howling with laughter. What is so G-D-damned funny? Fanon really has no idea. Is he high? Is he simply delirious from starvation and exhaustion? He doesn't know, and he doesn't care, he's having too much G-D fun to care.

"Everyone in our family has it," Fanon tries to explain between fits of laughter. "The patch of grey. It's genetic."

It must be the lack of calories. The alcohol has gone straight to his head. And all the stress from his journey is being released, endorphins spinning, all the muscles in his legs relax like warm jelly. Then there is the tantalizing smell of roasting meat, and a shank is shoved into his face. He is ravenous and doesn't hesitate to tear off chunks of flesh with his teeth. It is slightly charred on the outside and under-cooked on the inside, but it's the most delicious thing Fanon has ever tasted, and he isn't going to complain. It is food, and he is STARVING.

The merriment continues late into the night, they dance and twirl and sing all though the snowstorm which continues to gust outside the thicket. They are well stocked with food, and drink, and supplies. There are smiles all around. A delightful group of people. A pretty young girl has clearly taken a shine to him. The girl sits next to him, touching his arm as he talks and drinks. The woman has the most interesting shade of brown eyes, almost amber-yellow. So slanted they could have been oriental. Another young woman, with silver eyes—though no less captivating—sits on his right, and the two women tease and joke and compete for his attention. Not in a jealous way, instead they are playful and good-natured in their rivalry. Mischievous even. The way they share looks, and laugh at him when he asks, "What's so funny?" But they won't tell him. Maybe their interest in him is due to the fact that he is a newcomer to their group? He gets the sense they all know each other really well.

He is fresh meat.

Who knew that his near-death due to exposure would lead him to such an unlikely party? At some point during the night, the young women—who are both close to him in age—lead him a short distance away from the fire and offer to share a sleeping bag. "It will be warmer if we share." The girl with the amber-coloured eyes smiles. "It is a very cold night." The woman with silver eyes has a matching grin.

Fanon smiles back, and they climb into the blankets. The two women are beautiful. Their long hair is so soft and sleek, like silk flowing down their backs. Their eyes are like honey and moonlight, large and captivating. Hungry even. They smell of woodsmoke from the fire, and the softness of summer. They are gentle, but insistent, and neither one seems to mind sharing more than his warmth. In fact, they seem thrilled. Uninhibited. He's never met women like this. Afterwards they hold each other in a pile.

And Fanon is grateful for their warmth. It is a very cold night. He falls asleep in their arms, happy and content.

Fanon feels a light touch on one of his eyelashes. A rock is poking into his ribs. He shifts uncomfortably but doesn't want to withdraw entirely from the drowsy state of unconsciousness. He's enjoying his sleep. But the ground is hard. And he needs to pee. He's cold. The fire must have burned down.

He cracks an eyelid. Sunlight blurring through his lashes. So the sun has already risen. He opens them, sees the sky through the branches above. The sky is blue and clear of clouds. It's stopped snowing! The storm has passed. Finally. And then he remembers. *The party. The beer, the food—the women!* That's when he comes fully awake, realizing how cold he is. And alone. Where are the women who kept him company through the night? He sits up. Looks around the clearing. Everybody is gone.

And what's more, there is no sign of a party.

No empty beer bottles. No cigarette butts. No ashes where there should have been a cold fire pit, with a few embers still smoldering—no, there is nothing! No impressions in the ground where bodies slept, no footprints in the snow, or trail indicating the direction in which the people retreated as they made their way through the deep snow.

Correction—there are no human footprints. There are plenty of other footprints. Paw-prints. Paw-prints are everywhere in the snow. A swirl of paw-prints like a whirlwind in all directions, dissipating and concentrating in frequency as they change in distance and proximity from where he'd slept in the snow. He sits at their centre, the centre of the storm of paw-prints littering the snow.

Surrounding him in a slowly expanding concentric circle, like a galaxy of rotating stars.

Coyote paw-prints. He recognizes the marks. They aren't so uncommon that he couldn't recognize these tracks. And he is a decent tracker. This isn't his first hunting trip. He knows what a coyote print looks like. Four claws. Four large round toes, closer together than a dog's. And a rounded triangular palm.

And. They. Are. Everywhere.

Lying on the ground a short distance from him is what remains of the carcass of a deer. The sightless eyes stare at him. Glistening milky white. Ribs curve like the concave in a stringed instrument, flesh stripped from the bone. The deer has been unwrapped, torn apart like a flower. The snow is drenched in carnage. Red on white and red on white. And closer to hand, the shank of one leg, the hoof and some fur still attached. It's been gnawed on. The shank of the leg retains the impression of teeth. Human teeth. Fanon raises his hand to his mouth, and his hand comes away bloody where it dripped down his chin and congealed. The front of his jacket is stained. He remembers the steaming, delicious flavour of the meat, and realizes it couldn't have been cooked. There is no indication of a campfire.

No beer bottles. No cigarette butts. No sleeping bags.

Just the coyote prints everywhere, surrounding him in a galaxy radiating outward from his centre. *And oh god!* The thought struck him. *What he'd done with those women?* Did that happen too? Or was it all a dream? Was his mind concocting lies to protect his psyche from the horrors he was forced to endure in order to survive?

Fanon stumbles to his feet. Staggers from the thicket of trees and takes his bearings. From where he stands, he can see the tree-line. He'd been a stone's-throw from the relative safety of the forest. Who knows how many hours he'd spent, wandering, mere yards from reaching his goal? But the blizzard had hidden everything, with visibility next to zero. He was lucky to have survived. He was lucky he hadn't wandered in the wrong direction entirely. He should have hunkered down, and waited for the storm to pass, instead of expending all his energy in futile efforts, and becoming swallowed in delirium. Hindsight is 20/20.

Fanon walks, descending from the highlands, making his way back to the camp, where he knows his grandfather Giizis and the others will be waiting for his return, if they had not already set out searching for him. Someone would have been left at the camp, just in case he came back, while everyone was out searching for him.

He tries not to think on other things. Tries not to think of the party that he thought he'd crashed. Tries not to think of the people he'd met. Tries not to think of the night that didn't happen. Tries not to think of people that don't exist. It's all so confusing. Had they saved him? Fanon is certain, that if he hadn't stumbled upon that "party"—he would be dead. He wouldn't have survived the storm. Overcome by exhaustion and hypothermia.

When he gets back to camp, his grandfather Giizis leaps from his seat by the fire, and rushes to greet him. Wraps him in a large blanket, pushes a flask of Rusty into his hands to warm him. Owen and Zeno are out searching for him, and Giizis stayed behind with the other youths to hold down the fort in case he returned. They gather around him with a million questions, happy to see him alive.

Everyone knows how dangerous it can be out on the land during rough weather. They weren't sure if he would make it. Not even the most experienced hunters and trappers are immune to making mistakes, or getting caught out in a storm. Shit happens, and sometimes people died. But Fanon is lucky.

"I hope you realize that." Giizis's face is a mass of wrinkles.

In the distance, a coyote howls. And Fanon feels his face flush with heat.

What has he done? What has he done?

But, at least, he's still alive.

ÉDOUARD ITUAL GERMAIN

de *Ni kistisin / Je me souviens*

NI KISTISIN / JE ME SOUVIENS

Sur les murs gris
La gueule du requin câlin
Sa voix grave
Pleine de tristesse

Vous m'entourez
Au versant de l'abîme
Emmêlant votre plaisir
Où se cache l'enfer
Autour d'un étang
Où je m'enfonce
Pour sentir le poids
De vos excès
Comme un long fantôme

Livré en un lit nu
Pour amusettes
Ravivant votre image
À côté des ruines
Me frayant un chemin
Dans le grand cercle
Je remonte l'espoir sacré
Des grands sages

NI8INA8IN / MON PRÉSENT

Dans les contreforts du rêve
Je m'éveille
Scène du jour ou du soir
Je me rassure et m'effraie
Je vois l'ombre bleuie

Un bruit d'eau
Berce un enfant
Et ces tranquilles forêts
Qui m'accueillent
Bercent toute l'enfance

Sur ce tableau
Se forme mon JE

ICHK8TE8 / FEU

J'aimerais partager avec toi
Ce feu d'amitié
Balancé par la brise
Le vent vient en courant
Le vent fait chanter
Ce que je suis en train de vivre
Face à la lune
Je suis un sans-abri

Certains jours, mes larmes viennent
Du fragile
Sombrant dans mes vagues
Je hurle mes blessures
Mes verbes sont à l'imparfait

Les hauts et les bas
Comme un oiseau blessé
Dans les bas-fonds
Où j'ai tant traîné
Où je suis passé
Où j'ai laissé une trace sur le sable
De quelles langues sont tes mots
Pour la vie

TANYA TAGAQ

From *Split Tooth*

There are too many foxes this year. It usually happens in a four- to seven-year cycle, all dictated by the rains and melt. Plenty of rain means that the lemmings and their young are forced above ground, where they are easy prey for the fox pups. If too many foxes survive, there won't be enough food for them when winter comes along.

They populate the dump, and all garbage cans in town are full of them. I once saw five foxes in one rusted garbage can. Some become rabid and all the children need to walk to school carrying a stick, preferably with a nail in it. All of the houses in Nunavut must be built on stilts because the permafrost makes it impossible to sink foundations. The space under the house makes a perfect hiding place for foxes. Foxes are such steadfast and mysterious creatures. If a wolf and a lynx mated, perhaps their love child would be Fox, who seems to embody the uncanny agility and size of a cat coupled with the strength and durability of a canine. My friend Eugene had to get rabies shots in his tummy after being bitten; it did not look pleasant. I was proud of him for not crying. Let's avoid rabies.

My father and I go out with the handgun to kill some foxes. Satisfying dry cracks and snaps of sound as the gun goes off. I feel like a hero for an instant, saving the foxes from a slow death of starvation. My father is strong, self-assured. I hope that someday this fortitude emerges from my fragile psyche. The foxes run. The foxes die. I mourn them, but I understand that there is danger in mourning for those who would not mourn for you in return. Empathy is for those who can afford it. Empathy is for the privileged.

Empathy is not for Nature.

Our family had dogs that would have to be buried or put out of their misery. My father always took care of his work, even if it was mercy-killing our family pets. He did it without allowing room for regret. He just did it. Like how we are all born, like how we all die. No choice, only action. These foxes will die of starvation; better to put them out of their misery. These foxes will harm schoolchildren; better to put them out of their misery. These humans will destroy the earth; better to put them out of their misery. Right now we are Earth Eaters, but I want to be a blood lover, an oil spewer, someone with a great wingspan, a spirit sipper, a flesh licker. I want it all. I kill a mountain of foxes in my dreams. Mercy killings, but I do enjoy it.

Speaking of tonight's dream: the sky is the kind of orange that only happens in the fall after the midnight sun begins to retreat. Rolling hills of sandstone rock look like pages of books, making it impossible to walk except for thin paths of spines or else you lose your balance. The path is guarded by sentries, hundred-foot-tall polar bears, who are all facing south. I must pass them one by one. I'm terrified but know it must be done. These are beasts of Protection and Warning. I am thankful they remain still as I meekly seek passage through their domain. The sun is setting and the sky is crisscrossed with airplanes, each leaving plumes of thick grey sickness. None of the planes can fly past the line of sentries. Only half of the sky lives while the other half dies. Dead skies. The sentries can only hold the balance for so long.

We ARE the land, same molecules, and same atoms. The land is our salvation. Save Our Souls.

⁂

The storm has caused a whiteout. Thick flakes of snow coupling with ferocious wind. The snowflakes turn tiny and reveal seven sundogs on the horizon. The light is blazing. It's the New Sun. The flakes turn fat again and take the visions away. The snow begins to oscillate between thick and thin flakes in a breath like rhythm, causing chaos. I am a witness. I am naked but not cold. We are in spirit flesh form. We walk towards the sun. Wandering on the land, I slice some meat off my own bones to eat. It is the only flesh available and my spirit is starving. It doesn't hurt. I am hungry, hungry for justice, hungry for truth. My flesh keeps growing back but the scars are bad. The scars are too tough to eat so I keep cutting off pieces in new zones of fresh flesh. We reach bone on both calves. My spine is elastic. I am grey and numb, hungry. It's getting colder. I feel nothing.

The wind picks me up off my feet and places me near the shore. The wind wants to help feed my belly. What great fortune that Wind is in a good mood, for she can kill on a whim. The ocean is inexplicably open. There is never open water this time of year. I need to feed. We find some arctic tern eggs near the shore and suck them up; life sprouts new hope in my core. Golden fluid, so hot, travels and shines out of my throat like the sun.

The sun talks to my throat in recognition. I strengthen. I grow, spine straightening and gold spreading. My arms turn into tentacles and I whip the water, pulling eggs out of arctic chars' bellies with an alarming precision. The gold spreads to my eyes and down my fingers. My spine clicks together like Lego pieces and we grow ten feet. I am deadly. I am ravenous. The fish eggs tickle my throat and make my eyes slant and ears twitch. More gold. The horizon presents an electrical storm. Grey black blue rushing toward us. The sun grows afraid and throws some stars into the sky to distract the storm. The electricity absorbs the stars and grows stronger. The sun surrenders, taking her dogs with her into the ocean. I must leave. The only vessel available is a large ice floe. The wind shifts, and I am being swept out to sea.

Cast adrift, I am fat and windburnt. Then comes fear. The floe starts to break up. The ocean is eating the ice, licking and chewing on it. Large cracks form in the floe and the water is calling my name. I will die in the frozen ocean. Humans cannot survive in the frigid water, even in spirit form (most times). The ice breaks into small pieces and I am plunged into the water. It is so cold that it burns. Treading water and feeling the life leave my body, I accept.

I succumb. The pieces of ice have quadrupled in number and have become too small to grasp. These small pieces morph into miniature polar bears, dozens of them. They make mewling noises while they swim alongside my flank. It's an indecipherable language but I am aware they are attempting to comfort me. One bear grows large and swims beside me, his sphere of reality warming the ocean for me. He has given me his corporality. The ocean is like a warm bath.

I mount his back and ride him. My thighs squeeze him and pulse with a tingling light. We are lovers. We are married. He swims with incredible strength and we travel quickly. He keeps me safe and I am drunk on his dignity. The smaller bears shrink, only to be eaten by engorged shrimp. The ocean grows hot with life after the offering of food. My skin melts where there is contact with my lover. The ocean and our love fuse the polar bear and me. He is I, his skin is my skin. Our flesh grows together. His face is my pussy and she is hungry. My legs sprout white fur that spreads all over me. I can feel every hair form inside of me and poke through tough bearskin. My whole body absorbs him and we become a new being. I am invincible. Bear mother, rabbit daughter, seal eater. Bear lover, human lover, ice pleaser. I will live another year.

FÉLIX PERKINS

de *Boiteur des bois*

Plus je sais qui je suis
Moins mes proches me reconnaissent
Essoufflé de ramper dans les marches
On s'éloigne quand on m'entend suer

Je prends plaisir à être malheureux
Sinon je ne suis plus victime

La vraie douleur
C'est gagner 4 dollars au *Set for Life*

Je cours au dépanneur
Chercher mon dû
Je tenterai ma chance la semaine prochaine

Je fais monter les enchères
Avec les autres adeptes de ma discipline
Je dis : moi, c'est pire !

Comme le matador qui fait harakiri
Devant le taureau à l'agonie
Je mets mes racines à nu
Bénévolement

Rendre son âme
Sans remboursement
Payer le prix

J'ai prié pour être veuf
Cocu
Orphelin

C'est stylé d'être un rien qui n'a rien

Sur la route
Trainent quelques pommes
    et ta carte d'assurance maladie
Le doute bat ses propres records
L'abandon
Rien de plus que des métastases
Au marathon des condamnés

Ma vie se lit entre les lignes
Sur le rebord d'un café
Entre les fils de mon attrape-rêve

Meilleure chance la prochaine fois

Si je scalpe des roux
Pour m'en faire un pelage de tigre
Est-ce que je serai à la hauteur des romantiques

On trouvera refuge

Je m'accroche au fer rouge de la horde
Les amoureux désespérés sont des clichés
de merde
Ils puent tellement ils existent

KAITLYN PURCELL

From *ʔbedayine*

FAREWELL

I spit chunks of vomit out into the grass. Always hated goodbyes, the way they twist my stomach and need to be erased with a six-pack of tall cans. Smoke from Thana's cigarette dances with horseflies while her long black hair sways in the sun. Our green van is parked next to a little outhouse, and the dirt roads stretch out north and south from us. We are only four hours from home, but we still have maybe ten to go.

Thana passes me the water bottle from her backpack and asks, "Did I ever tell you the story about the first time I drank?"

"Was that when you gave yourself a fat lip?"

"No—I was probably eleven and I stole a strawberry cooler from my sister's room. Thought it tasted pretty good, so it went down quick. My mom found me covered in red puke in the washroom. And you know what she did?"

"What?"

"She laughed. Then she threw a towel on me, shut the door. I cried for a while before my sister came in and helped me wash the puke off. Never asked my mom for help after that. And you know what? We need to look out for each other, you and me. And always make sure to wash the puke off when it gets tough. Y'know?"

"I promise to wash the puke out of your hair, but you gotta promise you won't leave me for some cute guy again," I laugh, before gargling some water and spitting it out.

"We'll see who's talking once you have a guy crawling all over you, too."

Thana puts out her cigarette and jumps back in the driver's seat. As the car pulls back onto the highway, I pull out my notebook and write.

loss turns to vomit *can love bury these knots?*
in love and lost the way. *goodbye, family.*

Never meant to wander, but I always did. Dad told me I was a runaway kid from the moment I began to walk on two feet. I guess when I was a toddler I was playing in my parents' closet and they thought I'd walked out into the forest or'd been taken by a black bear. Never was a good time, two overreactive parents and a runaway kid like me.

My dreams have also captured me, causing me to wander into other worlds. Always did like my sleep. I remember lots of my dreams, even ones from when I was still in the cradle. There's this one dream-inside-a dream I've had since I was little. I first had it when I was just learning how to ride a bike—I remember, because I had another weird dream around that time where I lost control of the handlebars. But, this one dream-in-a-dream I keep having, it usually goes like this:

I wake up to the sounds of dogs barking and screeching. I go to the window, but it's still dark out. I walk down the hallway to try and find our dog, Bebi, but the front door is open. The screeching gets louder, so I run outside. As I step out the screeching goes silent. I become surrounded in light. A wind grabs me. It feels like I'm falling through heavy air.

That's when I actually wake up. This dream comes back every once in a while. It changes a little bit each time, but I always end up stuck in that blinding light. I always write down my dreams, and it's easier when they're bizarre. Sometimes they're so beautiful that it's hard to get out of bed. I live for the dreams about swimming in the ocean with the blue whales, orcas, hammerheads, and bottlenose dolphins.

Gravel turns to asphalt as Thana changes the CD with one hand on the wheel. She asks me to tell her a story.

"Hmm."

As the sounds of emo boys singing about broken hearts fill the car, I look out at the burnt-down landscape. Blackened skeletons of trees cast shadows over a ground green with new growth. I say, "Well, you know how my dad made me go to Sunday school, right? He thought it would be good for me, after Mom left. I would have to wear these dresses and these shiny black shoes. We would have to sit in the basement and read from the bible, and they would give us weird things to do, like colouring books of religious pictures. Well—this one week after Bebi died, I was really sad and I went to the washroom during Sunday school because I needed to cry. And while I was in there, I heard someone whistling outside the stall. But I looked, and there was no one there. I went back out and everyone was sitting silently, just working on their colouring. Creeped me out and I didn't know what to do, so I just went back to my seat."

"Did you tell your dad?"

"Yeah, he was upset. I didn't have to go back to Sunday school after that."

"Weird."

Thana's always loved my stories. I was pretty much a loner when we met, since I had a hard time speaking and most of the other kids thought it was weird.

We met in the tenth grade, around lunchtime. Instead of walking home, I walked toward my favourite place in the trees. That week, I had been hanging out with my cousin Johnny and I told him about the nightmares I was having, so he gave me some of his mom's painkillers to help me sleep. I took two, and I guess I ended up sleepwalking, or something, and my dad found me lying on the couch, drooling. A few days later, he found out that Johnny was stealing morphine from his mom, and asked if I had taken anything from him. I think I'm pretty good at making stories, but I'm also pretty terrible at lying. He yelled at me and told me not to turn out like my mom did. I spent that week afraid to say anything. I didn't want to be my mom. I couldn't even figure out how to be good enough to be anyone's friend.

That's when I met Thana. I was crying in the trees, throwing rocks at the branches, when I heard someone yell, "FUCK!" And saw her standing with a cigarette not too far from me. I held my breath, but it was too late. Her eyes found mine, and she started walking toward me. We became two strange, sad girls, sitting in the forest talking shit about the town and our families. After that, I was glad our families were messed up enough for us to become friends.

If not, we might have never left.

—

Pulling into the first big town in Alberta, we're greeted by flashing hotel signs and colourful fast food restaurants. It's probably the closest thing to Vegas that we'll ever get to see. We find a gas station, where I load up on Sour Patch Kids and Cool Ranch Doritos while Thana fills the car.

A thin guy walks into the store. The dusty blond colour of his hair reminds me of Dylan, from back in Smith. Dylan, the boy who had strawberry coolers and a copy of *Night at the Roxbury* on VHS. The boy who ruined high school.

In the tenth grade, Thana was all googly-eyes over this boy at the ice cream store, and he invited us both over. I remembered feeling weird about going, but I knew it meant a lot to Thana by how she smiled on the way to Dylan's house. In his basement, the white of the hallways was painted over in layers of grease streaks left by fingers. They turned on the TV and Dylan put on *Night at the Roxbury.* He cracked open coolers for each of us before he fell into the plaid fabric of the couch. Thana joined him, while I sat to the side in the recliner.

My hands were tight around the curves of the bottle while I strained to keep my eyes on the TV. The plaid couch seemed to move beside me, but I was too scared to look. Thana and Dylan's breathing seemed to get louder while my insides were shaking.

stars in thana's eyes create constellations
and the astrologers in her ears explain why
pluto has fallen into her heart and her
hands make their way to his
thigh   *his dick shivers while wind*
                           mourns past the windows

I put my cooler on the table and stood up. "You know, guys, I have to—I should go."

Thana stood up and grabbed my hand. "Just come sit with us. Relax."

She pulled me beside her, down on to the couch with Dylan, and my hands started to sweat.

"I always thought you two were beautiful," Dylan said. I kept my eyes glued on Will Ferrell and Chris Kattan, bobbing their heads and dancing in shiny suits. I gripped the edges of my shirt. Thana put her hands over my face. The shiny suits blurred into the dark and into the strawberry coolers. She pulled my gaze into hers, and then my lips onto hers.

After that day, it felt like everyone knew what we had done. They probably did. I spent more time avoiding people, spent more time in the trees.

I wave the junk food in the air before I jump back in the car. Thana laughs as I fasten my seatbelt. I pull out my astrology book and say, "So, your Venus is in Libra and my Venus is in Aries." Thana asks me what that means as we turn back on the highway.

JAYE SIMPSON

From *it was never going to be okay*

00088614

00088614 **/why/** 00088614/00088614/00088614/00088614
00088614/0088614/00088614000886140008861400088614
/000886140008861400088614000886140008861400088614000886140008
86140008861400088614000886140008861400088614000886140008861400
08861400088614/00088614
/didn't/ 00088614000886140008861400088614 **/you/**
00088614000886140008861400088614000886140008861400088614008861400
088614000886140008861400088614000886140008861400088614/00088614000886140008861
400088614000886140008861400088614000886140008861400088614000886140008
86140008861400088614000886140008861400088614000886140008861400
08861400088614000886140008861400088614000886140008861400088614
/000886140008861400088614000886140008861400088614000886140008
86140008861400088614000886140008861400088614000886140008861400
08861400088614/0008861400088614000886140008861400088614000886140008861
400088614000886140008861400088614000886140008861400088614000886140008
8614000886140008861400088614000886140008861400088614 **/say/**
0008861400088614000886140008861400088614000886140008861400088
61400088614000886140008861400088614000886140008861400088614000
886140008861400088614000886140008861400088614000886140008861400088614000886140
0088614000886140008861400088614000886140008861400088614000886140008861
40008861400088614000886140008861400088614000886140008861400088614/00088614000

88614000886140008861400088614000886140008861400088614000886140
00886140008861400088614000886140008861400088614000886140008861
4000886140008861400088614

    000886140008861400088614000886140008861400088614000886140008861400
08861400088614000886140008861400088614/00088614000886140008861
4000886140008861400088614000886140008861400088614000886140008
86140008861400088614

/my/   00088614000886140008861400088614

0008861400088614000886140008861400088614000886140008861400088
61400088614000886140008861400088614000886140008861400088614000
88614000886140008861400088614000886140008861400088614000886140
00886140008861400088614000886140008861400088614000886140008861
4000886140008861400088614000886140008861400088614000886140008
86140008861400088614000886140008861400088614000886140008861400
08861400088614000886140008861400088614000886140008861400088614
0008861400088614000886140008861400088614000886140008861400088
61400088614000886140008861400088614000886140008861400088614000
88614000886140008861400088614000886140008861400088614000886140
0088614000886140008861400088614000886140008861400088614000886
14
00088614

/name?/

urban NDNs in the DTES

had a dozen foster parents
tell me to run from my mother's truth
the track marks up her arm,
shy away from the streets
they said ate her alive.

wasn't until i had rewilded
unto the very streets
that i recognized that it kept her alive.

harm came from
the môniyâw men
lurking in the alleys asking for something more
(like ligament or limb)
wrap their fleshy
digits around ikwe throat
squeeze life like pressing
orange for juice.

most of my mom's sisters are dead
like her too now—
caught in the crosshairs
of murdered or missing;
their children are working
& i make sure to say hello to my cousins,
we all picked up our mothers'
work eventually.

i have become a regular at the funeral parlour on hastings.
burying parent & child every other week.

don't have tears left once home, save them
for longer nights

remember there are NDN children
who need to eat still.

i ran onto main and hastings
cried out in anguish, this place called cold
called heartless
called monster & maw
was never the culprit & the blame was never to be
my mother's or her sisters'—
rather machines of genocide
placed here by
the illegal government voted in
by our now-neighbours.

i've found truth:
the mythos was fabricated;
& there will always be
funerals to attend,
NDN children to feed.

decolonial pu$$y

i have been the storm
& the break—
the tumble
& the get back up again—
the one-time hookup
turned three-week tryst.

there isn't anything
more decolonial
than a trans woman's pu$$y.

i have been the shout
& the coarse dying cry—
i have been the blow
& the bruise—
the kiss turned
forbidden entanglement.

there is something
about the way
fucking a trans woman
sets men free.

i have been the aftermath
& the beginning—
the cliché in the hyperbole
& the metaphor in plain sight—

soft lips pulled
between his ravenous canines.

something about a cis woman
carrying child
that turns the warm between my legs
to salt, proud men tend
to bury seed in sand

pray to be fed into the fall
bite tender breast & beg for rain
by spilling our blood
as tribulation.

there ain't nothing more decolonial
than my pu$$y.

about the ones i want to love

when i planted my heart in the corner of the yard,
by the strawberries and rhubarb:
what did i expect to happen?

what did i expect
to happen when i tried to love &
my heart was buried ten years ago
by a house that was never home?

i want to go back now
i hear the garden was pulled up
stripped from the willing & giving soil
for strawberries & rhubarb were too much trouble
for her at her old age.

i wonder if my heart was unearthed
thrown into the forest behind the house with the rest of the compost
i wonder if some strawberry plants resisted her pull & still come up
through grass
or if some took root in the compost pile
& have crept down the ravine's edge.

a delicious half-breed settler in indigenous foliage.
i wonder if the bear cubs feast
on plump red berries & juices as an act of resistance.

i wonder if they feasted on my heart?
you see, i wouldn't mind that
i had gotten used to sharp teeth on my heart
before i cut her out of my chest
i even had to break a few bones to do it.
but if a cub ate my heart to grow up strong,
then i am at peace with that.

/but/

if not
i would like to dig her up
break the bones in my chest again
sew her back in
with red & silver thread & wooden beads
patch together with ribbons & cedar.
i would set the bones with ash & clay.

it will hurt more:
for scar tissue is protection & thickness
rough & tough
the body saying *not again*
scar tissue covers nerves
& you have to cut
a little deeper to get
to where you want.

this is my fault
no longer wanting to be a wandering ghost
in a community of other healing beings.

what did i expect
when i found people with hearts mending
& they handed me a chance
to hold their heart for a moment?
what did i expect
when i came face to face with my people
for the first time in my existence

what did i expect
when for once in my life touch doesn't have to be flinch?

what did i expect
when i heard the cherry tree & apple tree
got root rot,
died shortly after i left?
when the guilt of burying such a precious thing
under such carelessly nurtured fruit trees.

what did i expect
when every plant
that ever provided
for the inhabitants of the house ceased
to exist after i left?

i buried my heart in hopes my heart would be
enough to keep them fed in the winter

/but/

i see that sacrifice failed
ultimately i want her back now
i want to give more than just half-empty words
to the ones i want to love,
it is not fair for me to be such a living ghost
who can come & go as i please
all whilst holding their heart in the palm of my hand.

so now
i cleanse my body
mark where i am to cut
prepare the herbs and tools,

get ready to exhume her from her tomb
healing is sacred & i want to love & be alive again.

it's time.
been time for too long now.

can you hear that?

//thud thud/—/thud thud/—/thud thud//

//thud thud/—/thud thud/—/thud thud//
//thud thud/—/thud thud/—/thud thud//
//thud thud/—/thud thud/—/thud thud//
//thud thud/—/thud thud/—/thud thud// //thud thud/—/thud thud/—/thud thud////thud thud/—/thud thud/—/thud thud//

*//thud thud/—/thud thud/-/thud thud/ //thud thud/—/thud
thud/—/thud thud// //thud thud/—/thud thud/—/thud
thud////thud thud/—/thud thud/—/thud thud////thud thud/—/thud
thud/—/thud thud//*

*//thud thud/—/thud thud/—/thud thud// //thud thud/—/thud
thud/—/thud thud////thud thud/—/thud thud/—/thud thud//
//thud thud/—/thud thud/—/thud thud////thud thud/—/
thud thud/—/thud thud////thud thud/—/thud thud/—/thud thud////
thud thud/—/thud thud/—/thud thud////thud thud/—/thud thud/—/
thud thud////thud thud/—/thud thud/—/thud thud////thud thud/—/
thud thud/—/thud thud/—/thud thud////thud thud/—/thud thud/—/
thud thud////thud thud/—/thud thud/—/thud thud////thud thud/—/
thud thud/—/thud thud////thud thud/—/thud thud/—/thud thud////
thud thud/—/thud thud/—/thud thud////thud thud/—/thud thud/—/
thud thud////thud thud/—/thud thud/—/thud thud////thud thud/—/
thud thud/—/thud thud////thud thud/—/thud thud/—/thud thud////
thud thud/—/thud thud/—/thud thud////thud thud/—/thud thud/—/
thud thud////thud thud/—/thud thud/—/thud thud////thud thud/—/
thud thud/—/thud thud////thud thud/—/thud thud/—/thud thud////
thud thud/—/thud thud/—/thud thud////thud thud/—/thud thud/—/
thud thud////thud thud/—/thud thud/—/thud thud////thud thud/—/
thud thud/—/thud thud//*

let's begin.

PART III

INTIMACY

TYLER PENNOCK

From *Bones*

I wonder if my attraction to men
            is preceded by my understanding
            of their capacity for violence?

Or if the opposite is more likely?

Is my attraction
            to you
            dominated
            by my fear of the other side—
            the chaos it brought
            to the edges of our house
            and our imaginings?

(Sharp corners

            making us bleed)

•

I remember the laboured breathing coming from the basement—the slanted light that entered the house mimicking the breaths, until the house itself was moving. In there, the shadows were my solace, the light a threat.

I dreamt that I was being pulled into the basement, where the breathing pounded out all my memory. I remember the screams I knew were down there, that never made it beyond the door.

In a house where comfort was cannibal—

like prey, lying down and giving in to their pursuer

my safety was my ending

•

I dreamed of my sister. It began outside the house built by my mother's abuse. I ran into the house, through the back door.

The light through drawn blinds threatened to breathe me in. I remember running through the kitchen, toward a cellar door that was locked.

Through the back door, burst an angry white bear.

She came in through the kitchen, grabbed my left hand, and bit through the flesh. The blood warmed my wrists, but didn't make it to the floor.

Enough

I said.

I closed my eyes, and started again. This time, I ran through the back door, locked it, and started toward the cellar door.

The bear came through the door, bit my left hand, and pulled me away —bloody—from the cellar. The blood ran down the sides of her face.

Enough

I said.

I started again. Through the back door, locked several deadbolts and a chain before I started toward the cellar. Had the locks on the cellar door ready to keep her out.

The bear burst through. I think she had the keys to all my locks. She charged through the kitchen, grabbed my hand, and pulled me toward the exit. Again.

I did not bleed this time. She pulled me from the house, and onto the lawn. I looked at my hand, and wished for blood—blood is how I understood the world.

This time
there was none

•

BLAIR YOXALL

"Little Bull"

Today I comed home from school in exactly 7 minutes and 31 seconds, which is 1 minute and 18 seconds faster than I comed home yesterday. It's also 2 minutes and 9 seconds faster than I comed home last Friday. That was one day after Kokum bought me Timex for present because I did good in school. She always buys me presents on Thursdays when I do good in school. Timex is the best present I've gotten by far. Today I wanted to show Kokum that I can run fast like a buffalo, so I runned real fast the whole way home and it only took me 7 minutes and 31 seconds. And the best part was that it wasn't even lunchtime when I got home, so that meant me and Kokum could still go picnicking at Henderson Lake!

Thursdays and Fridays and Saturdays are my favourite days because that's when Kokum comes to Lethbridge to visit me and Mom and baby brother, Louie. Kokum lives in this place called Calgary, which is a million miles away from Lethbridge. Calgary's probably the second-biggest city in the world after New York City. They have skyscrapers so high that sometimes I think they'll come crumbling down on top of me and squish me like a pancake, *splootschke!*

I don't know if I like it there. The people look at me weird, but Kokum says it's getting better.

I don't know how Kokum can stand the drive from Calgary. It's probably because she's so old she doesn't notice time go by. Maybe if I had boughten Kokum a Timex for doing good at Kokuming she would learn that the drive from Calgary lasts forever. But, then again, maybe she'd stop coming if she knew that.

Yesterday was Thursday and Kokum gave me an ugly old set of pencils for present. I thought she must have thoughten that I did bad in school because nobody wants pencils. And nobody especially wants pencils with all their erasers chewed off. But Kokum told me I got these pencils because I did *especially* good in school. It made no sense! Then she explained: "Jaxon, these pencils used to be Mosom's."

"From the olden days? When he was a grade oner?"

"Well, no. Those pencils don't exist anymore. But these were Mosom's favourite pencils from when he was an old man writing stories in Meadow Lake."

"Why are they all chewed up?"

"Mosom chewed all sorts of things when he was thinking real hard. You know, Jaxon, he was the best storyteller in all of Northern Saskatchewan." I wonder who the best storyteller is in Lethbridge? Probably stupid Jenéa MacDonald. This one time she wrote a story about the wind blowing radiation into my brain and turning me into a zombie because I go for Stampeders and she's a Roughrider.

"Mosom would have really liked you, Jaxon. And I think you would have really liked him, too. You two would probably just sit around all morning and talk about words and stories and stuff like that. I think he would have told you all about the olden days, too."

Mosom died when I was a baby in Mom's tummy. Mom says when he was my age, we looked the exact same. She says we even had the same hairdo before they chopped off all his hair at this place called residential school.

I know Kokum really misses Mosom. She also really misses the farm up in Northern Saskatchewan. Kokum's farm was probably the biggest farm in the whole North. I know this because Uncle Wade told me. He used to live there with Kokum, but he moved away not long ago and lives in this place called Fort McMurray now. The last time we saw him was Thanksgiving when we went riding with him and Kokum on the farm before Kokum moved to Calgary. After Uncle Wade moved to Fort McMurray, Kokum moved to Calgary because Auntie Kathy lives there. Maybe one day Auntie and Kokum will move to Lethbridge. Uncle Wade, too.

Mom says Kokum didn't know what to do without Mosom around to feed the horses and play guitar for her. Uncle Wade used to look after the horses with Mosom, but he was almost never home after Mosom died because he worked so much doing oiling. But then Uncle Wade did so much oiling he just moved away for good, I guess.

Kokum and Mosom were born on a reserve called Flying Dust up in Northern Saskatchewan, which is right beside the Meadow Lake. Meadow Lake is a weird name for a town. How can a town be both a meadow *and* a lake? It makes no sense.

Kokum says sometimes on Flying Dust and the Meadow Lake they have bad water in the taps and you aren't allowed to drink it until you boil it. She says they have lots of dogs with no masters, but most of the old people try and take care of them. Maybe one day Kokum will get me a dog for present so we can both look after him. Maybe a husky! I like huskies because they look like wolves. I'd call him Barney. One time I seen a dead husky on the side of the road at Flying Dust. I'd never let that happen to Barney. Not in a million years.

Even though the water's no good on Flying Dust and the Meadow Lake is really cold in the winter, Kokum hopes to go back someday. She says you can eat all the moose meat you want and people don't look weird at you.

I don't know if you know this, but I'm the smartest kid in my grade. That's why Kokum gives me presents on Thursdays. I might even be smarter than my teacher, Mrs. Evanston, but I'm 53 years younger than her, so she knows more stuff than I do because she was alive for all of it.

I'm really good at math, too, but my favourite's reading and writing and drawing. Sometimes I like to write stories about the Meadow Lake. One time I wrote a story about this cowboy called Wyatt who wears a big cowboy hat and big braids and he rides paint horses to protect the Meadow Lake from bad guys. Sometimes I write about the great brook trout who swim in the streams that Mosom used to fish. I like to draw pictures of them, too. For a long time I was making this really cool picture of Mosom catching a big fish that leaped out the water into a net Wyatt holded for him. But that picture's no good anymore. Kokum says Mosom liked pictures and stories about the Meadow Lake when he was a little boy. Kokum says there used to be lots of stories about the Meadow Lake, but there aren't many left anymore. It made Mosom sad, so he started writing stories about the Meadow Lake before he died.

The reason I know I'm the smartest kid in my class is because I'm the best at reading. My favourite books have no pictures sometimes, but not all the time. Right now I'm reading this book Mom gave me about this boy wizard called Harry. He was supposed to be killed by You Know Who, but You Know Who couldn't kill

Harry because Harry's "the boy who lived." So now Harry has a scar on his head like a lightning tattoo. Mom says I'm not allowed getting a tattoo until I'm 18. Harry is the second-smartest person in Hogwarts after Hermione. Mom says if I had curly hair I'd be just like Hermione I'm so smart, but I don't think so because Hermione's eleven and I'm six.

Even though sometimes Thursdays are my favourite because I get presents, Fridays are even more my favourite because that's when Kokum braids my hair. Kokum is the only girl I let braid my hair into the really big braid that goes down my back like a horse tail because that's my favourite braid. Not even Mom is allowed to give me the big braid.

Today when I comed home from school, Kokum brung me into the bathroom and filled up the tub with hot water and bubbles. I climbed into the tub and tried swimming around, but I kept getting stuck like a goldfish. Kokum took the shampoo and scrubbed it all over my skull real hard to wash the grease and dust off my hair. She grabbed big chunks of hair and rubbed the shampoo real deep to get all them hairs squeaky clean.

"I need you to wash that shampoo off your head now. Okay, Jaxon?"

"I want to break the world record for breath-holding," I said. "Can you time me on Timex? I need you to time me on Timex."

"What's the record?"

"Easy-peasy. 22 minutes and 0 seconds. I just need one more second to win. I've done it a million times, I promise."

Kokum reached over the counter and grabbed Timex. She looked down her big Snape nose and squinted at Timex real hard—so hard you couldn't even see her eyes. She says old people like her go blind sometimes. That's why they have to look funny at things so they aren't all smudgy and washy.

"How's this thing work?"

"You just push this button until it goes *beep-beep* a million times and there's a bunch of zeroes on the screen. Then just make it go *beep* one more time and the timer'll start." I standed up to see what Kokum was doing better. The water tumbled down my body and splish-splashed back into the tub.

"Like this?"

"Yeah, just like that. And push this button one more time when I say 'ready.'"

I slooped back into the water and pinched my noseholes real hard so no water could squiggle up there and go behind my brain. I knew I had to breath-hold for a really long time, but I knew I could do it. No problem. I'd done it a million times. Only 22 minutes and 1 second to break the record. Easy-peasy, piece of cake.

"Ready, Jaxon?"

"Ready!" I gulped a bunch of air into my chest-balloons. "Go!"

I dived into the water and dunked my head real deep—deep as the bathtub, deep as the ocean. I holded my breath real hard and swam deeper and deeper into the bubbles like a big fish and shaked my head real fast to get all the shampoo off. But I still had 22 minutes to kill. I had to pass the time somehow. I had to distract myself so that I wouldn't notice I needed to breathe. But how? There was no TV underwater. No SpongeBob, no Nemo. Nothing. I thought, maybe I should sing? I *should* sing! It all made sense! I should sing and shake that shampoo off my head and sing! Easy-peasy! I whipped my head around and sang real loud, *I shake it off, I shake it off! I-I! I shake it off, I shake it off!*

But no matter how much I shaked, it didn't stop me from knowing how bad I needed to breathe. I could feel it way deep inside me like all the air was going stale. I need to breathe so bad, everything was going black.

I sensed it. I seen it. I knew it was true. I knew it was all over. This was it, it was the end, game over, finito, donezilla, no more Jaxon Little Bull, six years old, died of breath-holding in the tub, never even kissed a girl.

I flied out of the water like a big Saskatchewan fish and breathed so big I swallowed up all the air in the room. The room rocked like a boat. I felt my face for a beard and my belly for a gut. I looked around for old saggy skin. I stuck my hand in my face to see if I had gone blind. I must have been underwater almost as long as Kokum is old!

"Kokum, what does Timex say?" I needed oxygen, but there was none left in the room.

Maybe even the world. "Did we set the record? Did we do 22 minutes and 1 second?"

"You doubled the record! 44 minutes and 0 seconds, Jaxon!"

I felt my jaw hit the bottom of the tub. I was going to be rich and famous. I was going to be on the cover of *TIME Magazine*, on the cover of the 2016 *Guinness Book of World Records*. I imagined me hunched over a big table at the Chapters in the mall, signing millions of autographs for all my fans. Cameras flashing everywhere, big red carpets to protect my shoes. They'd make statues of me all over town. They'd come all the way from Timbuktu to take selfies with me. All the girls from school would want to be my girlfriend, even Jenéa MacDonald. But I'd never be her boyfriend. Not in a million years.

"Oh my god!" I said. "No way! Kokum! I don't believe you! We set the record?"

"Here, look!" Kokum handed me my Timex. I looked at it . . . I wanted to throw it in the water and smash it up! Kokum lied to me! I couldn't believe it! How could she lie to me? How could she not know? 00:44.00 means 0 minutes and 44 seconds, not 44 minutes and 0 seconds! How could Kokum not see that? I was nowhere near the record. Probably farrer from the record than Calgary is from my house.

"Kokum! That says 0 minutes and 44 seconds! Them back numbers mean seconds, not minutes!"

"Well that's gotta be pretty close, don't you think?" Kokum's face went all red and bubbly. I could smell her fib like a fart. "Sorry, Jaxon. I didn't know . . ."

Kokum kept looking away at the bathmat on the ground. I felt bad for getting mad at Kokum. She didn't mean to hurt my feelings. I think she might have been telling me what Mom calls a "white lie." You tell people white lies to make them feel good or to protect them from the truth when the truth is real mean and nasty.

"I'm sorry, Kokum," I said. "It's okay. I know you didn't mean to hurt my feelings. Maybe next time we'll do the record."

Kokum asked me to climb out of the tub after I twirled around for her so she could make sure she got my hair all squeaky clean and ready for braiding. When I popped over the ledge, Kokum grabbed the Harry Potter towel and scrubbed me dry, head to toe. Then she slabbered lotion all over me and helped me get dressed all nice and good for the day: white Stampeders T-shirt, Batman underwear, red shorts, yellow socks, Timex on my wrist. I looked like Jon Cornish, MVP.

Kokum sat me down in front of the mirror. In the reflection I seen all the ancestors standing behind me and Kokum, all of them looking after us and protecting us and smiling for us. They always came to watch Kokum braid my hair. I liked seeing them. I seen Mosom nibbling a pencil and holding his hat to his chest; I seen Kokum's Mosom wrapped up in the scratchy wool blanket he had boughten from the Bay a million years ago; I seen Wyatt from all my stories and drawings winking at me, puffing a smoke, the tassels on his leather jacket all burned off.

Kokum picked up the hairbrush and grabbed a handful of hair and worked out all the knots and tangles, top to bottom. I let my head fall back every time Kokum pulled with the brush. It's like we used to do with the horses' tails at Kokum's farm on the Meadow Lake.

I closed my eyes and thought about the Meadow Lake and Flying Dust and the last time me and Mom were there at Kokum's farm. It was Thanksgiving, right after we shampooed all the horses and braided their tails. We were riding Kokum's paint horses out in pasture, single-file—Kokum in the front, me in the middle, and Mom and Uncle Wade in the back. Baby Louie was on Kokum's back in a sort of knapsack. He was sleeping. I think that's why they're called knapsacks—so babies can nap in them.

I looked behind me and watched Uncle Wade talk to Mom. The sunshine bounced off his shiny bald head like a mirror and straight into my eyeballs. Him and Mom were talking about boring, newsy things and saying bad words, paying me no attention, not watching me kick my legs out the stirrups or anything.

". . . If that Ebola found its way up here," Uncle Wade said, "we'd be right fucked. We'd get wiped out faster than a wet asshole. And you know they wouldn't take us down to Saskatoon or Edmonton or anywhere like that. Not like they care we're up here, anyway."

"Uncle!" I hollered. "Stop saying cusses!"

"I think Uncle Wade should eat some soap when we get back," Mom said. "Don't you, Uncle Wade? Now don't eavesdrop on us, Jaxon. Just look ahead and keep being careful. And put your damn feet back in them stirrups. You fall off that thing and I'll have your head on a pike."

"What's a pi—"

"Jaxon," Kokum said real loud and teachery. I turned around and faced forward and put my feet back in them stirrups. Mom and Uncle Wade went back to whispering boring stuff again, but with less cusses. I bounced around with every step my pony made. Her name was Birdy.

Every time she walked, I moved around like I was a big tree blowing in the breeze. A leaf tumbling, tumbling, tumbling down to the ground. A big bobblehead. An old cowboy. The pasture stinked like horse poo and rotted leaves.

"Kokum?"

"Yes, nichi?" she said.

"Where're we going?"

"Say that again, Jaxon?"

"I said, 'Where're we going?'"

"Baby, you're going to have to speak up. I can't hear a dang thing you're saying."

"Nevermind." I looked at the rotted leaves in the pasture. It would take a million years to rake all these leaves. Would make for a sweet pile, though.

I heard Uncle Wade say another cuss, but I pretended not to notice like Mom told me to.

I'm not allowed listening to other people's conversations, even if I'm a stiff bored.

Kokum whistled a sad song. I rocked side to side on Birdy's back like the trees blowing in the wind, their leaves tumbling, tumbling, tumbling . . . A big bobblehead cowboy, rocking back and forth, back and forth, back and forth.

"Hey!" I heard a hushed, manly voice whisper at me from the side. "Hey! Jaxon!" There beside me rode Wyatt, his hands shackled to the reins. "Where you reckon they're taking us?"

I looked all around, seeing if these police people who arrested us were paying us any attention. Sheriff Kokum rode up front, gawking around like a bird, just whistling away.

Constable Mom and Constable Uncle Wade talked quiet to each other, pinning their big brown hats to their heads when a big wind gust blowed in. It was like they didn't even remember they had me and Wyatt under arrest. How could they forget? We were the most wanted men in the whole North—Robin Hoods of the Meadow Lake, Batmen in the bush. How could they forget about us? We could get away right then if we wanted to. The rope that connected all our horses was sliced. Constables Mom and Uncle Wade traded candies with each other. Sheriff Kokum kept whistling that annoying fiddle song no one likes, but people dance to, anyway.

"What you say we take off—right now?" Wyatt said. "I cut them ropes off our horses when them yahoos behind us wasn't looking. See? Long as our horses don't step on them ropes none, we can get away, no problem. Right now. You're wearing spurs, ain't you, Jaxy-boy?"

I looked over Birdy's ribs at the dull boots Kokum had boughten me at King of Trade.

"I don't need no spurs," I said. Sheriff Kokum whistled a different, less annoying song.

Wyatt spitted on the dirt.

"You sure you ready for this, Jaxon?"

"I was borned ready. Ready, Birdy?" She sneezed, so I said, "Bless you."

Wyatt holded his reins over his horse's neck and kicked her hard in the tummy. "Yip-yip-yip-yip!" He zipped onto the hill toward the forest, his hat flying off in a cloud of dust.

I turned my heels inward and kicked poor Birdy right in the ribs as hard as I could. I gave her the kissy-lips and clicky-clicks to go fast, "Smooch-ooch-ooch-ooch! Heeyah! Heeyah!" I holded the reins over her neck and whipped them at her and kicked her and kicked her to go fast like a bird, clicking my tongue for her like Kokum showed me. When I whizzed by Kokum, I seen her face go all scared and dusty.

"Hey, you come back here, boy!" Constable Uncle Wade hollered at me. His voice was behind me, small like an ant's.

I heard a whole herd of hoofs chasing me.

"Wyatt, Wyatt!" I hollered. I listened for his yip-yips and the sound of guns firing at him, but only the wind blowed in my ears. He must have fallen off, I thought. What if he's hurt? I standed up in the stirrups, hoping to see Wyatt over the hill. Mom squeezed in front of me, cutting me off. Uncle Wade cantered to the side.

Birdy tried to stop, but she was running too fast. She standed high on her back legs, howling. I pinched the saddle's horn with my fingernails, slicing through the leather. I fell onto her neck.

I grabbed a fist full of mane. I slided off Birdy's neck and onto her side. Her mane was all greasy from shampoo, it slipped right out of my hands. I slinked sideways. I watched the stirrups dangle and bang against Birdy's belly, getting farrer and farrer away as I came closer to the ground. The wind whooshed behind my ears. I made a big thud on a pile of leaves. Baby Louie screamed. Kokum holded Birdy's reins so she wouldn't go crazy and run away. The sky rocked like the leaves leaving the trees, tumbling, tumbling, tumbling . . .

"Alright, Jaxon," Kokum said. "I'm all done. Open your eyes."

I flung open my eyes and seen Kokum standing behind me with all the ancestors in the mirror. She holded my braid, tugging at it and playing with it, looking over each little hair, making sure it was A+.

"You look like a million bucks, baby," she said.

"Do I?" I sat up straight and made my face all cool and mysterious like Wyatt's. I looked in the mirror and tilted my head to the side, then to the other side, then over my shoulder. I definitely looked like a million bucks, alright. Not even Jenéa MacDonald could take me down.

"No, baby. Let me *really* see your braid." I squinted my eyes like an old person. I raised my neck. I lifted my eyebrows and flexed my shoulder muscles. A big bull moose modeling his antlers to the lady moose. A big grouse flapping his wings. All the ancestors smiled at me before they went away.

"You look tough," Kokum said.

"Yeah. I *feel* tough." I threw my braid back.

"I wouldn't mess with you none, Jaxon Little Bull. Only a fool would try and mess with you."

"Yeah, only a fool would mess with me. Not even Jenéa MacDonald can mess with me."

"No one can mess with you."

"Not even Roughriders people." I sticked out my tongue.

Kokum peered down her Dumbledore nose at me. ". . . You know, Jaxon. I'm a Roughriders girl. And I wouldn't mess with you one little bit, Jaxon Little Bull. You're way too tough for me."

"Way too tough!" I flexed my muscles and made my face all mean at the mirror. "Arrrrrgh!"

Kokum told me to stop modeling for myself and save it for the ladies at Henderson Lake. It was time for picnic. We walked to the kitchen like the Batman and Robin and packed up all the moose meat chili and bannock and cheese and salsa for Indian tacos. We put all the food and some juice boxes and plates and forks and slicers into Kokum's picnic basket and hoped Yogi Bear wouldn't be there to swipe our food. I made sure to bring some carrots and peas and cheese for Louie, too. Louie can't eat Indian tacos yet because he's still pretty little. I made sure Mosom's pencils and my drawing pad were in the basket so I wouldn't forget.

Luckily, me and Kokum can walk to Henderson Lake from my house because it's only 22 minutes away. I know this because I timed it on my Timex. It's easy to remember because that's the world record for breath-holding. Because Kokum had to push Louie all the way there in his stroller, I brung the heavy picnic basket. It must have weighed a million pounds. It cut real deep into my shoulder. I also brung the scratchy wool blanket Kokum's Mosom had boughten at the Bay back in olden days to sit down on. Kokum told me about how her Mosom had boughten the blanket in this place called Saskatoon. It was just like the special blanket that Kokum's Mosom's Mosom had boughten in pioneer times. He had boughten it with beaver furs because beaver fur was money back then. I asked Kokum why beaver fur isn't money anymore. "All the beavers would disappear if it was," she said. "And you'd also need a bigger wallet for all your furs, wouldn't you, Jaxon?"

When we got to Henderson Lake, I laid the blanket out on a big patch of grass right by the water so I could watch all the fishes swim up to the surface and make their fins stick out. It was really hot outside. Kokum had a little ball of sweat stuck on her eyebrow. We opened the picnic basket. I hucked little pieces of bannock into the water for the fishes to munch up.

"Those fish eating the bannock are called 'pike,'" Kokum said. "They've got them all over the prairies."

"Have you ever caughten one?"

"Millions," she said. "We'll have to fish for some one day, won't we, Jaxon?"

I grabbed my drawing pad. I flipped through it until I got to the drawing of Mosom and Wyatt out fishing with the two moose and the bear cub. I had worked on it all week. It was really good, but not done yet. Mosom's hat was all wrong and Wyatt still didn't have a face. Kokum's the real drawer in the family. I hoped maybe Kokum would give me tips on how to draw Mosom's hat because it looked like a sombrero.

"What are you drawing, Jaxon?" Kokum said. She was watching Louie flap his arms like a pigeon, throwing peas all over. "I see you're using Mosom's pencils." Louie got a pea stuck up his nose because little kids make no sense and do that sometimes.

"Nothing. Just Mosom and Wyatt."

"Who's Wyatt?"

"Oh, you know. He's the guy who protects the Meadow Lake from bad people."

"Are there bad guys in Meadow Lake?"

"Not anymore. Wyatt made them all go away."

"Is he a rodeo cowboy?"

"He used to be. He used to rope calves. He's real good at it because he ropes bad people so much."

Kokum scooted her bum next to mine and holded a plate with some bannock on it. She slopped moose meat chili all over the bannock for Indian taco. "Wanna hear something kind of funny, Jaxon? Every time we come out here, I imagine everyone around us is in the rodeo."

"What do you mean?" I put the drawing pad down and looked at Kokum goofy. She handed me the plate with Indian taco. Kokum sat so close to me I could smell the smelly smell of lotion on her hands.

"Usually I pretend there are barrel racers around and bull riders and stuff like that," she said. "Like—hey, come here. You see those two roughriders coming down the sidewalk there? That's our rodeo queen and her boyfriend. She's coming to watch the rest of rodeo with us."

"How can you tell?"

"See how they walk? Strutting their stuff. Flashing off them belt buckles."

About as far away as I can run backwards without falling came a pimply boy and his girlfriend. They holded hands, probably getting cooties everywhere. "Ain't they both something else, Jaxon?"

The rodeo queen sat her boyfriend down on a bench real close to where we sat. They wanted to watch dragon boaters out on the lake. The boy's belt buckle shined like Uncle Wade's bald head. He looked like a bull rider, alright. The rodeo queen stuck her hand up to get the sun off her eyes so she wouldn't go blind. It made no sense why they both wore big fancy jeans, it was so hot. But they looked nice, I guess.

I cut a hunk off my Indian taco and gobbled it up. The boy leaned into the girl's neck like a vampire and whispered a secret to her. They turned and looked weird at us.

"No, not now," said the rodeo queen, "not here. There's people here."

"No there's not," said the boy. His voice went all hushy like Mom's does when she says cusses. "You mean them? On the blanket? Just ignore them."

"No, Duncan. I can't. They're sitting *right there.* They make me uncomfortable."

"Don't worry about them. Just pretend they're not there. Maybe they'll get up and leave." I put down my Indian taco and picked up my drawing pad. I wasn't hungry anymore.

"Duncan, c'mon. Can we please just go somewhere else? What if they want something? They might come over here."

"No they won't. Just forget about them. We're just as entitled to sit here as they are. And, I mean, c'mon. It's not like we got a bunch of beer with us or anything."

I pinched the drawing in my hand, making the paper all scrunchy. I seen two little droplets fall onto the paper, making big streaks all over Mosom's face. I put the pencil eraser in my mouth and squeezed it with my teeth, hoping that maybe the lumpy thing in my throat would go away.

". . . Is that little girl wearing a Stamps shirt?" the girl asked. "You'd have to be blind to dress your granddaughter like that. I'd be so embarrassed if I was her."

"*Who cares.* Can you *please* just ignore them? It's a beautiful day."

I looked at Mosom and Wyatt on the paper and whispered real quiet so not even Kokum could hear. "Why are they talking about us? Why are they so mean? Please don't tell me any white lies, Mosom. No white lies, Wyatt. Please . . ." I waited for them to say something, but I couldn't hear nothing. Their faces were too smudgy and drowned with tears.

". . . I wonder where that baby's mother is," the girl said. She looked at my brother.

"Passed out in a ditch somewhere. I don't know. Who *cares.* Can you just forget about them for five seconds?"

"It's just shitty of mom to dump her kids on grandma like that. Like, why can't Native people just not have any fucking kids if they can't take care of them all?"

Kokum's arm went weak. Her plate tumbled like a leaf and spilled on the blanket. Her Indian taco sat on top of a big, bloody chili stain. She standed up. She stared at the people.

"Shit, Duncan. She heard us. Duncan, c'mon. Let's go. Duncan, c'mon, I think she's coming over here . . ." The girl tried to shove her boyfriend off the bench. "Duncan, move, now."

I took the pencil out of my mouth and tried to redraw Mosom's face, but the pencil sliced through the paper. It was too wet. I pushed harder. I needed to see Mosom's face so he could be here to protect me and Kokum.

The pencil broke.

Kokum walked over to the people on the bench.

I *beep-beeped* Timex. It started counting all the seconds and minutes. I tried breath-holding and singing to make the time go faster. *I shake it off . . . I shake it off . . . I . . .*

"We're so sorry, we didn't think you could . . ." said the girl.

"It's just—I mean, c'mon, get that kid a haircut! You're just inviting him to get made fun of when he looks like a girl! . . ." the boy said.

I stuck both halfs of the pencil in my mouth. I chewed it. I gnawed it. I tried to swallow the whole thing like a fish hook.

Kokum's shadow covered my drawing. I wiped the snot off my nose and pulled the two pieces of pencil out of my mouth. Kokum told me to get off the blanket. I packed up all the picnic stuff and throwed it back in the basket, not even looking how it went in. Kokum put Louie back in his stroller and pushed it back onto the sidewalk. I put the basket on my shoulder and speed-walked to Kokum. I looked back at the girl and her boyfriend, hoping that maybe they were watching some little boy catch his first pike with his grandma. They just stared at us.

Me and Kokum made it to the crosswalk. I dropped the picnic basket and wrapped my arms around Kokum and screamed into her lap.

"Why were they so mean? What did we do? Stupid Mosom and Wyatt for not being here to protect us. I thought you said my braid would protect me! I thought you said nobody could hurt me!"

All the people around stared weird at us. They stepped around us. They walked away from us.

I wiped my nose on Kokum's pants. She squeezed me hard and rubbed my back. "Why aren't they here, Kokum? What did we do? Why were they so mean?"

When Kokum opened the door to the house, she tossed the blanket onto the couch. She pushed Louie with his stroller into the bathroom with us. He started to cry. I dropped the picnic basket next to the toilet. I wished Yogi Bear had stolen it so there would have been no picnic today. Kokum holded my shoulder and sat me down in front of the mirror.

"Sit still," she said. We were all alone. Kokum's face was all smudgy and drowned.

I *beep-beeped* Timex to make the time stop. 44 minutes and 0 seconds. I would never breath-hold long enough, even if I stopped crying. I took Timex off and let it go thud on the ground. It landed on the button. The timer looked up at me weird and started over. I felt the tug of Kokum playing with my braid. She grabbed the scissors from the drawer. For the next 7 minutes and 31 seconds I listened to Kokum weep as she chopped off all my hair.

JAS M. MORGAN

From *nîtisânak*

The story of nikâwiy and nindede, woven together from stories told to me by blood kin, or who's to say what's lies and what's The Truth

Of course, there are two sides to every story, and the second portion of this one begins with nindede and nikâwiy (my Cree mom).

This story is made understandable through a warning. In the prairies, The Truth is a yt man. The Truth is whatever the yt man says, and whatever truth is said by the yt man is the ruling law of the *holy wild wild (prairie) west.* This story is made understandable by the admittance that when I listen to nikâwiy talk about her life, I've often wondered if she's lying—where her (our) truth lies. I've told people, nikâwiy isn't lucid, you see, I don't know what's lies and what's the truth. Ergo, I've told people, nikâwiy is just another crazy squaw; I'm just another crazy squaw. As if the real world doesn't integrate with the otherworldly for us Cree people. As if the whole prairie world isn't the ultimate gaslight to someone like nikâwiy, designed to make her feel crazy when she contends that perhaps her disappearance, her spiritual destruction, wasn't warranted. As if truth isn't relative and, if she contends that her experience is true, well then, isn't it, to her, at least?

I always felt like my dad was keeping something from me about my adoption, but I could never identify what. When I turned eighteen and pulled my papers, I realized that it was likely that I was millennial scooped. If I told my dad this, he would probably say, That's not the truth. I say, I have no adoption papers, only an admittance to foster care and a court order from my mom and dad to petition to adopt me. They found me in foster care and the courts convinced nikâwiy to sign the papers on me. I was adoptable, with squishy Cree cheeks, to boot. But these are the things you don't talk about: not in adoptee organizing that centres sixties scoopers, not to one of the most dangerous yts out there—yt lady social worker—who could bring trouble into your home, and certainly not to your yt parents.

All this begs the question, whose truth do we privilege as The Truth, in the story of nikâwiy and nindede? This story is made understandable by my assertion that nindede doesn't get a name—not father, not dad, and not even sperm donor. Nookomis (my Saulteaux grandma) says we don't say their names anymore, the men who chased us off the rez, terrorized us in the cities, and made us their emotional surrogates. I have always been caretaking beyond my capacity for the men in my life. For sexually abusive nindede who constantly reaches out, weasels his way around blocked numbers and profiles, wanting to "heal" me and my siblings, when he really just wants to get into our heads and fuck with us some more. For my brothers who are quick to anger and despise the way my face curves in the same way nikâwiy's does because it represents the love she could never give. So I take care of them, let them stay with me for free, buy them food, give them shelter, and listen to them talk about the woman they left behind in shambles, having made off with whatever money she had in her purse and what fit in a backpack. And, when I no longer do, then, of course, I'm a bitch, or so they say when they call from a pay-phone downtown just to let me know that if they kill themselves, it's my fault—this is the mess my father and older generations of men in my family left in the wake of their terror.

Uncles, dads, and grandfathers, except stripped of their titles. I don't know if giving nindede kinship is much better—but I have to call him something and, at the end of time, he'll always be my Saulteaux kin and the head of my clan. We can pretend that I have power over him in refusing his name, or we can accept the power he exercises over me within the dystopian now,[14] now that our kinship lines are sick with patriarchy. His unnaming is more of an unclaiming, anyway.

Other neechies will often ask me why I claim nookomis from Coté who married into the Ironstands of Tootinaowaziibeeng, and indebted us to this patrilineal lineage forevermore, and not my dad, even though he still lives on the rez—usually rez NDNs with sôniyâwak, or money, when they're trying to place me. The placing of me by rez NDNs is always carefully considered, or more accurately judged, by the rez I'm registered to. Of course, the rez I am registered to is a legal, and perhaps patrilineal-turned-masculinist, designation that was given to me by colonial legislators with no capacity to understand the fluidity of Cree, Métis, and Saulteaux identity within my community, and the kinship-based ways we shared lands—who sought only to number, categorize, and manage our bodies. My identity is never understood by rez NDNs who try to place me in terms of who loves me and claims kinship with me, as nookomis has taught me—the feminine and relational ways of understanding where I belong in this world. As nookomis has said, You (I) can never forget that you're (I'm) Cree-Métis, too—*first.* Tl;dr: Kinship is the original and most important form of Indigenous law and governance. Fuck the treaties.

But there's a little more to this question of where I'm from: the rez NDNs want to know if my people are those medium-poor NDNs from the rez, or maybe even some nouveau riche neoliberal upwardly mobile neechies from the rez, with ties to casino money or a money-laundering chief somewhere in the mix. Sorry to disappoint, we're those dirt-poor ones from the city, who the NDN bro ass-holes would beat up when we came to stay with our granddad for a while.

NDNs just want to be the fanciest, to suss out the *bad* families. An NDN will spend a lifetime making a name critiquing the state, only to turn around and be one of those what's-his-dollar-value-per-square-mile, looking-for-the-*good*-family-lines-in-your-family-names, give-their-name-to-any-colonial-machine-that'll-lift-it-up-and-pay neechies. Honestly, fuck the rez—our little plots of land KKKanada gave us to squabble over, to distract us. I'm honestly supposed to believe a rez like Kahnawake is *très refusal* because it's a self-functioning community that resists amalgamation under the state, when it's putting up eviction notices on its women's doors, and addicts are dying in its darkest corners because stigma about drug use and alcohol pushes them into unsafe situations. That's cool, K-Town—keep destroying one another over that little plot of land that the man gave you, calling it the holy land while dictating what NDNs are good enough to swim in your bourgeois waters, as if you could own the waters to begin with. Much teachings. Very tradish.

The rez ain't so pure. The women, gender-variant, and sexually diverse kin in my family fled rape and unspeakable abuse on the rez, another poorly funded, forgotten prairie rez with zero resources to sell out on, as early as they could and can only go back in groups now, and only as necessary to get payouts. How could you return to the place where your abusive dad's uncle is the preacher, and his cousin is running for chief and council—a nation ruled by men who are the lifeblood of my terror of a granddad? How could you return to a place where, if you entered alone, without the support of your male kin, rape and violence against you would almost be certain? Where, if you were lucky enough to be blessed with housing, which, on Toot, consists of a broken-down trailer in a field, it would likely be broken into and burned down by community members who knew you were an easy target? The treaty left its mark on our bodies, and then named us all after our Saulteaux male relatives we were trying to escape. But don't underestimate me by erasing this prairie hardness. There are multiple ways to warrior up, one such way being getting on toward those flashing city lights (*iskwêwak, iskwêwak, get that sôniyâwak*[15]).

The fancy rez NDNs tell ghost stories to scare one another. My family tells ghost stories to shield us from the truth by creating a protective barrier of lies—a mysterious skin.[16] nikâwiy is from Prince Albert, but has been living in the east end of Saskatoon since her early twenties. nohkom was in residential schools and married a yt man and moved to the city shortly thereafter. Much like nohkom, nikâwiy has never said my granddad's name to me. While I don't know much about what happened in that house, during nikâwiy's youth, I do know that the women who resided there left in pieces. nohkom has been a non-verbal shit disturber, a term I use with absolute respect and admiration, and more specifically completely snowed 24/7, for years. She has never been nikâwiy still can't believe she and my brothers survived that house and survived nindede. Whatever The Truth is about my family is now an amalgamation of my mom's assimilationist values, my dad's authoritative Truth, and nikâwiy's breaks from reality. What I do know is that nikâwiy was on the receiving end of some of the most terrifying abuse of her life, even after my granddad had left his mark. My health was in peril. She needed to put me in foster care, just for a little bit, where they could take care of me. I'd come back, she told herself. Just like my brothers, who they let come back all the other times. But this time, I didn't come back.

Don't mistake my words for trauma porn, because this is just how it went down for us. If these stories can't be told without a yt tear being shed, that's not my problem. No, my trauma is not a commodity, but my story doesn't always have to be uplifting, resurgent, or revolutionary to be my truth, either.

Notes

14. Molly Swain of the podcast *Métis in Space* has named it this. Indigenous Peoples are using our own technological traditions—our worldviews, our languages, our stories, and our kinship—as guiding principles in imagining possible futures for ourselves and our communities.

15. Missy Elliott, "Work It."

16. *Mysterious Skin*

SHAYNE MICHAEL

de *Fif et sauvage*

Quotidien

Lancer des avions de papier
Plonger dans la piscine
Sauter par-dessus la clôture
Couper des carottes
Se cacher dans le garde-robe
Kicker un ballon
Grimper à un arbre
Regarder les étoiles
Se faire traiter de sauvage

*

Courir dans un champ de fleurs
Tomber dans un trou
Faire un bonhomme de neige
Perdre sa première dent
Lancer d'autres avions de papier
Jouer du piano
Ramasser ses crayons
Se faire traiter d'osti d'sauvage

*

Souffler des bulles de savon
Regarder des feux d'artifice
Flatter un chien
Manger un gâteau de fête
Magasiner
Faire le plus gros des châteaux de sable
Se faire traiter de gros crisse de sauvage

*

Manger de la crème glacée
Se masturber
Aller voir un show d'humour
Tomber sur la glace
Conduire son premier vélo
Assister à un mariage
Cuire des guimauves sur le feu
Entendre un bébé rire
Faire le ménage
Se faire traiter de fif

*

Manger du chocolat
Dormir
Rêver
Ouvrir un cadeau

Écrire une lettre d'amour
Éternuer
Jouer de la musique
Pleurer dans son lit
Lire une bande-dessinée
Se faire traiter d'osti de fif

*

Aller à sa première *date*
Trébucher dans l'escalier
Acheter de l'alcool
Prendre un bain chaud
Écouter un film d'horreur
Faire un dessin
Se faire traiter de crisse de gros fif sauvage
Se battre
Arroser une plante

JOSHUA WHITEHEAD

From *Jonny Appleseed*

XXIV

Tias and I used to hustle Mush when we were kids. I liked my mushom, he was a gentle, soft-spoken man who loved Werther's caramels and Budweiser. He used to buy me party-sized chocolate bars, like those Jumbo Mr. Bigs that were twice the size of your head. He wasn't NDN like us, but Kokum insisted we call him Mushom. His real name was Pierre LeClerc and he was the luckiest, and only, môniyâw on the reservation. He won $100,000 on a scratch ticket when he was in his thirties and from then on out he became popular among the family and all the rez girls. He bought my mom a used Cadillac Seville and that forced her to call him Mush—half liking him, half detesting him. He used the remainder of his winnings to buy a gas station that was quite successful while he was alive. He liked to give all the NDN kids a piece of candy whenever they visited, and overloaded their bags with Twizzlers and Pop-Rocks on Halloween. He was a dandy fellow.

But there were better ways to get money from him than by simply asking. Sure, if you asked kindly enough, he'd throw you a few dollars, maybe ten bones if you were really lucky, and then shame you for it when he was on his benders. If there's one rule I've learned from hustling, it's never to put yourself into a situation where you owe somebody—always leave your clients owing you. Though, if you were patient enough, you could swindle forty to fifty bones from Mush by waiting for him to pass out and collecting all his empties. His house would be littered with aluminum: cans in his sink, cans in his bed, cans in the pockets of his coat, crumpled in his war chest. Tias and I used to wait at his place and listen to him and Kokum tell us stories about the good ol' days which would usually erupt into an argument about who had it worse—that's the thing about old folks, they think life is a competition of scars and suffering.

When Mush passed out and Kokum kept herself busy calling everyone she knew on the phone, Tias and I would begin collecting cans like the hermit crabs that cleaned the aquariums in those city pet stores. After we had loaded up two recycle bags' worth, we'd take them to the vendor and exchange them for forty dollars. After we split the cash, we'd go to Mush's gas station and load up on all types of candy: gummies, chocolates, peppermints, Eskimo Pie, and everyone's personal favourite, Nestlé Redskins. Usually, if we didn't have enough for what we wanted, one of us would distract Mush's cashier and the other would load candy into their coat.

With what little money we had left, we'd buy a few cigarettes from the junior high chumps who stole them from their moms. They actually made decent money by selling cigarettes for a dollar. Then we'd take our goods back home to gorge on the candy as we watched *Ren & Stimpy* late into the night. High on sugar, we'd then smoke the cigarettes to give ourselves a head rush and walk around the room light-headed and dizzy—it was the closest we could get to being fucked up as ten-year-olds. Sometimes we would take turns puffing on Kokum's inhaler too, until she caught on and gave us both a damn good slap with her wooden spoon. That's how we thought it was, that being drunk and high were natural processes to growing up.

There were times, if I looked pitiful enough, like a brown-skin Annie singing "It's the Hard Knock Life" sad, that my kokum would let Tias stay over on weekends. We would both sleep upstairs in my uncle's old bedroom, but before we did we'd argue about who got to sleep against the wall, which was always way cooler. To beat the heat, we'd jack the small fan from my kokum's bedroom and put it in ours, which also helped to drown out the clanging of their bottles downstairs—it disrupted our watching of *Boy Meets World.* While Tias raved over how beautiful Topanga was, I swooned over Shawn. And the real name of the actor who played him was so erotically charged for me: Rider Strong. I used to whisper it to myself to fall asleep because I liked the way it sounded when I inserted a heavy breath into the spaces between its syllables. I would lay my tongue down on the bottom of my mouth and let the air vibrate and stimulate them: "Riiide," "der," "Strawwng." A good name makes the perfect sex toy.

Sometimes there would be a party downstairs, and we'd sneak down and watch my kokum, Mush, my mother, my aunts and uncles, cousins, the gas station employees, a tribal officer, and a cavalcade of brown-skins dance around to Loretta Lynn. As Loretta wailed about her man not coming home a-drinking, I would tiptoe into the room and say goodnight to everyone. Funny, the people who loved me the most could only tell me so between two and three in the morning. Then, while they professed their love and pride for me, I'd sneak a couple beers into the pockets of my sweatpants. Back upstairs, Tias and I would crack them open and pretend we thought they tasted good.

"Damn good beer, eh?" Tias said on one such night.

"I've had better, you know?" I replied.

"No, that's the name," he said. "Damn Good Beer, Minhas Creek— wonder where the Damn Good Chips are?"

We buckled with a laugh that ran so deeply through our bodies that our abs hurt afterwards. Then we flipped through the late-night channels, mostly old white women trying to sell patches for varicose veins and Chyna wrestling in the WWF, until we settled on the Showcase channel and watched a show called *KinK*. There was a drag queen who was putting on makeup and kaikaiing with another queen. The taller of the two backed the other against the wall, slid her hand up the other's thigh, and slowly raised her dress, revealing the garters underneath. The shorter one then pulled the other's hands up against her body and wrapped her legs around her. We were both mesmerized.

Afterwards, while we both tried to sleep, Tias asked me if I thought that scene looked like fun. I giggled and said yeah. He laughed, but then he slid closer to me and I felt his hand on my leg. I rolled onto his chest and spread both of my legs over his torso. We started giggling, our bodies vibrating with each other's. It felt like we were a guitar and our lungs and esophagus were being strummed like strings. Fitting, I thought, as we made our own music and let our limbs dance their own ballet without ever moving. Downstairs, Loretta howled in the background that the squaw was on the warpath tonight. We fell asleep like buttons in buttonholes.

The next morning, when the sun was rising, my mom came into our room and nudged my shoulder.

"The heck you doing, boy?"

She put her arms under my pits and raised me up. I wrapped my arms and legs around her and breathed her in, the smoke, the booze, the sweat and tears that made up her perfume. She rubbed the wetness from my eyes, which she called sleepies, and kissed my cheek. I opened my eyes wider and saw a patch of blood on her dry lips, and the black mascara streaming down her face. Even in my half-asleep state, I was both afraid and concerned.

"What happened?" I asked.

"M'boy," she said, pulling my face against her breast and starting to cry. "I'm not the drink, I swear, okay? I'm not the drink."

She put me back into bed beside Tias, who was still asleep, and covered us with a blanket. She kissed us both on the forehead and said, "My boys, kisâkihitin."

I could hear Roger calling her from downstairs, his shout sounding more like the pitiful welp of a dog licking its wounds after a fight.

"Mom?" I said. "Can you lay with me until I fall asleep?"

She smiled and crawled in between Tias and me, pulling us tight against her body. Tias was stirring now, and both of us nuzzled our sleepy heads against her, until her heartbeat lulled us back to sleep. When we finally woke up later, we discovered that one of us had pissed the bed.

We never found out who.

XXV

It was midnight and I had just finished with my seventh client of the day. Some guy named TimOTron cheated me out of ten bucks because he wanted Masc4Masc. My body was stinging and my penis sore from the constant friction. Tired as I was, I was also excited that I had made one-fifty in a couple of hours; I really couldn't complain. If I were eager enough, I could wait a few more hours and get my European clients who were six hours ahead; they'd be finishing their work day soon and coming home horny as hell. But my body was saying I needed a break so I lit a butt and sat against the window ledge in my bathroom. I wanted to talk to the pigeon, have him listen to me, but he was asleep, tucked beneath a heap of garbage. I checked my phone to see if Tias had messaged me. The little box for "Message Sent" was grey, indicating his phone had received the message but he hadn't read it yet. Typical, I said, and sighed when I saw him posting memes on Facebook. I wondered what he was doing over at his mom's right then. I wondered, was he watching *The Walking Dead*? Was he touching himself? Was he thinking of me? Or was he texting her again?

Hungry, I decided to walk the few blocks over to 7-Eleven to spend a few of my hard-earned dollars and get a Big Bite. The place actually made half-decent hot dogs and they were cheap to boot. Once, before I set the rule of never meeting clients in person, I agreed to go out with this guy, corkdub78, who was some thirty-something mechanic at Crappy Tire. He said he was straight but sort of a "tranny chaser"; I told him I was Two-Spirit, not transgender, and that tranny was an out-of-date word. When he looked puzzled, I told him, okay, well, if you popped my hood you'd find that I'm a machine too. He didn't understand. Score one for The Vacuum.

He took me to a fancy dinner at The Keg, where the minimum cost for a meal was fifty dollars. I suggested we split a plate and he looked at me like I was the cheapest fuck he'd ever met. If life were a game of Monopoly, my mother would be the banker. She was as economical as they came; she could turn seven dollars into a meal for eight. A rule of thumb, she told me once, was to never put myself into a position where I would owe someone—"Too much power," she said. "You'll pay it over threefold." So I never let anyone pay for my meals, let alone a date. A slice of overcooked steak and a scoop of mashed potatoes doesn't buy me. I always split the bill, but if you really wanted to be strategic, especially if you liked the guy, you could take control and pay for the entire meal yourself—make them owe you.

I convinced corkdub78 that I wasn't that hungry and that we should split a main course and then grab a coffee afterwards. He agreed and we shared a sirloin steak and baked potato. I ate slowly and took little bites, thinking I would make it last longer. But to be honest, the steak sucked and the potato was undercooked.

But before I knew it my fat fuck companion had scarfed down every bit left on the plate. All I had eaten was a few slices of meat and a few bites of potato. To hell with this, I thought, so I grabbed my coat and excused myself for the bathroom. The guy wasn't all that bright, christ, he didn't even ask why I needed my coat to take a leak. I slipped out the patio door and dine-and-dashed his ass so hard. Afterwards, I hit up McDonald's and devoured two Junior Chickens. That's the problem with white guys, they think they can impress you with fancy meals and expense accounts if you let them. I really don't give a shit about how much money you make or how many bathrooms your condo has. If you want to impress a neechi, you need to take them out to an Applebee's or Montana's or even Foody Goody Chinese Buffet and let them enjoy a smorgasbord of food for $12.99. And if you really want to impress them you could swing by a Co-op and split a carton of white mini-donuts. No Cree boy gives a rat's ass for escargot or lobster tails. Shit's nasty.

Back at the 7-Eleven, I bought two Big Bites, a chocolate milk, and a pack of cigarettes, and sat on the curb outside, eating. The streets of Portage were lively with noise: cars thumping in potholes, snippets of hip-hop from a balcony across the street, the clang of bells from the Asian Food Market, the low thrum of a motorbike, a bottle smashing in the distance.

"Can't you read?" a voice shouted from behind me. "No loitering!"

I brushed the man off with my hand and felt him shove a corn broom against my back.

"Goddamn Natives, always sitting around here. Hurry up and leave before I call the cops." The store manager hit me with his broom again and held it there; the bristles dug into my back. It felt kind of exciting. I pushed back against the bristles. It felt good to be hurt like that. He pushed harder and knocked me off the curb. My milk slipped out of my hand and spilled down my shirt, pooling between my legs and seeping beneath the curb. I wondered how many bugs would drown and die down there.

"That's it, I'm calling the cops," he said. "Damn drunken kids."

I lay down on the sidewalk and spread my arms and legs like a starfish. I wondered if some alien up above was looking down at me thinking I was a constellation.

"Final warning," he said.

I lit a cigarette and puffed on it without any hands. Smoke slithered out of my nostrils. I winked at him. "You know," I stated between puffs, "this is my land, you ingrate."

"*Your* land?" he said. "Who the hell do you think you are, you punk? I pay the fucking tax here, the tax that pays for your welfare, you good-for-nothing—" He stormed off back into Sev as the ashes from my cigarette began to drop on me. They burned a little, singeing what little hair I had on my face—"Muskrat hair," Tias always said. "The blessing of being a Nate is that we only need to buy one razor per year."

I sat up and saw the manager talking animatedly on his landline, staring in my direction. I got up and threw my hood on. Good luck finding me, there are a million loitering NDNs in Winnipeg tonight.

There's something quintessential about being me and walking at night. Finishing a seven-hour wank session, feeling exhausted, overworked, burnt out, underpaid, sad, hungry, lonely, nostalgic, and strangely beautiful during a one a.m. Sev-run. I calculated that it took me two hundred steps to walk the block back to my apartment. On the front steps of my building, I lit another cigarette. I thought, if it takes two hundred steps to walk a block, then there are two thousand steps in a mile. I wondered, if I walked 600,000 steps, if they'd call me Navajo and let me be a real NDN?

An elderly woman shouted out her window that if I didn't get up and go, she'd call the cops. Cops, I thought, everyone's always threatening me with cops. I waved my keycard at her and rolled my eyes. She huffed and closed her window. I could still feel her eyes watching me from behind the blinds. I wondered who she thought I was. Do people think I'm another ghost on the boulevard? Am I a vanishing NDN? If I disappeared, would they look for me like they did that woman, Thelma Krull? Would they rally behind my death like they did for that dead lion, Cecil? Nah, I thought. I'd become another name on the registry. My head felt light but my chest felt heavy.

I wished Tias would come over.

BEVANN FOX

From *Genocidal Love: A Life after Residential School*

Nōhkom wore rouge and lipstick for special days. She was so pretty. Sometimes she let me put some on. Nōhkom's broaches, earrings, rings, and scarves were very beautiful. I loved the way Nōhkom smelled of perfume and Doublemint gum. She always had gum to give to me. When we were alone, Nōhkom let me look at her jewellery and play with it for a while. The pieces were mostly there to admire. Nōhkom wore different floral dresses for different occasions, and her thick beige stockings were held up above each knee with an elastic band.

Nōhkom often told me that I talked too much, but she would comfort me by rubbing my head and running her fingers through my long hair. I especially liked touching Nōhkom's arm to feel her skin. It felt so loose, flabby, and soft. I would ask Nōhkom if I could touch her flabby soft arm while she told stories about her younger days and sang songs in Cree. I remember her singing, *Edmonton* "ē-itoh-tē-yān," *automobile* "ē-pōsi-yān. Mōniyaskwēw ē-itēy-mi-soyān. Ē-cika ōma ē-otihko miya . . ." *Edmonton driving in an automobile. Acting like a white woman feeling good about it, but I had lice in my hair* . . . The way she sang that song was so funny. Her laughter as we joined in. It was hilarious!

Nōhkom would buy tubes of baloney and cut the slices thick, just the way I liked them. I loved baloney and ketchup. I dipped the baloney into the ketchup and looked at Nōhkom. Once again,

I noticed the skin above her elbows, hanging so loose, her hands and fingers bent up as she used both hands to lift her rolled cigarette to her mouth. But even with her bent and twisted fingers, Nōhkom cut the most perfect baloney slices and I thought the slices were beautiful because Nōhkom cut them, and Nōhkom was beautiful.

Nimosōm washed my hair once a week with a special shampoo called White Rain. This was my favourite shampoo, and I loved the scent. He used fresh rainwater from the barrel to rinse my hair and then he brushed out all the knots and tangles. "Respect your hair, for it is a part of you. Don't leave it lying around, it is sacred. Don't cut your hair," he said.

Every spring Nimosōm washed my hair in boiled sweetgrass water, when the grass was new, having just sprung from the earth. Nimosōm said my hair would grow like the grass grows. And it did grow very fast! Other times he washed my hair in cold black tea that had sat for days. All of this helped my hair to stay healthy and strong and it grew very long. Nimosōm kept loose strands of my hair in a bag and when the bag was full we burned it.

When it rained, Nimosōm prepared our home for prayer and smudged each room. Then he smudged the children with sweetgrass smudge. It was so comforting. The rumbling cracks of thunder came, and the rain showers followed. We felt safe in our grandparents' home as we listened to the thunder move across the sky. Our eyes grew huge at the sound of the thunder and we giggled together. Nimosōm talked about the thunderbird and how the bird's spirit protected us. I had a picture in my mind of huge, beautiful thunderbirds watching over our home. Sometimes, when the lightning stopped, Nimosōm let us run out in the rain and shampoo our hair with the raindrops. We laughed and ran in the rain, having so much fun!

Nimosōm loved listening to my stories. He would make tea and put sugar and evaporated milk into my cup before settling at the table to talk. Sometimes we argued over something but Nimosōm would smile and say, "Okay, Mōniyāskwēsis [*Little White Girl*], you win." He challenged me on everything, and sometimes I found it difficult to stay in an argument. But it was fun to talk and talk and to say what was on my mind.

The Jehovah's Witnesses and Mormon missionaries came around to visit, handing out pamphlets and reading materials. Nimosōm went outside to meet them and talked for a very long time, asking questions about their beliefs and their churches. He never sent them away. Sometimes I heard him arguing with the missionaries. Nimosōm believed in prayer anywhere. "Pray in your mind, talk to the Creator in your heart," he said to the missionaries. "You don't have to go to a church." Even though Nimosōm argued with the missionaries, he liked their visits and loved the debate. "A real good talking argument," Nimosōm called it. The missionaries always left frustrated with my grandfather. Yet they would come again to visit.

Every morning there was work to do and play had to wait until later in the day. Sometimes, when I was feeling lazy and did not want to work, I went outside to the outhouse and stayed in there for a long time, hoping the dishes would be done by the time I went back into the house. The toilet stunk, and I gagged as I looked through old catalogues. Toilet paper was a luxury, and it disappeared very fast so there was a box of newspaper, brown paper, and rags on the floor beside the toilet. Oh . . . and the flies.

"Those dirty rotten bastards!" Nimosōm swore at the flies every day. They were pests and germ carriers. I took a can of Raid, which Nimosōm kept hidden, and sprayed the toilet before I entered.

At nighttime a pail called the slop pail was put by the door. I hated the job of emptying it the next morning. The mess sprayed back in my face as I gagged and complained about the other kids using the slop pail during the night. I called them cowards for being scared to go outside to the toilet at night. Sometimes going to that toilet was a nightmare but, when I was in there, I screamed for privacy because my cousins and siblings would throw stones at the toilet to disturb and startle me. I would run inside the house to tell on the others, and Nimosōm and Nōhkom would try to calm me down.

The bush was a beautiful escape. I took comic books and a catalogue and set out on my journey alone. Sometimes I brought a jar of Kool-Aid and some baloney sandwiches for a picnic. I sat in the warm sun in the old cars abandoned in the bushes, looking at every page of the clothing catalogue. I dreamed of making and wearing beautiful clothes someday. On every page I saw myself wearing the clothes, and I said out loud, "That's me, there is me and that is me again."

I loved the smell of the trees and plants in the warm sun, the sounds of the birds. I could hear the other kids looking for me and wondered, "Why can't they just leave me alone?"

I knew every trail like the back of my hand and ran through them barefoot. Sometimes I would climb a tree and watch the others looking for me, calling my name. A butterfly would flutter by and stop to sit on my fingers; it was so delicate and beautiful. I told myself not to move or even breathe. I would look at its pretty wings and smell its dusty scent. "You're a sacred butterfly." The different blended colours on the wings were so amazing and beautiful! "Fly away, pretty one." I remembered Nimosōm and Nōhkom's words: "Never hurt living things; each has its own spirit. The trees and the rocks have spirits too. Everything has a spirit!"

The children weren't allowed to break branches off trees. It was disrespectful and hurtful to the tree. It was tempting at times to break off a branch filled with berries and eat from the broken branch, but the guilt that followed was not worth it. Instead, we picked the berries off the bushes with our fingers. It was sheer laziness if we broke branches, and we really got in trouble if we did.

I would smile and ask Nimosōm, "Why are you so mean to the flies?"

"The flies will always be dirty!" Nimosōm said.

"Don't the flies have a spirit too, since they are alive?" I asked.

"I never really thought of them, but I'm sure they have a place on earth too, maybe to bug us, drive us crazy and make us grouchy!" Nimosōm laughed.

Once I set the other kids on a race to the beehive and then threw a rock from a distance. I regretted destroying the bee's home, but I did it only to get back at the other kids and to try to get them to stay away from me. They were stung many times. I smiled with sweet revenge. When I got home, however, I paid the price twice over. My grandparents were so upset and disappointed in me. I explained that I just wanted to be left alone—not bothered or followed—but the other kids wouldn't leave me alone. The troublemakers were standing there with bee stings all over their faces, arms, and legs. "Respect life in the bush because if you don't, something will come back on you, you may get hurt.

TENILLE K. CAMPBELL

From *#IndianLovePoems*

#114

I love you
my Cree lover
you and your cheek-
bones that beckon my lips
day and night

I love you
my Cree lover
the way you stake your claim
on my body
day and night

I don't love
your mother

#64

Cree Man
you are the salt and pepper
in my moose meat stew
the one i need
for spice in my life

Cree Man
you are the loudest bingo
caller in the hall
your voice echoes through the rafters
of my urbanized heart

Cree Man
i wait for you
standing behind drum circles
listening to the high twangs
calling my name

Cree Man
i wait for you
a double
double in one hand
warm fry-bread
in the other

#209

okay I was faking
to make him feel better
moaning out loud in Dene
stuff like
esjie
dénįgha thot'įné chelekwaze
hey
that's the only Dene I remember
on short notice

pêyak nîso nisto nêwo
muttering out loud
so he knew
that he would drive me crazy
with his little *toogaloo*
tugey

I arched my back
saying things like
owieyahhhh
and *ooohhhh*
thinking
all the while
this was worth
at least two
Golden Globes

I grabbed fistfuls of pillow
screaming my latest release
rolling my eyes
as he grunted away
until his two minutes
of fame were finished

I rolled over
panting slightly
acting dizzy and giggly
kissing his lips

sëchazeh
you were the best I ever had . . .

esjie: oh my god / I'm so sure (Dene slang)
dénįgha thot'įné chelekwaze: go away, white boy
(Dene, pronounced *deh-nee-gha thow-tee-nay che-lay-kwa-zay*)
pêyak nîso nisto nêwo: one two three four (Cree)
toogaloo: penis (Cree/Métis/Dene slang)
tugey: "fuck" / swear word (Cree/Métis/Dene slang)
sëchazeh: my sweetie / my babe (Dene)

TENILLE K. CAMPBELL

From *nedí nezų*

the first time we fuck

I can't say make love
I don't know who your family are
but the first time we fuck
I expect
you to bless my sex
with prayers straight from your mouth
I want you to whisper your truths
with tongue
up and down my sacred being
where my moon and sun collide
where my power patiently waits

the first time we fuck
you need to recognize the ceremony
that my body holds
I'm your sweat lodge
bringing you closer to the sky people
eyes closed forehead against mine
I ground you to the earth
hands braced on either side of me
fingers clenched tight as I tighten around you

the first time we fuck
you need to recognize your blessings
hold me in your arms fingers trailing
curves the Creator made to hold power
feel my heart beat slow breathing deep
before you slip out of bed
covering me with soft blankets

the first time we fuck
you may recognize
the possibility within me
a safe place to land a welcoming
but understand this
I may be your ceremony
but my bed is not your home

I wonder

if you would love me

if my thighs had gaps
to let in the setting sun

if my curves were rolling hills and shallow lakes
instead of mountains and oceans

if my skin ran smooth over muscles
instead of water rippling over rapids

I wonder
if you would love me

if my bones were delicate and hollow
sustained only on your compliments

if my stomach lay flat and unscarred
untouched by birth and life

if my feet were tiny like a hummingbird's
instead of flat and wide to grip the earth

I wonder
if you would love me

if my breasts were a dainty handful
instead of spilling through your fingers

if my mouth was only used for your pleasure
instead of reciting poetry aimed to cut

if my mind only thought of you
setting aside decolonization and language reclamation

I wonder if you would love me
if I wasn't me at all

sex sex sex

one-trick pony she is
        baby
        I got tricks
        for generations
the biggest trick
is still being here
surviving thriving organizing

we still here

we echo and ripple descendants pouring
down concrete over pavement
babies cradled on hips snug within cradleboards
wrapped in starblankets under protest signs
#JusticeForColten
#TinaFontaine
#IndigenousResistance

we don't have the luxury
of not explaining to our babies
why we don't wear black hoodies
why we don't take cabs alone
and why we don't trust cops

but

we still here
hands holding mukluk wearing
tears spilling laughter flowing
medicine in our very bones
ancestors in our eyes
as we gaze and catch feelings
across citywide marches
seeing us in them and them in us
just tricks
surviving thriving organizing
yeah
we got tricks for days

PART IV

MEMORY

AVIAQ JOHNSTON

From *Those Who Run in the Sky*

Giant

By the time Pitu felt sure that the creatures were not going to follow him, he was exhausted. Though he knew he could still be in danger, he could no longer find the strength to build a proper shelter. His adrenaline from the last fight had worn him thin. He began to build an iglu, but the snow was not hard enough to cut blocks. The boy instead dug a shallow hole the length of his body, with a measly wind shelter on one side to protect him slightly from the elements.

Normally, Pitu had trouble falling asleep in shelters of this kind; they were uncomfortable and dangerous. Though they provided slight cover, the soft snow was no protection from animals. Pitu knew that if the wolfish creatures reached him, he'd have no chance of survival. With no energy to fight, he'd be killed in a moment.

Let them kill me, Pitu thought. *I'm never getting out of this place anyway.* With that realization, Pitu fell into a dead sleep. Curled into a ball, he dreamt of the fox and the old man.

The landscape was summery, the tundra covered in moss and lichen. A caribou-hide tent was propped in the middle of a gravelly area. The fox was skirting around the edge of the campground. Its coat was a spotty, dirty black colour to blend in with the black lichen-covered rocks, its eyes dark and focused in the direction that Pitu was watching from. There was a small fire directly in front of the tent; a rack made of flat rocks was lying on top of it, holding up a stone bowl full of boiling meat. The old man sat on a boulder the size of one of Pitu's huskies. Thoughts of Miki sprang to Pitu's mind. His stomach twisted with the thought of his dog.

The old man tended to the bowl of *uujuq*, cooking meat, in silence. When Pitu began to walk closer, he looked up and sighed. "You again?" he asked. "Why do I always see you? What do you want?"

"Who are you?" Pitu asked.

"I am Taktuq," the old man answered, spitting out the words. "'Fog,' that is what the spirits call me."

"Why do I keep seeing you?"

"How should I know?" Taktuq said irritably. "Didn't you hear my name? I sit here confused in the clouds all day."

"Taktuq . . ." Pitu thought of the shaman that Tagaaq had told him about. The shaman had vanished. No one heard from him or saw him ever again. "Taktuq . . . Are you the shaman that was once revered by all?"

"Revered?" Taktuq growled out a laugh. "Hah! Never. I am the shaman that could never find peace."

Despite his dismissal, Pitu was sure that this was the old shaman he needed to find. He asked, "Where are you? I need you to help me."

"You aren't very smart, are you?" Taktuq replied. "I don't know where I am. I'm LOST."

"How can you be lost?" In his frustration, Pitu began yelling at the old man. He'd moved closer to where Taktuq sat, but felt that if he went any closer he'd be sent back to his mind and awoken from the sleep he so desperately needed. In the distance, now that he thought of his real body, he could hear a thunderous thump that sounded only a short distance away. Pitu focused on the old man again. "You're a shaman. You can't get lost—the spirits are supposed to help you! You can't be lost! You have to help me!"

"The spirits cannot help a soul that is broken, young shaman. That is why you are lost, too."

"Don't talk to me as if you know what is happening," Pitu spat. "You were guided here by your spirit, weren't you? I've been thrown into chaos! You have no idea what it's like in the open land of spirits. You sit here in your comfortable summer."

"That may be true." Taktuq shrugged. "It's been a long time since I left this place. The air feels too hungry when I step onto the snow." He shivered as the thought of the frozen land made him cold. "I will try to send someone to help you."

Taktuq looked at the fox and whistled lowly. It turned in the opposite direction and dashed away, disappearing from sight much faster than it should have. Pitu heard another thump not too far away; this time he also felt it. He tried to step closer to the summer landscape that was just beyond his reach. The ground beneath his feet splintered as the world around him began to quake. He stopped, spreading his arms wide in hopes that the world would stop quivering under his feet. There was another loud thump, this time only a short distance away. The old man didn't seem to notice.

Suddenly, the fox was back in view. The earth under Pitu's feet quaked again, making him topple onto his back. His eyelids became heavy, and just as he emerged from his dream, he heard the shaman say, "Your guide will find you soon. Don't move from where you are when you wake!"

However, this was easier said than done.

When Pitu opened his eyes and was back in his body, he was looking right into a humongous face. He jumped at the sight of the giant, holding back a high-pitched scream. He calmed himself to hide his fear. He played cool, like a cornered lemming would, until he could think of a plan to get away.

The giant was staring at him in amused curiosity. The eyes were a dark shade of brown, almost black. Greasy shafts of hair hung around the sides of the face; a giant nose was less than an arm's length away from Pitu's own. There was a grinning mouth with only a handful of brownish teeth full of dark black spots around their roots.

And the smell! Pitu tried to hold his breath, but the smell was atrocious. He couldn't remember a worse odour filling his nose. His eyes watered at the stench. Even a thousand caches of *igunaq*[1] did not smell that awful.

The giant's mouth moved and a high-pitched voice bellowed, "*Kinakuluugavit?* Who are you?"

Pitu shrieked, trying to squirm away from the giant. It towered over him, laughing at his fright. His attempt at escape was quickly thwarted as the giant grabbed Pitu around his midriff and called out, "You are so TINY!" The giant's laughter filled Pitu's ears, making his eardrums ring. "Who are you, TINY ONE?"

"Who are you?" Pitu shrieked back.

The giant laughed again. "Aaah!" it said. "Ah! You are so cute! Even your voice squeaks like a little lemming!"

Pitu was offended. "I am a great hunter!" he yelled in his deepest voice. "I do NOT sound like a lemming!"

"Oh, little lemming, I will keep you!"

He thrashed against the giant, trying with all his might to squirm free. The struggle was useless. Pitu decided that it would be more frugal of him to save his strength. The giant picked him up and shifted his arms and legs as if checking to see how well they could move. As the giant inspected Pitu, he began to inspect the giant, too.

He couldn't tell whether it was male or female. Though the voice was high and relatively soft—for a giant—it had prominently male features. It was large enough to make a fully grown beluga appear as a seal, a polar bear as a puppy. The clothing was shabby; the upturned caribou hide fading with age and the residue of a thousand messy meals and unkempt days. Pitu wondered how many caribou it had taken to make the parka in the first place. There were stitches all over it.

The giant smiled widely, its breath fuming out of its mouth in stinking wafts. Pitu almost gagged on the smell. The giant spoke in an ancient dialect of Inuktitut, so Pitu struggled to understand all that was coming out of its mouth. To distract himself, he again asked the giant, "Who are you?"

The giant chuckled with pure mirth. "Ah! When you speak it makes me so happy!" The giant stomped its feet in a giddy fashion, then it began to walk away from the little shelter Pitu had made, leaving Pitu's knife and harpoon behind. "I am Inukpak!" the giant said. *Inukpak*, thought Pitu, *a giant named Giant.*

"Tiny Hunter, that is you, and I will keep you to hunt for little things!"

"Inukpak, my tools!" Pitu shrieked. "I cannot be a little hunter without my tools!"

He felt his cheeks flush with embarrassment as he referred to himself as a "little hunter."

Inukpak laughed again, bouncing Pitu around in a disorienting jaunt. The giant continued forward, moving with incredible speed. "Silly little hunter!" Inukpak cooed. "I will make new gear. Ones that are not so sharp. I don't want you to hurt yourself."

"How can I hunt without a harpoon sharp enough to pierce a seal?" Pitu countered. "Or a polar bear?" *Or a giant?* he thought to himself.

"It's okay!" Inukpak still seemed far too cheery for Pitu to truly believe. No one could be that happy. "You're just going to be playing!"

Pitu tried to think of more ways to convince Inukpak that he needed to get his weapons, but he was still tired from the day before and his mind was slow. He couldn't come up with a plan that would leave him in one piece. He knew that if he could just get out of Inukpak's grip, he could run back to his makeshift shelter and retrieve his tools and find a way to outrun the giant.

Pitu looked over his shoulder and was disheartened to see that his shelter was no longer anywhere in sight. They had gone much farther, with much greater speed, than Pitu had ever thought possible. Suddenly, he grew incredibly tired, without any energy to become angry. With careless abandon, he let Inukpak take him deeper into the land of spirits than he could ever truly begin to understand. *I am never leaving this place*, he thought. *I will never go back home to see my family again.*

❋

By the time the giant stopped walking, Pitu had lost feeling in his lower body. He looked up into the sky to try to gauge the time, but it remained an unshifting overcast grey, revealing nothing. However, he knew they had been travelling for a long period of time because his body ached as though he'd been on a day-long *qamutiik*[2] ride. They were near the distant mountains that Pitu had been trying to reach since he arrived. With the large steps that Inukpak took, it dawned on Pitu just how long it would have taken him to journey that far with just his two feet. The trip had taken Inukpak hours, yet the giant was still jaunty and annoyingly cheerful.

Inukpak climbed through passages in the mountains with ease, following a path that no human could see simply because of the great distances cleared by each step. Pitu thought of the glaciers back home, how they seemed to crush mountains with their weight and the endless stream of melting waters that slid down to the ocean in summer, following a path that was large and wide. Did giants create those paths in the past? Were giants somehow responsible for the glaciers that brought so much life to his world? Pitu shook his head, the thoughts jumbling his mind.

They came to a full stop in a valley surrounded by a bowl of mountains. There was no iglu, but there were plenty of other things that would make living here comfortable. *Do giants feel the cold?* Pitu thought. This one didn't seem to.

In the valley, there was a herd of caribou that made Pitu's mouth water. There were other animals, too. Their arrival woke a polar bear from a doze; wolves (that were, thankfully, normal wolves) wagged their tails in greeting. They all swarmed around Inukpak, little pets greeting their master. The sight perplexed Pitu.

The giant put a hand into the pocket of its parka, bringing out a giant handful of other animals. The giant dropped the lemmings, hares, and foxes into the middle of the wolves, and then took a seal for the polar bear to eat on its own. Pitu's stomach grumbled as he watched.

"Oh, little hunter," Inukpak said, "Are you hungry, too?"

"Yes," Pitu grudgingly replied.

"You can have a caribou!" Inukpak said. "What do you want? The ribs? The leg? The head?"

Pitu perked up at that. The head was the best part of the caribou, with its brains, eyeballs, and most of all, its tongue and jaw. Inukpak laughed again. "The head it is, little hunter!"

Notes

1. Fermented walrus meat.
2. A sled made from many materials, such as frozen fish, moss, driftwood, and animal bones, which carries supplies and families, usually pulled by dogs. Modern *qamutiit* are made of wood and typically pulled by a snowmobile.

JOSHUA WHITEHEAD

From *Full-Metal Indigiqueer*

DOUWANTTOKNOWWHATMAKESTHEREDMENRED[QUESTIONMARK]

pe: ::::ter:: :::: ::: ::p(l,0)an: :: :: :: :::downloadingdisneysoftware: :: :: :: ::: :::: : :: : ::: : :: :

: ::::pleasewait:: :: :::: :::: :::simulacrumsimulationsequenceinitiated: ::: : :: :: : :: : :: :: :: : :

: :::::removecookie[questionmark]: :: :::1: ::: :: :0:: ::::: : : :1:: ::::: : :securitybypassed: :: ::

::: ::downloadlostboys[questionmark]: :: ::: :Y: :: :: :: :: :: :installationcomplete: :: :: :: : ::

makes me red
in the cheeks when you piss me off
in the scalp for the economic mnemonic warfare you ack[cost]
me with
in the gut for feeding me kfc & deep-fried things
in the fingerpad for the daily diabetes prickings
in the esophagus for the burning from drinking herbal essence
between the toes for always walking west
in the vulva for all our babies in cfs
in the veins: quotidian quantum qualification
this is a brand of blood: tm
blood | mihko
red | mihkwâw
red is embarrassment
red is shame
shameiam | iamshame

shame makes the red | man | red
makes him injun; makes him feel
makes him real in pictures & in the mirror
in the blacktopscreenofanimacpixel
talk to us, they say, talk | pîkiskwewin
confess to us your shame
confess to us your sin
receive a gold medallion
virtual as your skin
thin as frybread
thin as fried bologna in your sandwich
shoddy as a promise
this is your [treat]me
confess; they say; confess
this isnt a day school now, its trc
express in detail
the feeling of fingers digging in your abdo[men]
the taste of [neu]trition & shoal water
can you feel the metal on your tongue[questionmark]
the stick that pushes down your buds[questionmark]
tell them how it felt to have someone rub your hair
rub you down there
tell them how it felt to be hit&whipped&beat
for speaking your name in full regalia
tell them in vivid detail
so they can masturbate in their seats
ejaculate history into a two-ply klee[next]
pay off these little red injuns
heres fifty dollars for your shame

to work through, they say, we need to work through
move beyond, undo, assimilate, associate, incriminate
nation to nation is the new assimilation
move b[ye]ond the priests who hold our sermons
say prayers on thanksgiving & columbus day
but for you: we need to work through *you*
move beyond; undo; work through
confess until theres nothing left
maybe a scar
maybe a virtual participatory ribbon
confessionnotacceptedpleasetryagain
maybe a thread or two of your ribbon skirt
maybe a word or two in the air
nepewisiwin | pakwâteyitam | nepewisiwin
shame | hate | shame
i am here
crawling on the floor
spotlight down & feathers annulled
still tasting sunny boy on my tongue
burning hot sensation of fingers
sham | shame | mask
have i not worn this face youve given me
for two hundred years or more[questionmark]
when you strip away the thread
take away the paints
bake away the clay
chip away the sham
i am the man with no face
the woman without hair

(you would have liked me when i was nikâwiy)
i am nothing
anymore
confess
history
shame
story
me
i
[period]
there is shame written on my bones—
where my mother etched my name
onto my sternum she wrote
"kisâkihitin"
right beside where a priest wrote
"this is mine"
there is shame here
but there is family too
there is indigeneity
there is truth
& i need these all to survive:
hereIamhereIamhereIamhereIam
in the space between the breast
iam
the beating of my heartdrum
iam:wondrously amused
iam:inthiscell
iam:[injun]
iam:[unity]

iam:myshame&thatsokay
iam:wheremisery
becomes:[my]story
iam—
iam
iam

—h/er[e]

NAZBAH TOM

From "The Hand Trembler"

The barking dogs alerted me to a car driving towards the house.

"Grandma, someone is coming."

"Oh, it's our visitors," she said as she wrapped up her spindle and wool. She carefully placed them to the side and brushed lint off her clothing. "Go see what they want, will you?"

I walked out of the house and headed to the driver side window to greet them.

"*Ya'ah'teh.*" I could feel the heat from the engine as he turned off his truck. The man's skin was the shade of hard work in a corn field.

"*Ao, ya'ah'teh,*" said the driver, smiling in my direction. His hair was in a neat bun and around his wrist was a turquoise bracelet. His wife sat next to him, a thin nylon head scarf tied around under her chin. I looked down and rolled a pebble underneath my shoe waiting for him to say more. After a few moments, the man asked if my grandma was home.

"We're from down the way. Your grandma knows my parents. She's my *naali* by clan."

"Mmm-hmm," I said as I continued to play with the pebble underneath my shoe, not looking at him.

"We're wondering if your grandma can see us today?" he said hopefully. When he smiled, I caught a glimpse of his front teeth outlined in silver.

I walked back inside to find the radio had been shut off. Quiet. Grandma was putting on a pot of coffee. She had already changed into a clean red cotton skirt and a light grey flower-printed polyester shirt; her hair in a neat bun.

"I can see them today. Go let them know and bring them in here. You know what to do with the dogs outside. Make sure they are not around the house, *shi yazhi.* When you come back into the house, stay on the couch until I call you back in."

I returned to the waiting couple to let them know the good news and they entered Grandma's house. I closed the door behind me and did as I was told.

The dogs jumped up from where they were lying and ran away from my voice and waving hands towards the sheep corral for shade. I checked around Grandma's house to make sure other animals weren't lingering. The horse was penned up eating hay and oats. I quietly opened and closed the side door and made my way to the couch. I sat down and closed my eyes trying to listen in on what Grandma was doing with this couple. I could hear them talking in Grandma's bedroom, their voices muffled. Then silence.

Suddenly, the air shifted. I looked around the living room slowly. Outside, the horse stopped chewing for a moment and cocked its ears. It swatted its tail at nothing, the sound of coarse horse hair falling across its rounded rump. The dog with its head on its paws looked up suddenly and whimpered quietly. I caressed the poised hair on my arms slowly with my thumbs to the rhythm of my heart thudding. I sat and listened to my grandma's muffled voice singing in the next room, remembering stories I had heard about her and her magic hands. Grandma's trembling hands.

Grandma's conduit work between this world and the next. There was a landscape only she knew, between the couple's reports of their dreams, body aches, and animals that had crossed their paths. After several minutes passed, my grandma cleared her throat and I could hear her talking again. I heard the man's voice acknowledging what my grandma had learned. I heard them shuffle around before opening the door to the room.

I escorted the couple out to their truck. The woman said to me, "*Ahe'he'he*," with a warm look. I caught her eyes for a brief moment and nodded. The man climbed into his side of the truck and offered me his thanks before driving off. I knew our family would help with the ceremony they'd plan after their meeting with Grandma.

I headed back into the house to find Grandma tired, as if she had travelled on a long journey.

"I need to rest a bit. Can you bring me some water?" she said while undoing her bun with one hand and taking the pins out of her hair with the other. I did as I was told.

"*Ahe'he, shi yazhi.* Okay, I'm going to nap for a bit. We can eat the blood sausage when I wake up, okay?"

"Okay, Grandma."

I closed her door and returned to finding words in her crossword puzzle book. I settled into grandpa's chair, legs swinging, and empty coffee cup nearby.

RELIEF. I circled the word.

DREAMS. I circled the word.

I looked out on the rain clouds and I could smell rain many miles away to the west. The dogs were slowly making their way

MICHELLE PORTER

From *Approaching Fire*

On the plains when you watch for a fire, watch what the animals are doing, monitor the wind. You have to look at the earth you're living on. Learn how to notice what's growing and what's been burned before. Learn to anticipate how it might respond to heat and to flames. Build that information into your response plans. You read the history of the land you're walking on and ask about the last burning. When did fire last eat/feed this land? If it's been a long time between burns, you may get the urge to run. But you know you can only outrun the little fires and only for so long. When the large fires come, they chase you wherever you go and they eat/feed everything. The signs will be there. I see them everywhere. Mother, brothers, aunts and uncles, sisters on the run all the time. We're living through the years when fire suppression policies finally catch up with everyone.

Louis Goulet, my great-great-grandfather's brother, in the summer of what was probably the year 1868, was living through the final years of the Métis buffalo hunt, with a caravan of Métis families and Red River carts. Buffalo were scarce that summer. There was smoke. They watched for signs, for what they needed to know about the approaching fire:

> *Prairie chickens began flying over very high, downwind and away from the fire, only to fall to the ground here and there, suffocated. The*

windspeed increased day by day and the fire moved faster and faster. Deer, antelope, elk, large hares, little prairie dogs, foxes, wolves, even the buffalo we hadn't seen since the day we left, came out of hiding as if by magic, all of them fleeing at full speed.

My dear Pépé,

How did you tell the story of your Métis identity, my dear Pépé? Was it for you the same way it is for me? This word describes your membership to a nation of people and it is a braid between you and relations you know only in stories; between the cousins, the uncles and the aunties who raised you and the relations you never knew in places you hadn't visited yet?

Maybe Métis for you was an entry into stories that you weren't supposed to have, not anymore, not if the Métis had gone away like the government wanted them to. This word Métis is a story between you and me, Pépé, more so than the words great-grandfather. This word is a story we are telling each other, each from our own places on the land and in time, and that word is a story that will invite the next generations into our circle.

Louis Riel's great-grandniece, Jean Teillet, wrote that he preferred the word Métis. It was a European word, but one claimed by a nation. She wrote that in her book, *The North-West Is Our Mother*, a book about our people. I've already told you her name, I know, but there must be so much going on where you are, you must be playing so many gigs up there, all day and all night, that I'm sure you're not keeping track of the books I've been reading about our history, here where I'm living, here where I'm bending over my desk every day and every night.

You don't need a lot of books where you are, do you? All your questions have been answered. That is such an alien idea to me, a person who is so often weighted with uncertainty and with doubt. To have all your questions answered, even the ones you didn't know enough to ask, what does such an existence feel like, Pépé? I imagine a lightness, as if a wing had rooted beside each scapula, into the dense site where the muscles attach. We need the books to be written, they are critical, and we also need the traditional Métis music to stay with us here to answer questions we don't even know need answering.

Your music, you would tell me if you were here, is a muscle. We all of us need it here in this living world, so please don't take it with you. Let me keep some of it here to share.

In the 1930s in Manitoba when you were performing with the Red River Echoes, the word Métis was a dirty word. Your family was so well-known that you couldn't escape the meaning of your last name, not in Manitoba. To hold the last name Goulet and to be the son of Maxime Goulet in that province and in those years was to be Métis in a way that carried you along like a fast-moving river.

"The Métis Nation has always been a people of many names," Teillet wrote in the book you don't need to read where you are. It's in the second-last chapter of the book and when I read it, it struck me how you are also a man of many names, how I am a woman of different names, too, in my own way. I have to laugh at myself, Pépé: it took me almost to the end of the book to see that. Here are a few of the names for the Métis Nation, some given by outsiders and some that we gave ourselves: Bois-Brûlés, Michif, Âpihtawikosisân, Métis, the flower beadwork people, Freemen, gens libres, half-breed, and Otipêyimisowak.

Fire leaves its story in the earth, though sometimes what's left behind after a fire will look crooked. If you can work out the details of a fire's relationship with a given place, you can read the stories. Fire creates so much of the world—that's my interpretation of Kira Hoffman's aching and beautiful work on fire ecology. Seems like the world's on fire, like the world's burning itself up.

DANIEL SIOUI

d'Indien stoïque

IL FAUT RÉGLER LE PASSÉ

La première chose qui me met en colère et qu'il faut régler au plus sacrant, c'est la suivante : est-ce qu'on peut arrêter de vivre dans le passé ? Est-ce qu'on peut enfin arrêter de faire comme si notre vie avait pris fin à l'arrivée des Blancs et cesser de se morfondre avec ça ? Donnez-moi deux secondes.

Est-ce que la vie était vraiment mieux avant l'arrivée des Blancs ? J'ai des doutes. OK, c'est vrai que nous vivions cent fois mieux que les paysans en Europe, qui se faisaient siphonner leurs avoirs par les rois et les seigneurs, mais notre vie était loin d'être parfaite. Oui, nous avions un semblant de « libârté », l'accès à un territoire magnifique, qui nous fournissait ce dont nous avions besoin. En plus, il y a pas mal de maladies qui n'existaient pas chez nous à l'époque. Il allait nous manquer amèrement, ce temps-là, plus tard . . .

Que voulez-vous, les Blancs ne se lavaient pas ben gros, pis ils nous ont apporté toutes sortes de cochonneries pour lesquelles notre corps n'était pas prêt. Mais, tsé, on ne vivait quand même pas jusqu'à deux cents ans. Notre vie n'était quand même pas si jolie-jolie. Est-ce qu'on pourrait régler ça, une fois pour toutes ? Comprenez-moi bien : je suis loin de dire qu'il faut tout oublier du passé, ce n'est pas ce que je pense. Nos ancêtres (je ne peux pas parler pour l'ensemble des nations, mais au moins mes ancêtres à moi, les Wendat) ont probablement créé la plus belle philosophie de vie qui soit. Pas une religion basée sur des dieux en manque de confiance en soi qui ont besoin de se faire louanger sans arrêt, non, mais plutôt une philosophie de vie basée sur le respect. Le respect entre tout ce qui est vivant, des singes pas de poils à l'araignée au plafond. Non seulement il ne faut pas l'oublier, cette philosophie, mais il faudrait vraiment la remettre de l'avant. Les anciens avaient compris que tout est relié. Que la vie fait partie d'un cercle. Que les humains comme le reste de la création font partie d'un tout et que tout doit être respecté. Le contraire de la pensée chrétienne, finalement, où le reste de la création est là pour servir l'humain. Nos ancêtres étaient peut-être plus intelligents, en fin de compte, et avaient compris un des mystères de l'univers. Pourquoi les cons existent ? Parce qu'ils sont aussi importants que les personnes intelligentes ; les uns n'existent pas sans les autres. Ils devaient sûrement avoir autant de misère que nous autres à se rentrer ça dans la tête, mais c'est ça, le cercle. On doit accepter les autres comme ils sont ; tout le monde a un rôle à jouer. Je sais, c'est difficile à gober, surtout avec les covidiots qui ont fleuri en ces temps de pandémie, mais c'est ça quand même. Les êtres humains et la création sont aussi importants l'un que l'autre. Malgré tout, n'oublions pas que les ancêtres étaient des humains, et c'est bien beau la philosophie de vie, mais personne n'est parfait. Pas mal sûr qu'il devait y avoir des intolérants dans nos rangs aussi. Il s'agit pour s'en convaincre de se rappeler la façon dont on pouvait traiter nos ennemis. Il y a de bonnes chances que la jalousie et l'envie faisaient aussi des victimes dans les villages.

Ce que je veux dire, c'est qu'il est temps de déboulonner le mythe de l'Indien hollywoodien sur son cheval, en parfaite communion avec la nature, qui a l'air plus fort que l'univers : c'est de la bullshit (excusez mon français). Oui, nous avions une relation respectueuse avec la nature, mais le maudit orignal ne venait pas de lui-même s'offrir en sacrifice. Avant l'arrivée des Blancs et de leurs super fusils, il fallait lui courir après en tabarouette. Et les chances de l'attraper étaient bien minces. Les peuples autochtones ont connu de nombreuses famines et il arrivait quand même assez souvent que le monde meure de faim.

Avant de penser à notre avenir, il faut donc commencer par démolir le mythe que la période précolombienne était notre âge d'or. Sérieusement, il m'arrive de penser que c'est une tactique perverse pour nous faire croire que notre temps est révolu, que notre vie avait l'air bien plaisante avec la liberté, l'absence de stress, et tutti quanti : maintenant qu'il ne nous est plus possible de retrouver notre mode de vie, on serait mieux de laisser tomber et de s'assimiler à la société occidentale. Le pire, c'est que la plupart des Autochtones sont d'accord avec ça. J'entends sans arrêt dire qu'il n'y a qu'une façon d'être un vrai Autochtone : il faut vivre de la trappe dans le bois comme dans le bon vieux temps. Bon, premièrement, même à l'époque, on n'était pas tous des nomades vivant uniquement de la chasse. On dirait qu'on l'a oublié ça, aujourd'hui. On entend seulement la rengaine du territoire de chasse, qui nous permettrait de retrouver nos traditions. On entend ça même chez nous, les Wendat, alors qu'on se nourrissait presque exclusivement de légumes ou de poissons. Oui, on chassait de temps en temps, mais c'était vraiment pas notre pratique préférée. J'ai l'impression qu'on préférait bien plus commercer ou bien faire la guerre plutôt que de perdre notre temps à courir après une grosse bête poilue. Sérieusement, mettez-moi seul dans le bois et je meurs en deux jours max, en tournant en rond et en paniquant parce que je me suis perdu. J'exagère quand même un peu : je sais que, si je me perds, je dois rester sur place et attendre que quelqu'un me trouve avant, je l'espère, qu'un orignal me mange. Je suis un pur Indien des villes, je ne suis même pas capable de digérer la viande de bois. Est-ce que ça fait de moi un « fake Indian » pour autant ? Sûrement pour beaucoup de monde . . . Personnellement, je ne le vois pas comme ça. Au contraire, je suis un Indien de son temps et ce que j'essaie de dire, c'est que, si nous le désirons vraiment, la période que nous vivons pourrait être notre fameux âge d'or. Vous allez me traiter d'innocent, me dire que la vie d'un Autochtone aujourd'hui est plutôt moche, que la vie dans une réserve n'est pas une vie, à cause de la surpopulation, de la maladie, de l'alcool, de la drogue et des autres cochonneries qui font des ravages. Tout ça, c'est vrai. Ça fait quatre cents ans que ça dure. Nous avons survécu aux maladies, aux guerres— entre nous et contre les Blancs—, aux déportations, aux maudits pensionnats et à toutes les autres mardes et nous sommes encore là. Si ça ne fait pas de nous les peuples les plus résilients de la planète, ça, qu'est-ce que ça vous prend ?

L'État a tout fait pour que nous disparaissions, mais nous sommes toujours là, plus forts que jamais. Nous commençons à comprendre la façon de jouer des Blancs et nous savons que nous pouvons les battre à leur propre jeu. La preuve : les satanés traités, enfoncés de force dans la gorge de bien des nations, commencent à se retourner contre le gouvernement. Quand la Couronne les a signés, elle était persuadée que les Autochtones allaient disparaître et qu'elle n'aurait jamais à les honorer, mais (surprise !) nous sommes toujours vivants et le temps est venu de payer. Certains peuples ont même réussi à prouver les vols de territoire qui ont eu lieu bien avant nos naissances et ont reçu des compensations. Je sais que ça ne compensera jamais la vraie valeur des terres, mais il ne faut quand même pas rêver.

Là, je rêve en couleurs, mais voici mon souhait le plus cher : ne pourrait-on espérer que le temps écoulé nous permette d'oublier les vieilles chicanes ? Les maudites chicanes qui ont permis aux Blancs de nous monter les uns contre les autres. Les Wendat contre les Iroquois, pour un genre de guerre sainte incompréhensible. Les nomades contre les sédentaires, parce que les deux se prenaient plus pour de vrais hommes que les autres. Sans oublier les affrontements entre nous pour les maudites fourrures à vendre aux Blancs.

Est-ce qu'on pourrait enfin espérer s'unir et former un seul groupe souverain ? Arrêter de tirer sur la couverte et de penser seulement à sa petite nation. J'entends déjà bien des Autochtones me dire : « Moi, je suis un Wendat... », « Moi, je suis un Innu... », et ainsi de suite. Je les entends me rappeler que nous sommes des peuples distincts. Mais il reste que nous ne réussirons jamais à reprendre le contrôle si chacun reste de son bord. Si les Européens ont réussi à former l'Union européenne, pourquoi ne pourrions-nous pas nous aussi créer l'Union des Premiers Peuples ? Chaque nation resterait indépendante, mais nous aurions une plus grande force de frappe.

Nous devons absolument arrêter de vivre dans le passé et commencer à réfléchir à une structure qui nous permettrait de retrouver notre place dans le bal des nations. Ça n'arrivera pas si nous restons chacun de notre côté. C'est notre division qui a permis aux Européens de venir s'installer ici et c'est notre division qui nous empêche de sortir de la colonisation, tant que nous n'aurons pas choisi la façon de faire. Si ça continue comme ça, on pourra dire que nous nous sommes fait coloniser de force en en mangeant toute une et que nous nous sommes fait décoloniser de force en perdant ce qui nous reste.

ELAINE McARTHUR

"Brush of a Bustle"

A river of noise flows around the harbour
voices and laughter lap at the unsettled shores
of my nervous stomach rejecting their happy jostling
as they endlessly circle the dancing arena
I stand strong in their tide watching
waiting for my category

Announcer broadcasts the next round
"Next up ladies fancy shawl!"

Spectators settle in for a night of colour and dance
children on chairs are cocooned under blankets
adults bundle against the evening
teenagers have donned warmer fare in their quest
for summer love
my beadwork adorns me like a colourful painting
I check it for loose ties, crooked pieces, and straighten my shawl

"Ladies fancy shawl come on out!"

Butterflies in my stomach begin to flutter
His bustle breaks away from the silhouetted crowd
tiny wings madly pound I blush at the familiar shape

one I've watched for every weekend
his face and body darkened by the harbour lights behind him
he passes by so near his bustle brushes my eyelids
cheekbones and forehead in a tension set stroke

I close my eyes and breathe his space
the rhythm is silenced
lulled for one magnified second
no sound, voices nor laughter
just a liquid slowing of movement and noise
touch and secret whisperings left unsaid

"Last call ladies fancy shawl!"

The clamorous flow comes rushing back
I carry his message into the arena
spoken in the language of a dancer
a bustle's caress unnoticed
in a jostling busy powwow night

KEELY KEYSOOS SHIRT

"I Will Never Be Happier"

I will never be happier than to bend
to every stretch of land
and thank it for my time being
where your voice is never far.

And I need not look to the heavens.
If all the gods want is goodness,
they must have killed the fatted calf,
and ate in honour of your mother,
in her labour, in her giving of you.

In our time, we are wet with dirt and saliva.
For no mind about rubbing my face in the sod,
reminding me of flesh and hair.

Coming to the edge of my love,
wading deeper into the waters of what is,
knowing the only infallible one is you.

And after we will lay in the gardens, surrounded

by the flowers from which this knowing all bloomed.

Crawl back to you and lay my head on your chest when
I see the warmth of your summoning hand.
My head makes its home in you.
I have not loved until I met you.
I'll say it once more, to a shaded face
on a walk in the heat, somewhere further down the path,
to one who resembles both
me and you.

AMANDA PETERS

From "Waiting for the Long Night Moon"

It's quiet out here except for the sounds we were meant to have. The wind through the trees sing their songs in the voice of my mother. The roar of summer thunder bouncing off the lake is my father's booming laugh. Only the sound of the coyote causes me to tremble. It's the sound my sister made when they took her words, replacing them with their own. The sounds of my parents are imagined memories, age has robbed me of them, but her cry is cemented in my mind until the day comes when my old ears will hear nothing at all.

Despite the occasional howling of the coyote, I find comfort here in the woods, in my cabin by the lake. I know every rock, every tree root, every path used by the deer, the skunks, even the occasional bear, those animals so familiar to me that they've become my family. A red fox with a missing foot, an unfortunate encounter with a trap I assume, or a bear with a piece of her ear missing. I know them and I grieve when they stop wandering past my cabin. But still when the sun comes up in the morning, I wander out to greet those seeking food, or pray for a pleasant slumber for those ready for sleep. I sit, my legs crossed and my back against a big steady tree, my old body resting on the soft moss, and I watch as they pass.

"Good morning," I whisper, seeing the doe approach, her coffee-brown eyes focused on my face. I know this one, she has white hide scattered throughout her brown, her uniqueness a birthmark imparted by nature but a target for hunters. My sister was marked, white skin on her arm colonizing the dark. She covered it with long sleeves, even in summer. I never understood. To my young mind, a birthmark etched on skin the shape of a giant pine would be something to boast of. She told me I would never understand. I was just a boy.

Each time the doe appeared relief would wash over me. I feared that she would stop wandering past my door, that the last time she visited would be my last time with her. A couple days in a row and I would begin to fear that she'd joined the others who stopped wandering past my door and I knew that my grief for her would be different, darker and heavier. But she would always reappear, quietly taking notice of me.

I see her begin to approach and stay still until she's within a few feet. Slowly I raise my hands and she stops, her long neck extended, her nose high, picking up my scent. We're frozen, living statues locked in a battle of quiet and stillness, until my old arms began to shake.

Comfortable with my weakness, she approaches, sniffing my outstretched hands. Her nose is wet and her scent is musky, like mud after a heavy rain. She never takes her eyes off mine, even when I lower my arms. I feel like she's looking straight through them to the forest behind me. We stay that way, looking at one another, her nose in my palm until a pine cone falls, sending her bounding through the trees and my hands sink into my lap.

My weir has a few trout this morning. Breakfast will be good. My little cabin has a small garden that gives me most of the food

I need. It took time to get anything to grow here, where the trees shield the ground from the sun, but my rows have been planted in between the shadows cast by the tree branches. The garden looks like a labyrinth for small creatures. The trout will taste good with the wild carrots stored under the floorboards of the cabin to keep them fresh. They're not as sweet as the ones that come from the seeds bought in town, but with a little wild sage, they are tasty. When the food runs low, I force myself to go into town. I am anxious for days before, puttering and mumbling, trying to discover some clever trick that will allow me to stay home. But there is never a clever trick to beat hunger and I give in to my human need for food and set aside my need for solitude.

I don't like the town. It's loud and full of strangers. But it wasn't always that way. When I was a boy, it was nothing but a wharf and a trading post, small and inconsequential. But then someone found gold and the white people started to arrive to dig the veins out of the earth. I knew some of them, liked some of them. I even attended the school, the stone building with six rooms and a toilet that flushed and faucets that thumped and groaned before spewing water. I wasn't there two full days when one of the teachers used a long measuring stick to lift the skin off my palms. She was angry when she found me turning the faucet off and on, watching the water come from nowhere. I cried when the stick cracked, the whistle of its downward motion breaking the air along with my skin. I probably shouldn't have cried. I was nine, after all. But I cried and the boys teased. I couldn't get to my sister, she was on the other side of the building, separated by doors with locks. So, my hands bled and blistered and I cried alone. In the right light, you can still see the white scars where the skin didn't heal properly. A week later, my hands still wrapped, the green infection leaking out around the edges of the torn bandage, I crawled under the broken fence and ran back to the woods.

"You'll stay here with me, work with me. I never thought much of their teachings anyway," my father said as we sat around the fire that night, lit on the edge of the water, the full moon admiring its own reflection. We liked it out here on the water's edge, the winds lifting the tiny waves in the summer, capping them with crowns of white foam and quieting them in winter, freezing them solid, mid-peak. Mother washed my hands with lake water boiled over our fire, her delicate fingers gentle and eyes wet while she used a small knife to remove dead skin.

He went for her the next day, to bring my sister home. Instead my father emerged from the path alone. We never imagined that she wouldn't come home and I never believed that I would see her only twice more before she was gone for good. Her photo from a local newspaper, saved for me by the first Mr. Johnson, sits tacked above the fireplace in between drying herbs and rabbit furs. The story ripped to pieces and thrown in the fire so many years ago that I can't even remember the season or the phase of the moon when Mr. Johnson read it to me. An obituary, he called it. A recalling of family and friends, of good deeds and sacrifice. There was no mention of me.

DALLAS HUNT

From *Creeland*

Cree Dictionary

the translation for joy
in Cree is a fried bologna sandwich
the translation for bittersweet in Cree
looks like a cows and plows payment
eight decades too late
the translation for patience
in Cree is an auntie looking after four of her own children
and two of her sister's
the translation for evil
in Cree is the act of not calling
your mother on a Sunday

the translation for expedition
in Cree is travelling twenty minutes
to the only gas station in Faust, Alberta
to buy a Hygaard pizza sub
the translation for success in Cree
is executing the perfect frog splash
on your younger brother
the Cree word for white man is unpaid child support
the translation for conflicted in Cree

is your deep, steadfast love
for country superstar
Dwight Yoakam (or, depending on
the regional dialect,
George Jones, Patsy Cline
or Blue Rodeo)

the Cree word for constellation
is a saskatoon berry bush in summertime
the translation for policeman

in Cree is mîci nisôkan, kohkôs
the translation for genius
in Cree is my kôhkom muttering in her sleep
the Cree word for poetry is your four-year-old
niece's cracked lips spilling out
broken syllables of nêhiyawêwin between
the gaps in her teeth

Nathan Apodaca

1. the dollar store down the street in Kitsilano sells ninety-eight-cent abalone shells with maple leaves stickered all over them. heal me
2. i don't want to be cremated. just place my corpse in Fort Edmonton Park so some unsuspecting settler can find me and i can ruin their day
3. fireworks are explosions; they disrupt networks of kin, hurt birds and perforate my dog's eardrums
4. settler colonialism. *See* "the crime you see now, it's hard to even take its measure"
5. a thing i'm rationally afraid of: the raised voice of an entitled white man
6. multi-generational hurts are also fireworks; they paint an endless black expanse, bleed against a backdrop before fading into it; they are graffitied pain
7. i keep mistakenly reading "self-isolation" as "self-immolation"
8. occupation: a hoarse whisper, an accusation unevenly distributed and yet true nonetheless, a faculty lunch conversation best avoided
9. i'll eat Stove Top stuffing every day of the year, until sodium fills my lungs and my heart implodes, before i'll celebrate thanksgiving earnestly
10. March 12, 2020: i read that Justin Trudeau "self-isolated" and i let out a soft, involuntary moan
11. a fictive coherence. *See* Canada; a *Globe and Mail* comments section; life as deferral, as survival with an open invitation toward death

12. i wish i cared about anything as much as white people care about toilet paper
13. my white grandfather lived and settled on the lands my Cree great-grandfather gave up so his daughter wouldn't have to attend residential school
14. Sir John A. Macdonald was a drunken white supremacist, something i'll scream into the soft arches of your feet as they press into my temples
15. a niece of mine was born so premature that my mother described her as being so small that you could fit her in your hand like a pound of butter

SELINA BOAN

From *Undoing Hours*

the plot so far

ask / what is the history / of a word / a lake of commas /
a pause in the muscle of night / a dry river and the snow it
holds / i am afraid of getting this life / wrong / a thick-
rimmed fence / coins settled in a drawer for food / eat half
a lemon and you'll feel fine / i promise

in the dictionary / the nêhiyawêwin word
mahtakoskacikew / translates to / s/he settles or lays
on top of everything / i'll tell you a story / i stained my
hands as a kid in the backyard where i grew / peeling open
walnut shells / trying to find the part i could eat

at sixteen / i scaled the green water tower / settled at the
top for a better view / dreamt mother wasn't young /
driving a vw van cushioned with gas / hands on the wheel
/ wearing fire / *she was* / and i wanted to believe

from the ground up / growing / i never learned the
hul'q'umi'num' name for the place i lived till i was gone /
there are earned stories / names you don't share / i once
slipped into the bay / cracked my feet on dock barnacles
and bled / i wanted so many ways / to settle / our hearts
/ a window / a plot / a piece of land we wanted to call our
own but was / not ours to name

how to find your father

1. peel his name like an orange. like the skin on your hands. peel hours apart. sit so long in that cafe your tea gets cold. pick at your thumb till there's blood.

2. when the landlady's dog barks, shrug your coat to the floor. roll your head across the computer keyboard. stretch your arms to form a muscled y in the air before beginning your message.

3. odds are, if you use his name, cousins will emerge from the grass, from beaded felt, from twitter, they will appear like nîpîy, spilling into the shape of angled mirrors.

4. as a kid, learn quick that being *native* is *okay* as long as you aren't *too native*, as long as your skin is as yt as it is, as long as you're *pretty*, and you fit in with the other yt kids, and you don't talk too much, don't make ppl uncomfortable, read fantasy books at lunch against the portable.

5. google the definition of *find.* as a verb, it is to meet, to perceive by chance or with effort. as a noun, the act of "discovery," typically of archaeological *interest.* laugh at this. google your own face. google his name, over and over again until he appears in a profile photo, holding a fish.

6. begin with hello. begin gently, without anger or expectation. begin with what you think you know.

7. the day after one of your cousins gets married, there will be strings of lights coiled along the railing of the porch. eat leftover food, heated in the microwave. in the kitchen, scrape silver skin into the compost with your mother. anger will sear what you cannot yet touch. when you growl with shame, it will claw inside your stomach.

8. repeat his name. where he was last seen. all your aunties and uncles. all your cousins. sibling. nieces and nephew. his name.

9. the hardest part. get yourself onto a bus. pull calm from your jacket. when he walks out of the elevator, be prepared for the way time will speed up like eyes following earth through a car window. peel awkward laughter back. watch it blister and gush onto the sidewalk. let it carry you both.

in cree there is no word for half/brother

had i grown up with you, maybe we would've learned
to talk first in gesture, watch words form
from the end of our hands like bubbles
babbling wave after wave of kid-speak.

today, in my ~~vancouver~~ apartment
where tub water runs orange & silverfish slip
through book glue & tile cracks,
i learn the cree word for older brother
& wonder how to say it out loud.
nistes, i still can't say for sure

how we were kids, red
halved by waniyihcikewin.
my best guess is you know
the hook of survival,
how to laugh when a room needs it.
you can sink the eight ball in pool with side spin,
know kohtâwinaw's stories like revolving coins.

in the past beside this one,
you tease me   because i don't like eggs without ketchup
because when you're out late, i worry
you still remember the toque i stole from you in grade eleven,
the one you'd pulled down close to your eyes.

i know now that ohi in cree
looks like, oh, hi, but means
relative; or these ones here;
these things, here,

where kohtâwinaw worked at a bed & breakfast
up north   the place i first meet you
my hands shaky a gesture toward your name
a way to say hello.

have you ever fallen in love with a day?

that senselessly beautiful way light filters through a forest—all
gold body, all quiet sway
so soft on the inside u get drunk on it
pine cones hanging   from ur brain
a shelter from the teeth of animals, morning ice, love's shadow

ur learning ur language on twitter googling the weather in
nêhiyawêwin
tânisi ê-isi wêpahk
how is the weather being flung?
copper wires of rain heaved like a body touching itself
over this day, drowning all undershirts and sorrow

most days u hate urself   play online poker with the currency
of skittles
enter anonymous chat rooms to meet other women
u leave band-aids in the river dye ur roommate's hair
with blue gloves on the back porch leaves starting to brown
the ends of her in ur hands

if sadness is a legacy so is joy
and so, payipâstêw—the sun shines through a hole in the clouds
and in this forest, moss crawls up ur legs tinted with heat
curled like eyelashes under metal

how to be as lovable and dangerous as the sun?
how to love like a day?   not endlessly but with care
for every forest or room u touch   every spot there is light

BRIAN THOMAS ISAAC

From *All the Quiet Places*

Headlights lit up the faces of Eddie, Grace, and Lewis at the cattle guard. They stood shivering in the cold air that was thick with tumbling snowflakes.

"It's not coming, Eddie. They wouldn't send the school bus out on a night like this. This is crazy. We're all going to freeze to death," Grace said. "If it's not here in five minutes, we're going home. I'm gonna look like a fly in a sugar bowl anyway around all them *summas*."

A snowflake landed on Grace's eyelash and she swatted at it as if it were a bug. She shook her head. "This is what happens when you're poor. Always waiting for somebody else to do something for you, like they are doing you a favour, and you better be thankful. And if you bugger it up, they're going to have something to say.

"One time my mom made me a nice white dress. First time she ever done that. She made me wash off my horse's back and even gave me an old shirt to sit on because I rode bareback to the day school, and she didn't want the dress to get dirty. So I hopped on and loped down the road. Well, the horse spooked, and I fell onto the wet ground, and the dress was covered in mud. Got a good lickin' that day. But it just shows that sometimes, no matter what you do, people think you will prob'ly just land on your dirty ass anyway."

Eddie looked up at her. "You had a horse?"

"What? Oh Jesus, never mind about the damn horse. Just saying that if we coulda taken the truck we coulda driven in style to the concert. Just needed winter tires, new battery, windshield wipers, gas, and oil. That's all. Damn truck put us on our asses, just like that horse did."

Eddie hoped the bus would hurry. His mother rocked from side to side on her feet and groaned with each passing vehicle, ready to give up any minute.

"You said you'd go to the Christmas concert and watch me sing, Mom," he said.

Grace didn't answer. Rubbing her hands together, she looked back to the trail where snow was quickly covering their tracks.

"That's it," she said. "I waited long enough."

Just as she reached for Lewis's hand, Eddie heard the light bump of tires hitting the bridge decking, and the lights of a large vehicle waved up and down. The amber lights on top of the bus came into view, and the driver changed gears, swung off the highway, and did a wide U-turn in front of the cattle guard before coming to a stop. The doors flapped open.

The unsmiling driver nodded at them. As if it were just another day at work, he was wearing the same clothes as earlier that day, the lined denim jacket, the toque, and the green pants Eddie had seen gas station attendants wear. Grace took a seat behind the driver by the window.

"Can I sit in the back?" Eddie asked.

"No. You stay with me," she answered.

The bus pulled back onto the highway. As they drove over the bridge, Eddie crossed the aisle and rubbed the frost from the window. In the Cluffs' driveway under the barnyard light, Eva and her family were getting into a station wagon. When Eva looked up, Eddie waved to her. She looked away and opened the door to the back seat. Eddie was disappointed. Maybe when he saw her at the concert, he would ask her to ride home on the bus with him. But any courage he had to even imagine asking her left him, and he settled down in his seat.

The wipers could barely keep up with the snow gathering on the windshield. If it weren't for the tracks left behind by other vehicles, it would have been hard to see the road. At the outskirts of Falkland, Grace grabbed Eddie by the arm.

"Look, out there," she said.

Electric Christmas lights were strung around windows and doors of some of the houses. Eddie and Lewis rubbed the frost off the bus windows with their palms to see. On one house the lights blinked off and on in red, then yellow, then blue, then white, and then green. In the living room of another house stood a Christmas tree lit up by smaller lights.

"How can people afford to buy stuff like that?" Grace asked.

"Can we get lights like that, Mom?" Eddie asked.

"Sure. But we'll need a really long cord to plug into one of these houses."

The bus pulled to a stop in front of the Falkland community hall. When the driver opened the door, the noise coming from inside the hall sounded as if people were yelling at each other. Parents with children dressed in costumes streamed in through the wide doors. Just as Eddie was about to go into the hall, he was hit on the back by a snowball. He turned around to see Rodney Bell grinning at him. He turned and followed Grace and Lewis inside.

A ten-foot tree covered in decorations stood to the right of the stage. The large star on top of the tree rose above the cigarette smoke that stretched from wall to wall in a thin cloud. Men leaned against the walls on each side of the hall in a line that ran up the stairs to the balcony. Some people bunched together in small groups talking with one another while others stood by themselves looking uncomfortable. Eddie noticed two men looking at his mom. One leaned his head back as if to ask the other man a question. The man looked away, shrugging his shoulders. A spotlight swept back and forth across the folds of the blue curtains.

An older student approached Grace. "What grade?"

"What?"

"What grade is your kid in?"

"Grade one."

"The grade one class is at the front. I'll show you," he said.

As Grace followed down the centre aisle of the hall, Eddie saw people turning in their seats to watch. Their eyes went from head to toe, but his mother looked straight ahead.

A woman was motioning Eddie over to where she stood at the side of the stage.

Grace asked, "Who's that waving?"

"Miss Ferguson, my teacher," Eddie said. He felt important when Grace patted him on the back as he walked by.

Eddie and his classmates were guided onto the stage behind the curtain. They giggled as they waited. Then the curtains slowly drew back, and the house lights went down. The spotlight shone in Eddie's eyes as he looked for his family in the crowd. Miss Ferguson walked to the microphone to introduce her class before she sat at the piano.

The choir sang three songs, the audience applauded politely, and Eddie and his classmates took a bow. The curtains came together as Miss Ferguson led her group offstage. Just before Eddie walked down the steps, he saw his mother smiling at him and couldn't wait to hear what she had to say. When he stepped onto the floor, he lost sight of her because of all the people crowded around the bottom of the little stairs. As he made his way toward his seat, he saw Eva through the backs and legs of the grown-ups. She was holding a sheet of paper in her hand as she followed her teacher toward the stage. When she saw Eddie, she smiled and reached out. Suddenly Eddie felt someone push him hard from behind, and he tripped and fell to the floor. He looked up at Eva, who stood with a surprised expression. A man grabbed him by the arm and helped him to his feet.

Eva's teacher, Mrs. Stanley, rushed over. "Are you okay?"

Eva pointed behind Eddie. "Rodney Bell pushed him. I saw it," she said.

Eddie looked around but couldn't see Rodney.

"Mrs. Stanley, I saw what happened. I saw the whole thing."

Mrs. Stanley held her finger to her mouth. "Hush now, Eva. We don't have time for this now. It will be dealt with at school. You join the others and get ready to do your presentation."

The dirty melted snow on the floor left two dark patches on his knees. Eddie tried brushing his pants clean but gave up and made his way through all the legs back to his seat.

The bus stopped in front of the cattle guard, and after its door closed, spun its wheels in two feet of new snow. Rocking back and forth, the driver changed gears from forward to reverse until he made it over the slippery spot. The bus drove back onto the road, backfired, and sped away into the night.

"Let's take the long way around. It'll be easier than going up the hill by Grandma's." Grace walked ahead to break trail with Lewis on her back. Holding two bulging paper bags, Eddie found it hard to step in the holes she left in the snow.

It had stopped snowing, and the light of a half-moon lit up the snow-blanketed road ahead. As they walked, Eddie began losing the feeling in his unprotected fingers, and his back tightened when a light wind blew from behind. Snow slid off a drooping tree branch that sprang up, relieved of its weight, and the spilling snow freed more snow from the lower branches until the air filled with a swishing, sparkling mist.

Grace opened the door and swung Lewis down to the floor. He let out a cry as he slumped against the cupboard pantry. Eddie shut the door with his foot while Grace felt along the wall until she found the match holder. Then she struck a match and lit the coal oil lamp. After putting Lewis to bed, she opened the fresh-air grill on the stove, opened the damper, and filled the stove with wood. The fire crackled to life, and an orange glow appeared on the side of the stove.

She sat down at the table and noticed Eddie's fingers were bright red. She blew on his hands and rubbed them until Eddie felt his fingers tingle.

"That better?" she asked.

"They hurt."

"You'll be okay after you get warmed up. Next time I go to town, I need to get you guys a good pair of mitts with wool lining and maybe even lined pants. I seen how the *summas* dress their kids, and I'm gonna make sure you have what they have."

"And a new lunch kit too?"

"Darn rights. You know you can tell me what you need, and if I got money, we'll get it. I don't want anybody saying how poor we are." She smiled at Eddie. "Let's have a look inside one a them bags."

She laid the bag on its side, spilling the contents onto the table. There were candy canes, hazelnuts, almonds, walnuts, hard candy, chocolates, and a ball wrapped in green tissue paper. She pulled off the tissue paper.

"Look at this. That's the best-looking orange I ever saw. We didn't have these when I was a kid. Boy, if I was rich, I'd have one of these every day."

She peeled the orange, broke it into pieces, and handed one to Eddie.

"You know when the principal called your name and you took Lewis up to Santa Claus, you grabbed the bags from him like you didn't have a care in the world. You weren't scared at all. You're a lot braver than me, Eddie. I guess old Santa does know everything. He even had a bag for Lewis."

"My teacher asked me if I had a brother or sister at home."

"Anyway, it was good seeing you up there on the stage singing. Like I said, you're a lot braver than me. And I'll tell you something else: this year we're going to have a good Christmas. We'll get a better tree than Alphonse got last time, and we'll all have presents under it too. You wait and see."

Grace used pliers to break open the nuts and put them in a bowl. Eddie picked out the hazelnuts and chewed as he watched the smoke from the chimney swirl around the window. He looked back at Grace and caught her smiling at him. Neither spoke. Earlier that evening up at the road, waiting for the school bus, she didn't want to go to the concert. Now it looked like she'd even had fun. But there was an ache in Eddie's stomach he couldn't explain. Christmas or presents or even decorated trees weren't on his mind. All he could think of was Rodney. And he didn't feel very brave.

PART V

KINSHIP

CODY CAETANO

From *Half-Bads in White Regalia*

Applied

That winter I did my best to live quietly in the townhouse. Leacock's constant and booming presence in the living room served as a deterrent to entering it. After the bus dropped us Walker Village kids home from school, I felt unwelcome entering our foyer and zipped by the main floor, heading straight upstairs to my bedroom until I was hungry enough to come back down after everybody went to bed.

I jittered and trudged through my final year at Monsignor Lee. My eighth-grade teacher insisted I apply myself so that I could enrol for academic rather than applied courses when I got to Patrick Fogarty, despite the fact that multiplication and the Pythagorean theorem troubled me deeply. After a night of kicking serious locust ass in Gears of War, I showed up to school in trembling, helpless fear of all eyes on me. I would have done my homework, but the buckle always came through to save me from the effort that persistent application requires, zoning me out with the little think. When I got to class, with a pickling stomach digesting itself and the white and fuzzy tongue of dehydration curdling that last-second glass of milk, I entered the classroom with my head down. It wouldn't be long before the teacher, backdropped by the green chalkboard, was erasing yesterday afternoon's game of hangman and saying "Okay, guys, take out your math homework." Then all at once my fellow students would abandon me, whipping out a kaleidoscopic rainbow of binders and Hilroys flipped open to invaluable solutions and neat little numerical relationships, which might gather enough merit to land them a path to the good life.

But where I faltered in math, I had hope in reading proficiency. I could always read fast, and never struggled like some of my classmates or Muchachi's brother come reading time. And even though I wouldn't say it back then, I can partly thank Leacock for that. When I saw the Paul Auster novels in his move-in box, the cover of *Mr. Vertigo* worked some magic on me, enough to bring it up to Leacock one afternoon while Mindi prepped dinner. He said that he didn't like reading very much but loved reading Paul Auster books, especially *Mr. Vertigo*, said it was smooth the whole way through and that he'd be happy if I read it. So I did.

For days in the middle of that winter, when I came down with a mean case of the flu, I sat down with Walt the Wonder Boy and Master Yehudi, who taught him to levitate. Those two kept me company while I was bound to the mattress, even took me beyond it, around the universe and back. Walt was Harry Potter was Maniac Magee was Charlie Bucket. We all wanted to be Master Chief. In a sitting or two I read that book from cover to cover. Not all half-bads got this lucky.

Announcement

It was in the early days of spring when Mindi made her discovery. The heavy rain outside muddied up the dirt path that connected the townhouse rows together. I relaxed on the couch with my feet up on the coffee table. The carpet needed a serious vacuum and dishes filled the sink. Fruit flies and real estate flyers and the *Packet & Times* overtook the kitchen table.

I put on MTV's *The Real World: Brooklyn* and dreamt once again about living in a sunny penthouse in Red Hook, where the fridge and cupboards got stocked endlessly and housemates could follow wherever their ambitions took them. The buckle had just come for one of them, who'd just shattered the glass coffee table when Mindi came downstairs with a serious look on her face and said she had to tell me something.

"What?"

"I'm pregnant."

"You're pregnant? What do you mean you're pregnant? How?"

"I don't want to talk about it right now."

After that, Leacock came downstairs and into the kitchen. He opened a cupboard and filled a glass with tap water. I heard the suction of the freezer and out came a tube of ground beef he threw on the kitchen table. Then he went back upstairs to their bedroom and closed the door.

Meu Velho Homem

In the spring I spent a weekend with O Touro, and a pregnant Mindi dropped me off at the motel that doubled as cottages for Hydro One employees. O Touro had a new tattoo, which said "live to learn / learn to live" on either side of barbed wire that wrapped around a walrus-white bicep. He showed me his room with its single bed and a duffle bag of clothes and construction boots on the floor and the few silver-framed photos of us three on the dresser. It was peaceful. I hadn't seen O Touro since he was staying in Debbie's spare but felt comforted to see he kept close what mattered most.

Since his room was too small for us both, we slept on the couches in the living room, and at night he snored. I watched *Shrek* for the millionth time and ate as many bowls of Lucky Charms as I could in one sitting. The Hydro One dudes he didn't introduce me to ghosted around us and it was clear O Touro had asked to borrow their common room that weekend.

On the morning of the last day, we took a canoe out of the motel shed and walked down to the lake. We plopped it down into the water and hopped in without life jackets, paddling out to the middle. Our paddling stayed mostly consistent, steady, unnoticed in the breeze. O Touro's rowing drove the canoe and compensated for my shaking contributions. But no matter how much I struggled, he never complained or gave me shit. He just kept rowing and working out his shifted discs, just learning to live.

After ten minutes, we tossed our shirts at our feet and listened to the water birds clacking, telling us to keep going. We kept going.

CARLEIGH BAKER

From *Bad Endings*

Moosehide

It's the middle of the day, who cares when exactly, grey on goddamn grey. According to the GPS, we just passed the Arctic Circle. People get out their iPhones to take pictures of each other—Sean takes mine since we're paddling together—and when I smile for the camera I feel a little bit happy. Or I tell myself I feel happy. Technically, this is an accomplishment, paddling a million kilometres in the cold, past an arbitrary line on a map that raises eyebrows when you mention it to your fellow urbanites.

Sean and I both have to reach as far as we can across the canoe when he passes me the phone, to give my approval of the photo. The skin on his hands is cracked and scratchy; not the accountant's hands he had two weeks ago. The gaunt face glowing back at me from the iPhone looks pretty happy. I've lost weight. I guess that will make me happy when I get back to Vancouver and put on my skinny jeans. When I only have to wear one layer at a time, and people can see how skinny I've really become. For now, in all these layers, I'm a skinny face popping out of the Michelin Man. I take Sean's picture with the phone. He looks handsome. Of course, there's no Wi-Fi, so I just save the photos. If you're in the Arctic, and you can't Instagram it, does anybody care?

I'm tired.

Early in the trip, the river was all crusty whitewater. I was always paddling a canoe into a bunch of waves that looked like they were beating the shit out of each other. The water roared, and I could hear it all the time. I was excited by the noise at first, but I got used to it. At night, it was a backing track for Sean's evening banjo serenades. The guides had glanced sideways at each other when he'd added the bulky case to the packing pile, but everyone is happy to listen to him pluck away most evenings.

It's all couples on the trip: three couples and the guides, Jan and Eric. Also a couple. At night, besides the sound of the river, I can hear people rolling around in their tents, groaning like whales. Sean and I tried to get busy the first night, but my back muscles felt like they'd been run through a food processor. Same thing the second night, and the Thermarest deflated, so I was being pounded onto the rocks. Ugh. Around day six, I pulled Sean into the trees, away from everyone and down into a valley dotted with little white flowers. There was this spot with moss so thick, we had to climb up onto it. The whole thing was so badass; we weren't supposed to stray out of sight of the group, and we weren't supposed to go anywhere that might mess up the nature. The tundra is fragile, that's what the guides told us. We were stomping around, ripping out chunks of moss, and when I pulled him down to me, the sanctity of nature was the last thing from my mind. But the cold rose up from the ground, deep and penetrating. Sean put his jacket underneath me. We kept as many layers on as we could, his hard dick poking out of wool long johns, my own base layer pulled just low enough to let him in. But we couldn't stop shivering. A handjob under the majestic northern sky just seemed sad, and besides, we'd forgotten to bring wet wipes.

"We'll get it," Sean said. Kissed me on the forehead.

"Yeah."

The other couples are from Toronto, a zillion times more urban than us. I don't know why they don't seem to have any trouble getting it. From the sound of it, they're getting it constantly.

The river has slowed since we left Aberdeen Canyon, it's big and sluggish and muddy now. For the most part, the only sound comes from the nattering of our fellow travellers, and this only happens when we're rafting, boats tied together. Sometimes the wings of birds make a *whoop whoop whoop* sound when we startle them into flight. The couples don't mingle much anymore, and I'm not sure if that's because we're comfortable with each other now, or because we've given up.

When we pull off the river, the moosehide is just laying there. God. Big, inflated lungs laying next to it, jiggling like jello. Intestines, veiny grey tubes.

"Why is everything inflated?" I ask Sean.

"Botulism," somebody says.

"Don't poke a hole in them," somebody says, "or the worst smell will come out."

How bad, I wonder? The worst.

Brown-winged birds of prey circle over us.

Everybody loves the hide, prodding and poking it with sticks. Stretching it out so they can see the full length of the inside, mucus membrane and pink blood, a skin cape cut ragged around the edges. I can't look at it. I don't see a dead moose, I see a live moose in the final moments of suffering before its life ends. That kind of empathy is stupid. I know. The moose is dead, and it's feeding someone.

Somebody's going to notice that I'm the only one not looking, and ask me why I'm such a wuss. So I make a big show of looking at other things: tiny plants at the river's edge with ice globes surrounding the fruit, broken willow branches, rocks. Scarred rocks that look like patients in the sick ward; what makes them look like that? I toss a few in the river. Each lands with a fat *plunk.*

Sean's talking to Eric about taking the moosehide with us and I'm pissed at him for this. Surely bears would smell it and come looking for us, or lynx, or—what else is out here waiting to kill us? He wants to make something out of it. Whatever. I remember somebody in my Aboriginal Studies class saying that scraping a hide is much harder than it looks, even with expert hands, and we're no experts. We have no tools for this. I may be a mixed blood—Sean and I are both Cree-Métis—but we were also both raised white. All we know are white-people things. But I do know that a perfectly good moosehide shouldn't have been left here. Why did the hunters leave it? Skin it and leave it?

"I think it's a female," somebody says, poking around the ass end, playing the expert.

"You're not supposed to kill females," somebody says.

"That's sexist," somebody says.

"The females make more moose, dumbass."

"Not without sperm they don't."

"Maybe she attacked them?"

God. It's like reading the online comments section on YouTube.

I'm hungry.

Somebody passes around a snack, just a big block of cheese cut into a million pieces with a dirty Leatherman. It clogs and sticks in my throat. We get "fun-sized" Mars bars too. Chocolate and cheese. I put the Mars bar in my PFD pocket. My fingers can barely get the zipper down. My fingers, dirty for days despite a river of hand sanitizer. Bloated and pus around the nails, one finger swollen so big I can barely move it. Rub Polysporin in the cracks before bedtime, and hope for the best. I can still paddle just fine. I may have lost weight, but my shoulders are strong now. I can feel the muscle through my merino wool bottom layer, though I haven't seen much of my actual skin for fifteen days.

"Can you help me with my PFD?" Sean asks. He looks like a little boy when he asks, and for some reason I choke up a little. Get it together, lady.

"Sure," I say. Tug the zipper down hard, even though my fingers might break off.

"Do you want my Mars bar?" he asks.

"Don't drag that moosehide along with us," I say.

"I could make a drum from it."

I turn around so he doesn't see how hard I'm rolling my eyes. A drum. We're *accountants.*

Now it's pictures around the moose remnants, eight of us lined up like so many soldiers.

Someone's found an antler, too. Not from the carcass, this one's older. And probably caribou, Eric tells us. People take turns with it, more photo opportunities.

Sean's arm around me, the other holding the antler up to my temple. We'll get back to Vancouver and show this photo to our friends, and they'll be jealous of us. I can't even count how many times people used the word jealous, like we were going on an expenses-paid five-star Mediterranean yacht cruise or something. You'd have to be a masochist to want to trade places with us right now. There is nothing easy about being here, and there was nothing easy about getting here. Sean and I trained for months, saved for months. I guess it was good for us to have something to focus on. We barely fought at all. I'm not sure if we picked the right kind of vacay. I'm not sure if it's just the tour we chose, because I've never done anything like this before. But I definitely didn't expect things to be this hard. I pictured myself drinking wine, looking out at the river. I'd imagined calm, and a clearing out of my mind that might make the future easier for me. Anyway. We're doing it now. We're committed.

MARIE-ANDRÉE GILL

de *Chauffer le dehors*

T'es la talle d'épinettes noires
qui brûle mon cœur full de super

C'est juste impossible que tu viennes plus
t'abreuver à mon esprit ancestral
de crème soda

Comme si de rien n'était, les lacs continuent
de faire des moutons, les gens de sniffer des images
et les machines de créer le vertige de la fabrication
du baloney.

Je pleume les oies pour souper, comme je voudrais
le faire pour toi mais à l'envers : te greffer des ailes
qui marchent et des cris plein la gorge, que tu puisses
voir les fleurs sauvages de mon cœur cru, la médecine
millénaire qui nous enveloppe.

Même si le futur hausse les épaules et démêle
son filage tranquillement pas vite, je sais que
la disparition sera ailleurs que dans le ciel qu'on
a dézippé à grandeur pour l'habiter.

JESSE THISTLE

From *From the Ashes*

Tradition

"This one here looks nice, try it on." Grandma handed me a preppy white button-up shirt to go with the black slacks she'd pulled from the good section of the Hudson's Bay men's department, over near the Polo clothes. The shirt fit slim around my torso and snug around my neck when she buttoned it up. She turned me to look in the mirror, but before she did, she licked her fingers and slicked my eyebrows into place.

Spiffy.

"Well, look at you! My baby boy all grown up and ready for work!"

I fixed my collar and stuck my chin up slightly. I knew this was a special occasion because Grandma usually took me to Bargain Harold's or Zellers, and we'd go to the Skillet Restaurant and eat hot dogs in a basket afterward. Not today, though.

I thought of those Skillet hot dogs as I admired myself, and said, "But, Grandma, these pants and shirt are nearly $200. We can't afford that."

She wagged her head and scoffed. "You better believe we can. When it comes to work you gotta knock 'em dead."

I'd never seen her so excited or generous before, except when it came to Grandpa's work boots and overalls. He always had the best. Even his lunch pail and thermos. Work was important to the

Thistles, and Grandma made sure her man looked good and was well-fed when he made our family its money.

Grandpa, too, had acted differently since he'd gone across the street a month ago to talk with our neighbour, Mr. Q. He'd come back whistling, Yorkie by his side, and the dog appeared just as gleeful as he did.

"Good news, Jess," he said with a huge smile. "You've got a job." Mr. Q. was a manager at the produce department at the grocery store in the biggest mall in town, and Grandpa told me I'd start in a few weeks. "You'll be a produce clerk. $3.75 an hour."

He walked past me into the house to announce the good news to Grandma, who was watching a soap opera. She gasped with joy—I could actually hear it through the screen door, from where I was on the driveway. As I pulled out the lawn mower, she waved to me from the balcony. Like those old pictures of when men went off to war on battleships or trains and their women saw them off. I could feel my face flush, and I flashed a smile at her. I knew it looked weird. Grandpa didn't drink that day, and I caught him singing to himself later in the garage as he organized his bits and bobs for his job on Monday.

I examined myself in the mirror. I was now receiving the same treatment as Grandpa, and I smiled. Grandma hiked my pants up, exposing my socks and squaring my nuts in the process. "They fit nice," she said, "but up here, around your waist. I don't want to see you with them hanging low around your ass like you do with your jeans, that godawful rap style."

I thought I looked like Urkel on *Family Matters*, and I grimaced but somehow managed to keep my smile.

Grandma pivoted, grabbing one paisley and one striped tie from the shelf beside me. I covertly pulled my pants back down. *Relief.*

The ties in Grandma's hand weren't the wide-bottomed ones Grandpa wore to the elevator awards once a year that were the worst shades of brown and green, putrid remnants of the 1960s that he refused to replace. The same colours as those hippy flowers on the bath tiles in the upstairs bathroom. No. These ties were royal blue and black, thin at the bottom—actually fashionable.

"Calvin Kleins," she said as she turned them over to show me the labels. She lassoed one around my neck and had it bound up before I could say go, pulling it tight. My eyes bulged in the mirror and she patted my bum. "A lady killer, you are. Tall, dark, and handsome."

I looked at myself in the mirror with doubt. I was tall, but lanky as a daddy longlegs, and still covered in zits.

But I had just started grade nine, and Leeroy and I were taking a drama class, and, to our surprise, discovered it was filled with beautiful girls who found us funny. And in one of the photography classes I took, a girl named Heather asked to take my headshot. She had a crush on me, or so I'd heard from classmates.

"Sure," I said. "As long as I get a copy."

She made a bunch of prints and posted them on a wall near the gym—I saw them when I walked past. By the end of the day all the girls at school had stolen them. I knew because they'd been waving them at me in class. I couldn't be angry—I was more flattered than anything.

"No facial hair, though," Grandma said. She rubbed the back of her hand against my cheek and then pinched it hard. I pulled away, rubbing it with my fingers.

"Toughen up, sunshine!" She waved it off like it was nothing. "Native men don't get hair the same as others," she added. "Maybe you'll be lucky and never have to shave, like me." She hiked up her fuchsia slacks, exposing her leg. "It just didn't grow. That's the Algonquin in me."

The thought of never shaving upset me for a brief second. I pictured Grandpa dipping his razor in the sink before work every morning. I loved watching him shave when I was small. Sometimes, he'd lather up my face and we'd shave together. It was serious business. The silence between us was only broken by our laughter when he slapped on aftershave and screamed from the sting.

"Your granddad is as hairy as a Scottish musk ox," Grandma said, as though she could sense what I was thinking. "He hates shaving every day." Not wasting time, she wrangled a black leather belt from over by the till and fastened it around my waist. It fit perfectly, its chrome buckle reflecting light into the mirror. I felt like a millionaire.

"That's it," Grandma said. "That's your uniform."

We stood admiring the ensemble, Grandma holding my shoulders. I loved her so much at that moment—she was a good grandma, I knew that. I leaned over and gave her a big hug. I did look good, in a grown-up kind of way. My new job represented a real step toward adulthood. Most of my friends, like Derick down the street, only had paper routes. But here I was with a real-deal outfit and, soon, a real-deal paycheque. I suddenly felt confident and handsome.

When we got to the front desk to pay, Grandma turned to me.

"Grandma Clara King, my grandmother you met last year that's over one hundred. Her grandpa was a chief factor of the Hudson's Bay Company up on Lake Timiskaming during the fur trade one hundred and fifty years ago. He ran that fort. Our family built this country, Jesse."

The teller scanned the goods, and the total of $374.87 popped up on the register. My heart jumped. Grandma opened her ancient purse and handed over her credit card.

"That's why we shop at the Bay. Tradition is important—remember that."

Grandpa was running the van just by the store entrance. He had "El Paso" by Marty Robbins blasting on the radio when we got in, exhaust fumes flooding around us as we buckled in. Grandma promptly blazed up a Du Maurier and sucked in a massive drag. I coughed, waving my hand in front of my face, but I took in what smoke I could—I needed a cigarette myself. Grandpa leaned over into Grandma's cloud of death, peeking inside the bags.

"What you got there, little lady?" he asked.

"Never you mind, Cyril!" Grandma snapped. She snatched up the receipt, pushing his hairy paws aside, and folding it into the wad of other receipts in her purse. He let out a loud yelp, and they both laughed. "The boy looks like a million bucks."

SMOKII SUMAC

From *you are enough: love poems for the end of the world*

ka pałkinin̉ tik
or
there are things our women have taught me:

1. give generously without worrying where more will come from;
2. laugh deep and hard with each other more than you cry;
3. learn everything you can and teach it freely;
4. know where you are going and go all the way—get the doctoral degree, get on council, hell, don't stop there, you can be nasukin—you can lead your nation;
5. speak softly walk gently rock your babies to sleep;
6. raise your voice in song or anger—never be silent in the face of injustice;
7. feed everyone, including yourself;
8. light the fires, call in the drums, join hands—you never know when you'll need a friend—honour your relations;
9. share the good stories alongside the tough ones—share whatever story feels right, from the you light up my lifes to the ain't it awfuls, and especially the sexy ones—on that note
10. fall in love and celebrate every orgasm;
11. hold your loved ones close and breathe in the scent of them;
12. grieve loss as deeply as you love, without shame or fear;

13. carry the hearts of your sisters your grandmothers your daughters born or yet to come your aunties and nieces and cousins—carry them in your heart;
14. keep going. This is not the end.

"do you want to take the Cadillac for a ride?" Or: a love letter to Transthetics the company that made my prosthetic dick

From the first time I saw your video I knew that this was *the One.*

Ordered it on the next weekly release date and felt butterflies driving to shoppers to pick up the package I had missed at my door when it came.

Chase Ross, youtuber and trans 101er said he cried when he used his for the first time.

A trans friend once said it best "being trans is expensive" as they waved their hand gesturing to their shelf of dicks.

I ordered two new binders that day, too. I mean why not? if you're gonna do it . . .

Right for me was binder and shirt on. I shudder as I think of cis dudes with a shirt and no pants on, but this is the body I'm working with and I currently feel sexiest with a binder on under a button down.

I've already prepped three pairs of fancy new underwear (also ordered online) the way you showed in the video, elastic sewed in to hold my new body part in place. As I fit the elastic around it I can feel the gentle rise of anxiety and . . . adrenaline? That sense of impending adventure like sitting in a cart waiting for a rollercoaster to start, or filling up at the gas station, your last stop on the way out of town.

self love is a revolution for an NDN
I say out loud and think of Quill Christie Peters.

"self love is a revolution for an NDN"
and I hear Tenille Campbell's laugh.

"Self Love is a Revolution for an NDN"
and i take a deep breath
and I look down

and I am transformed.

*

I didn't cry after.
but I did text my friend three days and countless orgasms later

> "I'm having the best sex of my life. By myself."

Chase Ross said the first time he used his with a partner, he cried again.

at some point I start telling people
> "I've got the Cadillac of dicks."

I shudder when I think of a cis dude professor I know drunkenly repeating over and over to a room full of colleagues

I have a huge dick.

I consider what it means to write erotic poems about my dick.

I wonder if it's the same.

My best friend brings me to the reason I write: "But would you want to hear another trans poet read that poem?"

Yes.
I would.

And then there's a moment of electricity between me and a woman.
She's on my couch. We've been friends for awhile, but I hadn't considered

This.

There's a need so deep in my body to lean over and lie my head in her lap that I'm nearly shaking in the effort to stop it. I hold back. Other people in the room. We begin texting incessantly later on. For eight days we text incessantly.

And then we are meeting in the city. And then we are kissing. And then?

I'm explaining the nuances of queer sex and telling her about

the Cadillac.

I shake my head and laugh because what man has this much confidence about his dick in the hours before he's about to lose his virginity?

It was kind of like losing my virginity again.

Of course, never assuming it would happen I just kept kissing and asking and she kept kissing and saying yes and asking me and I kept saying yes until she smiled

You know that smile.

The one with the raised eyebrow that says there is nothing in this world I want more than to do this next thing I'm going to do to you

And with that eyebrow and her eyes that have flecks of gold in them like when the sun hits the water just right sparkling she leans in and asks

"can we take the Cadillac for a ride?"

and with her,
I am transformed.

JOCELYN SIOUI

de *Mononk Jules*

5 Au 10 Juin 1944 : Scission[1]

Ottawa avait un as dans sa manche.

Au premier jour de la convention, le département offre de discuter avec six leaders autochtones sous conditions contraignantes.

Bien décidé à faire taire Mononk Jules, le ministre des Mines et des Ressources (affecté également aux Affaires indiennes[2]), T. A. Crerar, promet de venir discuter avec les chefs si et seulement si Jules Sioui, le fauteur de troubles, est exclu de la réunion. Jules se braque, des murmures de mécontentement et d'indignation en fond sonore. Le département déploie son jeu en affirmant que Crerar ne discutera pas avec un homme ayant fait de la prison.

Un silence.

Jules croise les bras, sentant les regards peser sur lui. Les représentants du département quittent la réunion. Les jeux sont faits. Les quatre as sont sur la table. Jules perd sa mise.

Certains leaders sont furieux, d'autres dubitatifs. Plusieurs croient à une autre manipulation du gouvernement. Comment croire quiconque ment comme on respire ?

Jules sent qu'il est dans une impasse. L'enjeu est plus grand que lui. Ses ambitions ne peuvent se mesurer à ce qu'il considère comme la seule priorité : le droit des Premières Nations. Il abdique et avoue qu'il a effectivement déjà fait de la prison. Vent froid sur l'assemblée. Le changement brusque de la température fait rejaillir des divisions dans le groupe. Mammouth Jules se retrouve pris dans la glace.

Cette douche froide met en lumière les divergences d'opinions dans la façon de négocier avec le gouvernement. Plusieurs n'aiment pas le style cinglant de Mononk Jules. Une scission irréparable apparaît lentement dans le groupe. Andrew Paull, le leader squamish, collaborateur de la première heure, devient l'un des meneurs du schisme. Il n'y a plus l'ombre d'un doute. Pour faire avancer la cause, il faut discuter avec le gouvernement.

Jules est écarté de la convention.

FLASH-BACK

Octobre 1943, première convention.

Une légende dit qu'à la fin de la première convention, l'organisation voulut se doter d'un chef. On procéda donc à une élection en bonne et due forme. Mais Jules ne le voyait pas de cette façon. Il ne voyait pas pourquoi on ne lui concéderait pas la direction du groupe puisqu'il en était l'initiateur. C'était lui le chef, nul besoin d'élection. Sauf que la délégation préférait la voie démocratique. Et Mononk Jules n'avait jamais connu un énorme succès avec les élections…

C'est Andrew Paull qui fut élu à la tête du groupe.

Je ne connais pas la séquence des événements, mais ce que je sais, c'est que Jules, à la suite du résultat, s'est autoproclamé chef de tous les Indiens du Canada. On peut penser qu'il avait soif de pouvoir, mais mon hypothèse est tout autre.

Andrew Paull est sans doute l'un des politiciens les plus importants de l'histoire des Premières Nations. Son influence sur la lutte pour les droits autochtones est indéniable. Après avoir livré le combat auprès des siens en Colombie-Britannique, il devient le symbole de la résistance dans les années 1940 et contribue à la révision de la *Loi sur les Indiens*. Pour Andrew Paull, il était préférable de discuter avec les dirigeants du pays, de travailler à modifier les lois, de faire un inlassable lobbying. Jouer le jeu et parler le langage de ceux qui dirigent. Lutter d'égal à égal.

John Tootoosis, leader cri de la réserve de Poundmaker, relate dans un entretien qu'Andrew Paull n'aimait pas beaucoup la position souverainiste de Jules, qu'il n'a jamais aimé son style, qu'il trouvait cinglant et contre-productif[3].

Pour Jules, il était trop tard pour la politique. La lenteur et les courbettes qu'elle implique nuisaient considérablement à tous ceux qui souffraient dans les réserves. Lui privilégiait la guerre. Jules n'était pas un politicien, c'était un activiste. De ceux qui se jettent devant un baleinier avec un Zodiac. Andrew, le chef. Jules, le guerrier. Les deux sont absolument nécessaires pour faire avancer une cause. Je ne crois donc pas que Jules ait voulu le titre de chef pour savourer le goût du pouvoir. Il n'en avait cure. Simplement, il ne souhaitait pas que les Autochtones lèchent les bottes du gouvernement une fois de plus. Il craignait la politique et sa fourberie. Pour lui, l'heure n'était pas au compromis, mais à l'action radicale.

En 1944, la délégation a dû trancher : opter pour la guerre ou la politique. La révélation du ministre Crerar sur les antécédents judiciaires de Mononk Jules a eu raison de son titre autoproclamé.

6 juin 1944, 20 heures, après une longue journée de réflexion et de doutes.

Je quitte, mais je suis sûr que Crerar ne vous donnera pas ce que vous demandez. Je sais ce qu'il va faire avec vous. Il sait ce que j'allais lui dire, il sait ce qu'ils ont fait aux gens par le passé, c'est pourquoi il ne me veut pas ici. Mais je quitte la convention et ne rejoins pas le groupe (...).

Vous ne gagnerez rien en allant voir le ministre, mais je ne veux pas être blâmé après ça. Allez-y mais soyez très prudents. Pour ma part, je ferai ma réunion comme prévu à 8h dans le YMCA (...)[4].

Jules

7 juin 1944, 14 h 10.

Comme convenu, une délégation de six Autochtones a été choisie par la convention pour rencontrer le ministre Crerar. Ce dernier exige d'eux qu'ils ne discutent pas avec lui. Muselés, ils l'écoutent.

Tant que la population indienne augmentera, et elle augmente, le fardeau du gouvernement augmentera ... Je suis certain que les Indiens, comme tout le monde, sont anxieux de gagner leur vie, de devenir des citoyens utiles dans un pays qui après tout est notre pays commun. Il est indéniable que vos ancêtres il y a plusieurs siècles erraient dans ce pays et le possédaient (Crerar fait volontairement fi de l'histoire récente), mais au fil du temps, cela a changé, et je crois que nous avons une obligation de montrer au reste du pays que les Indiens sont bien traités, et que nous devons faire tout en notre possible pour les assister à devenir des citoyens utiles dans la communauté ... Votre obligation est de faire votre possible.

Les Affaires indiennes porteront une meilleure attention aux besoins en santé, en éducation et en économie (...)[5].

Ministre Crerar

Après avoir demandé aux délégués de ne pas avoir d'idées subversives, le ministre Crerar leur enjoint de quitter Ottawa, de retourner dans leur réserve et d'attendre trois semaines pour obtenir les réponses du gouvernement à leur requête. Il part en ajoutant : « Vous pouvez devenir des citoyens utiles ou continuer à vous languir dans l'obscurité collective[6]. »

Et pour sortir de cette obscurité, le gouvernement ne propose qu'une issue : l'assimilation.

Je ne sais pas comment le groupe d'Andrew Paull a réagi à ce flot de mots simulant l'ouverture et le progressisme. Je ne crois pas qu'ils aient célébré une victoire ce soir-là. Il faut beaucoup de diplomatie et de maîtrise de soi pour ne pas cracher sur quelqu'un qui ne vous considère pas comme un « citoyen utile ». Il faut fermer les yeux, respirer et se mordre la lèvre pour ne pas hurler quand on tente de vous faire avaler que votre histoire s'est arrêtée il y a plusieurs centaines d'années, alors qu'à peine soixante-dix ans auparavant, les colons britanniques et les Américains tuaient les bisons par centaines de milliers pour affamer les nations de l'Ouest, dans le but avoué de s'approprier leur territoire.

Jules écrira par la suite :

(Crerar) savait qu'il n'y avait pas un seul délégué pour se lever et lui dire : tu es de la gang des menteurs, des voleurs et des tueurs, veux-tu bien débarrasser la place le plus tôt possible, hypocrite et sans-cœur que tu es[7].

Le ministre était venu à cette rencontre dans le but d'étouffer le désir d'autodétermination des Premières Nations. La nouvelle stratégie d'assimilation du gouvernement canadien allait porter le masque de la confiance. Une idée simple et efficace : se montrer bon, investir dans des programmes en éducation et en santé, stimuler la confiance des peuples pour accélérer l'assimilation et les transformer en citoyens utiles. Pourquoi mordre la main qui vous nourrit ?

Mais le groupe d'Andrew Paull et de Jules avait au moins une chose à célébrer ce jour-là. Après 77 ans d'Affaires indiennes, pour la première fois, un ministre s'adressait directement aux leaders des Nations. La relation entre les Autochtones et le gouvernement canadien allait changer indéniablement.

Durant la soirée, Andrew Paull est élu chef de la Fraternité des Amérindiens d'Amérique du Nord (*North American Indian Brotherhood*). Considérant leurs objectifs atteints, de nombreux délégués quittent la convention et rentrent à la maison. Trois semaines plus tard, malgré la promesse du ministre Crerar, aucune nouvelle du gouvernement n'arrive par la poste.

Jules avait vu juste : « Vous ne gagnerez rien en allant voir le ministre[8] . . . »

Crerar leur avait signé un chèque en blanc.

6 juin 1944, 20 heures, au YMCA d'Ottawa.

Dans une salle presque vide, 33 délégués n'ont pas quitté la convention. Ils attendent patiemment, sur leurs petites chaises de bois inconfortables, que commence la présentation de Jules. La réunion débute.

En réaction à son exclusion, il fonde la Nation indienne de l'Amérique du Nord, un groupe plus décidé, plus radical, qui ne prône rien de moins que l'indépendance des Premières Nations.

Il veut un pays.

Dans la grande salle presque vide du YMCA, il fait la lecture de la déclaration de la Constitution de la loi de la Nation indienne de l'Amérique du Nord.

LA CONSTITUTION DE LA LOI DE LA NATION INDIENNE DE L'AMÉRIQUE DU NORD

Le premier pas des délégués des chefs indiens, à la Convention qui a été tenue, à Ottawa, dans l'édifice du Y.M.C.A., le 7 juin 1944, fut de nommer un Président d'Office : alors, l'élu a été le chef James Fox.

Le Président d'Office a demandé au Leader de la Convention de prendre la parole et de faire l'exposé des commandements et des règlements de la Nation indienne, lesquels doivent être la base fondamentale de la Loi de la Constitution.

Le Leader de la Convention, Jules Sioui, a fait l'exposé suivant:

1. Le Président d'Office devra, à l'ouverture de chaque grande réunion, faire appel au Chef Suprême de la Nation, lui enjoignant de réciter une prière spéciale, pour demander au Grand Esprit du Très-Haut de lui venir en aide pour le grand succès de la Nation indienne de l'Amérique du Nord.
2. Que les Autorités de la ligue de la Nation indienne de l'Amérique du Nord devront prendre toutes

les mesures nécessaires afin d'avoir la certitude que chaque Indien doive appuyer la Proclamation royale du 7 octobre 1763, qui a été signée en faveur et dans le grand intérêt de la Nation indienne.

3. Les Autorités de la ligue de la Nation indienne de l'Amérique du Nord seront tenues de garantir le plein respect du droit de la loi ; de faire connaître aux membres de sa Nation leur entière liberté et leur indépendance dans toute l'Amérique du Nord.
4. Les Autorités de la ligue de la Nation indienne de l'Amérique du Nord seront tenues de garantir le plein respect du droit de la loi ; de faire reconnaître que la Nation indienne est une nation qui a le droit d'exister sur le même pied d'égalité que toute autre nation dans tout l'univers.
5. Les Autorités de la ligue de la Nation indienne de l'Amérique du Nord seront tenues de garantir le plein respect du droit de la loi ; de faire en sorte que tous les traités qui ont été faits et passés soient reconnus et respectés afin de garantir la liberté et l'indépendance de la Nation indienne dans toute l'Amérique du Nord.
6. Les Autorités de la ligue de la Nation indienne de l'Amérique du Nord seront tenues de garantir le plein respect du droit de la loi ; de faire comprendre aux membres de la Nation qu'ils seront tenus de se procurer un certificat d'identification, afin qu'ils soient reconnus comme Indiens appartenant à

telle tribu, ayant par conséquent droit à toute la protection découlant des privilèges que renferment les droits de la Loi de la Constitution.

7. Les Autorités de la ligue de la Nation indienne de l'Amérique du Nord seront tenues de garantir le plein respect du droit de la loi ; d'acquérir les pouvoirs de négocier avec le gouvernement fédéral de Sa Majesté au Canada, au point de vue des ressources naturelles pour le bénéfice de la Nation indienne.
8. Les Autorités de la ligue de la Nation indienne de l'Amérique du Nord seront tenues de garantir le plein respect du droit de la loi ; de ne jamais déclarer la guerre contre aucune autre nation et de ne jamais participer à aucune guerre, peu importe qui sera en guerre.
9. Les Autorités de la ligue de la Nation indienne de l'Amérique du Nord seront tenues de garantir le plein respect du droit de la loi ; de faire savoir que tout Blanc ne devra pas avoir le droit de résider sur les réserves, sans s'être muni d'un permis spécial venant de la part des Autorités de la ligue : ce qui veut dire que chaque tribu devra avoir un plan officiel de la limite du territoire de sa réserve.
10. Les Autorités de la ligue de la Nation indienne de l'Amérique du Nord seront tenues de garantir le plein respect du droit de la loi ; de voir à ce que les Indiens aient le privilège d'aller chasser, pêcher et

trapper là où le gibier (c'est-à-dire les animaux à fourrure) se trouve, peu importe l'endroit, et bien entendu, qu'aucune des autorités soit provinciale ou fédérale n'auront le droit de les empêcher ni de les poursuivre, en autant que l'Indien le fasse pour son propre besoin personnel ou pour le revenu de sa nation.

11. Les Autorités de la ligue de la Nation indienne de l'Amérique du Nord seront tenues de garantir le plein respect du droit de la loi ; de se réserver le droit d'avoir des maîtres d'école qui devront être capables d'enseigner la langue nationale, suivant les tribus, avec l'obligation d'avoir le livre d'histoire de la Nation, ce qui permettra aux enfants des générations à venir d'étudier et de mieux connaître leur race, leur peuple et leur pays, et de mieux obéir aux Autorités de leur nation.
12. Les Autorités de la ligue de la Nation indienne de l'Amérique du Nord seront tenues de garantir le plein respect du droit de la loi ; de faire comprendre au peuple de toute la nation que le 5 juin de chaque année devra être reconnu comme la grande fête nationale dans toute l'Amérique du Nord, c'est-à-dire dans chaque tribu, ce qui permettra à chacun d'avoir un jour de congé ; alors, ceux qui travaillent à salaire devront être payés quand même ; c'est ce qui permettra aux générations qui vont nous suivre de se réjouir de leur droit d'être Indiens et d'être fiers de leur nationalité et de leur idéal.

Signé par le Chef Suprême : Jim Horton / Assistant Chef Suprême : John Tootoosis / Secrétaire de la ligue: Jules Sioui[9]

Le 6 juin 1944, sous la gouverne du chef suprême Jim Horton, de l'assistant chef John Tootoosis et du secrétaire Jules Sioui, un pays autochtone est né.

Quand un peuple connaît ses richesses,
il devient fier et grand.
—Jules Sioui, *Qui est ton maître ?*

Et pour mordre un peu plus le gouvernement canadien, les trois leaders vont jusqu'à créer une carte d'identité qui redonne le droit de pêche, de chasse et de territoire aux Premières Nations. Deux mille Autochtones achèteront cette carte en Amérique du Nord.

Entouré de combattants ayant les mêmes objectifs que lui, Jules acceptera d'être leader de la convention sans en être le chef. Il demeurera secrétaire jusqu'à la fin du mouvement, en 1969.

Aucun doute, son rejet de la deuxième convention a radicalisé Mononk Jules. Son exclusion a exacerbé sa détermination à lutter contre l'oppresseur. Les guerriers du gouvernement indien ne feront plus de compromis.

En quittant Ottawa, Jules met dans sa valise des restants de succès. Mis à l'écart de l'organisation qu'il avait créée, il reprend le train comme on se remet d'un lendemain de veille, avec un goût rêche dans la bouche. Sauf qu'il n'avait rien fêté. Assis côté fenêtre, il regarde défiler lentement le paysage défiguré par la ville. Il ne peut pas trouver ce pays beau. Les territoires extorqués, dépouillés de leur histoire, se succèdent d'Ottawa à Québec.

Ils étaient si près d'une petite révolution. Tous debout comme un seul homme, comme Jules l'espérait, ils auraient pu confronter Goliath.

Mononk descend à la petite gare derrière chez lui, celle dont le petit flot de voyageurs quotidiens lui permet de gagner sa vie, un Jos Louis à la fois. Sur le quai, il est seul. Il est tard. Il traîne les pieds jusque chez lui. Il entre dans sa petite maison blanche. Sa femme, Clara, dort à poings fermés, elle ne vient donc pas l'embrasser. Il dépose sa valise de cuir brun, se déchausse et se rend jusqu'à son petit bureau d'un pas lourd. Un fouillis de feuilles et de livres s'empile pêle-mêle près de la dactylo. Il s'assoit et fixe le vide. Son regard se pose sur une icône de saint Jude, accrochée au mur.

Jules prie jusqu'au petit matin.

Au lendemain du lendemain de veille, il est toujours assis à son bureau. Les touches du clavier, brûlantes d'avoir martelé le rouleau sans relâche depuis des mois, allaient noircir le papier de nouveau. Jules écrit *Qui est ton maître?/ Who is Your Master?*, un autre pamphlet qui résume avec lucidité la suite d'événements qui ont mené à la création d'un gouvernement indien, lors de la dernière convention. Jules profite du compte rendu pour publier la déclaration de constitution du pays et tente de rallier d'autres Autochtones à la cause.

Dans la première partie du livret, Jules donne une leçon d'histoire. À la lecture, on se rend rapidement compte qu'il n'était ni historien ni auteur. Mais, au fil des pages, sa clairvoyance éclipse ses maladresses et toutes les bondieuseries qui occupent les premiers chapitres. Il clame avec perspicacité que l'histoire des Autochtones doit être enseignée. Qu'on doit cesser de cacher la vérité pour pouvoir vivre d'égal à égal.

Cesser d'occulter l'Histoire. Affirmation tellement visionnaire que, 75 ans plus tard, cette question n'est toujours pas réglée.

« C'est un crime que de bourrer le crâne des enfants avec des erreurs et des mensonges. C'est une grave injustice que de forcer les maîtres à enseigner le mépris des Indiens à leurs élèves[10]. »

Enseigner l'Histoire, dépoussiérer les traces qui ont été volontairement cachées pour faire disparaître des nations, les assimiler, les transformer en « peuple invisible », comme le dirait Richard Desjardins, n'a jamais été plus d'actualité qu'aujourd'hui. Nombreux sont ceux parmi les membres des Premières Nations qui exigent que l'Histoire enseignée s'attarde davantage sur Donnacona, Kondiaronk, Riel, mais aussi sur les pensionnats, la *Loi sur les Indiens* et ses répercussions, la ségrégation, en passant par les héros contemporains qui ont changé la face de notre histoire. Des gens comme Andrew Paull, William Commanda et même Jules Sioui, pourquoi pas. Il ne faut plus que cette Histoire s'arrête au mode de vie de jadis, aux maisons longues, à la guerre contre les Iroquois, au commerce des fourrures... Cela perpétue l'idée que les Premières Nations n'existent plus. On nous répète inlassablement qu'enseigner l'Histoire, c'est choisir.

Je suis bien d'accord.

Est-ce qu'on peut seulement choisir ensemble?

Notes

1. La suite des événements de la deuxième convention est amplement relatée dans le manuscrit *Qui est ton maître?/Who is Your Master?* de Jules Sioui, ainsi que dans Hugh Shewell, «Jules Sioui and Indian Political Radicalism in Canada, 1943-1944», *Journal of Canadian Studies/Revue d'études canadiennes*, vol 34, n. 3, automne 1999, p. 229-31.

2. Que le ministre des Ressources soit également celui en charge des Autochtones en dit long sur les intentions du gouvernement de conquérir toujours plus de territoire, pour avoir plus de ressources. Il ne peut s'agir d'un hasard…

3. Hugh Shewell, op. cit., p. 230. [Traduction libre].

4. Ibid., p. 229.

5. Jules Sioui, *Qui est ton maître?/Who is Your Master?*, op. cit., 53. Hugh Shewell, op. cit., p. 232. [Traduction libre].

6. Ibid.

7. Jules Sioui, *Qui est ton maître?/Who is Your Master?*, op. cit., p. 22.

8. Ibid., p. 15.

9. Ibid., p. 23-25.

10. Ibid., p. 5.

SAMANTHA MARTIN-BIRD

"the indian (adultery) act" and "fanon"

the indian (adultery) act

boujee ndn
with a house in maui and miami
sadder than fuck

brags of thirty-million-dollar deal
with the feds

good fer u sad ndn
good fer dose cree kits
who'll finally git a school

boujee cree
straight from the bush
married a 6(1) indian
raised overseas

i shoulda married
a cree girl
he laments

his 6(1) iskwêw was more at
home in munich

than treaty eight

boujee ndn
with big brown eyes
lonely as hell

even now cautions
be sure to
marry a 6(1) indian

still reckons
our sovereignty
requires status

good fer u sad ndn
so sovren u sleep nex
to me

fanon

do you think of me when you read
        frantz fanon
                audra simpson
                        glen coulthard
                                basil johnston

does it remind you
of the
        one
                real
                        indian
in your life

does it make you consider
every paradox of
indians in modernity

do you wonder if i’m interested
in a settler like you

while critiquing colonialism
        while complicit in capitalism
smudging at daybreak
        brunching on avocado toast

do you think i’m a fascinating
object of study

the most contradictory of indians

send me every article
that makes you think of me

I won't read it
            send it anyways

ANDRÉE LEVESQUE SIOUI

de *Chant(s)*

ITUAL

Le vent, dit-elle, lui a-t-il dit, dit-on
Aurait retenu son chant par cœur en l'attrapant

Hier, tu as rêvé si fort
Que les esprits des animaux sont venus
C'est l'automne, ils sont prêts
La porte du songe s'est ouverte
Tu y es entré, tu as vu ton rêve devant toi
Atalukan
Ton corps de contes portait loin sa parole
Ton corps de poèmes libre à jamais

Puis les Tikéans ont soufflé
Aux oreilles des tihchiont* en dormance
Réveillant la Gardienne du ciel
Et ses tihchion'* en résonance

Tu sens alors l'odeur des fraises
Puis le goût du sucre en bouche
La salive de ce qui s'accomplit
La médecine

Léger, souriant, tu traverses l'allée
Bordée de tihchiont
Celle qui mène aux anciens jusqu'aux tihchion'
Tu es l'oralité qui fraie le passage
Des mots féconds à chaque pas
Un chant personnel te revient de la forêt
Un soupir humble comme ta vie
Ta parole est semée
On te lira à voix haute
Itual, haut perché
Des champs d'étoiles aux chants d'Itual
Des champs de fraises aux chants de phrases

Les vertèbres du poème à la verticale
La dernière adresse en nehlueun
À l'horizon de l'ouest, ton corps s'allonge
Accordé
Où les champs de fraises innumérables
Se mirent aux champs d'étoiles
Dans le plus beau reflet qui soit
Le cercle est complet
Nous pleurons aux rafales, bourrasques
Et sifflements
De t'entendre nous raconter à l'infini

Hommage à M. Édouard Itual Germain

*Tihchiont: fraise
*Tihchion': étoile

JE VEILLE MON ENFANT JE VEILLE

Je veille mon enfant je veille
Pendant que tu joues
Sous les décombres de la mort
Dans le carré de cendres
Entre les ruines des grands tabous
Des gestes ratés et des mots ravalés

Je veille mon enfant je veille
Pendant que tu te rebelles solitaire
Que tu manges ta folie
Que tu te noies dans l'amour flou
Pansant la blessure éternelle
Que les autres ont traînée avant toi

Je veille mon enfant je veille
Du matin au soir et la nuit encore je veille
Décelant la souplesse de ton esprit pétrifié
À l'affût des vagues qui te remontent le cœur
Je cherche le timbre posté derrière ta voix éraillée
Sous le voile du palais

Je veille mon enfant je veille
Pendant que tu songes au pire
À l'orée du bois brûlé
Pendant que tu pleures
Beau temps mauvais temps
Trahie par les oracles d'hier
Et les horoscopes du jour

Je veille mon enfant je veille
D'est en ouest
De l'abandon à l'humiliation
Au nord de tes frilosités
Au sud de ta timidité
Là où tu passes sans te faire voir

Je veille mon enfant je veille
Comme on a veillé sur moi
Dans l'ombre, à distance, en prière
Des yeux aux couleurs de celles qui voient
Des veilleuses infatigables et insoumises
Vouées à sauver des cœurs d'enfants

À tante Monique

MICHAEL HUTCHINSON

From *The Case of the Missing Auntie*

Heading in One Direction

"So were you freaked out when you had to figure out how to get home?" Sam shoved a spoonful of sugary cereal in his mouth and eagerly leaned toward Chickadee at the breakfast table. The Muskrats were alone in the house with their auntie at work and the little kids at day care.

Chickadee poured her cereal and waited for Atim to finish with the milk. She had a new attitude today. Yes, she got kind of lost and walked over an hour in the rain, but she had figured out how to get home, and she had pushed their case forward. Last night, she was still mad at the boys for not taking their missing auntie more seriously. She went to bed as soon as she got home without saying a word to any of them. This morning, she decided she was going to find Auntie Charlotte, whether the boys helped her or not.

"I followed the bus stops and walked home. No biggie." Chickadee shrugged.

"You looked pretty wet when you came in last night," Atim remarked. "Maybe even like you had been crying."

Chickadee rolled her eyes at her cousin. "I was mad at myself for getting off the bus in the wrong place. That was all."

"That was it?" Otter arched his eyebrow.

"Well, I actually fell off the bus." Chickadee giggled picturing herself in her panic. "But then, there was some guy who called me a 'stupid Indian' and told me to go back to the rez."

Little drops of milk shot-gunned across the table as Atim coughed out some of his cereal.

"You're kidding me!" He was angry.

Chickadee shrugged. "No. I tripped coming off the bus, so I was lying there in the mud. And then he shaded me as he got off." Chickadee quietly wondered if she'd be able to handle it the next time she was close to so many strangers. She knew she wouldn't even have to face that again if she stayed in Windy Lake.

"If I was there, I would have hit the guy." Atim shook his head angrily and then slammed his fist into his palm.

"Settle down, big guy. No reason to get upset about what some idiot racist says." Sam lightly slapped his brother on the shoulder.

Chickadee was thoughtful as she spoke. "It was different from when someone calls me an Indian at home. I didn't know the guy, not even a little, but he hated me just for who my family was. It was . . . sharper for some reason. Made me angry . . ."

"I think that's natural." Otter gave Chickadee a half-hug. "Sorry you had to go through that, Chickie."

"I'm mad just thinking about it!" Atim spoke through gritted teeth.

"Well, you shouldn't get more upset about it than Chickadee, it didn't happen to you." Sam shook his head at his brother.

Atim was about to retort when Otter spoke.

"Chickadee wasn't the only one who had a bad day yesterday."

Otter gave the biggest Muskrat a little nudge. Atim looked at the ceiling, then rubbed his eyes.

Sam told Chickadee about the mugging and their escape.

"Are you serious!?" Chickadee was the next one to cough and spit cereal across the table.

"If it hadn't been for the old, scraggly cab driver . . ." Sam shook his head.

"Cabbie John saved us!" Otter declared.

"Can't judge a book by its cover, that's for sure." Atim pursed his lips.

"So . . . is there any money left?" Chickadee asked the group.

Atim pulled out his pockets. Samuel shook his head. Otter shrugged.

"Brett and his buddies took it all," Atim admitted sadly as he swiped the hair away from his eyes.

Chickadee's heart fell when she heard it. "Brett?"

"Yeah, Brett." Samuel nodded slowly.

"But . . ." Chickadee was speechless. She couldn't figure how this was possible.

"He scammed us!" Atim threw up his hands. "His buddy punched Otter." He threw a hand out in his cousin's direction. "And Brett took them there."

"The big bully from the pool game said that was a scam too. I thought Brett hooking himself seemed kind of strange. I guess, for me, that's when the doubts started," Samuel recollected.

Chickadee's mind went over the past few days and all the little things that told her Brett had changed. He wasn't the Brett she liked in Windy Lake. She decided to put it behind her. Like the walk in the rain yesterday, she wasn't going to let it bother her today.

"So, what are we going to do then?" Chickadee raised an eyebrow at her cousins. The boys squinted hard but couldn't seem to squeeze out any new ideas.

"Okay," she said. "I propose we focus on Auntie Charlotte. I spent yesterday looking for Grandpa's sister. I've hit a dead-end, but I've got a lead on another place where we may be able to find info."

"It would be pretty cool to find Grandpa's sister after all this time. Why the dead-end?" Samuel was pinching his lower lip.

"We need her exact date of birth or else we can't go any farther." Chickadee slurped the last of the milk out of her cereal bowl. "I'm pretty sure the lady at the adoption registry knew more than she was saying, but she's using the date of birth as the key for unlocking the information."

"Is that what they call red tape?" Sam's brow furrowed.

"I don't know, but her assistant was helpful. She told me to go to the National Centre for Truth and Reconciliation, the N-C-T-R, she called it. That's where they keep a lot of the information on residential schools." Chickadee looked around at her cousins, who nodded.

"I want to go down there and find out as much as we can. If we can find out more, it might unlock the archives info, and we may actually get somewhere." She stood and gathered all their dirty dishes and put them on the counter near the dishwasher.

After using the computer to find the NCTR's address, the Mighty Muskrats headed out. The bus dropped them off in the middle of a large university campus.

"Who knew the NCTR was in the same location where Harold is going to school?" Atim looked around at the maze of different buildings.

"We're the new ones figuring things out." Sam chuckled at his brother. "Probably everybody else knew it was here."

"Could be." Atim nodded sagely.

Samuel looked at the map they had printed off at Auntie Sadie's. "I think, if we head . . . that way," he pointed down a path that led behind a cluster of buildings, "we'll find the place we're looking for."

The Muskrats walked between the buildings. When they got past them, they saw a large brick house tucked quietly away at the back of the university. It had once been a home, but it had long been converted to offices. The building had obviously been on the university grounds for many, many years. Its three stories looked tiny beside the huge buildings full of classrooms, libraries, and labs. The comfortable bundle of bricks now stored all the research brought together by the Truth and Reconciliation Commission of Canada as it delved into the history of residential schools.

DAWN DUMONT

From *Glass Beads*

The City of Lights

Nellie had a rip-roaring dream. She was in Paris with her mom and they were poor and ragged like those peasants in that movie that was based on a musical that was based on a book. They were searching for food because they were hungry and then at some point Nellie realized that she was pregnant. Pregnant in Paris with no money. That was a shitty scary dream.

"I thought you wanted to have a family," she mused, staring up at the ceiling at 3:30 a.m. "Apparently not." But she did, she just wanted it on her terms, with a husband who would be a good father. She didn't want to be like those single moms she saw waiting at the bus stop in the middle of winter, struggling with their strollers, their heads wet with snow because they didn't have coats with hoods.

Nellie tried to go back to sleep. Failed. And so was out of the house by 5:00 a.m. standing in line grabbing a coffee. She almost smiled at a tall, nice-faced, silver fox but she couldn't see his hand to check if he had a wedding ring so she decided not to bother. It was strange though, before she hit her thirties, men with grey hair were invisible and now almost magically, they had appeared—to ignore her like every other type of man.

In the car she pressed her blinking message alert on her cell and listened to the first onslaught as she wove through traffic, always driving faster than everyone else, even though logically it didn't matter. They always ended up at the same red light where the driver would shoot angry looks at her while Nellie stoically stared straight ahead.

The messages were short. Lots of requests for call-backs. Two of the calls were from chiefs and so her blood pressure immediately jumped.

Then three low-priority calls, a councillor, an Elder and a provincial politician's assistant. The last call was from her mother reminding her of supper the next day and then finally her assistant calling in sick.

"Fuck."

Nellie closed the door to her office and fell into her chair.

She looked up again after noon. There were no meetings scheduled and Taz was out of town so she had the luxury of concentrating on a brief she was writing about the lack of policing services in northern communities. It would have been a perfect day except that her stomach was raging at her.

She hit her phone.

"Hey you eat already?"

"Nah." Julie's voice had sleep in it.

Must be nice, thought Nellie.

They met at a health food place that neither of them was crazy about. Julie never saw the point of eating healthy and Nellie only paid it lip service.

Nellie picked the sprouts out of her sandwich as she described to Julie a play she'd seen on the weekend. Julie nodded at the right spots.

"How was the date other than that?" Julie asked.

"He's really nice."

"And?"

"I don't know."

"Can you imagine sucking his dick?"

Nellie choked on her coffee and looked around before answering. "Jesus Christ no."

"There's your answer," Julie said.

"I need to date different kinds of guys. I can't only pick guys who are hot. That hasn't gotten me anywhere."

"Yeah, you need someone smart."

"Everett is smart, just not in a book way. Maybe now he is, I heard he's getting his GED or something. I dunno. Probably has a young girlfriend he's trying to impress."

Julie shrugged.

"She's probably naturally skinny and one of those free spirits who goes where the wind blows and her name is Aurora, or Skylar, or Shenoah."

"Shenoah?"

"And now all he does is talk about spirituality and getting to know the wisdom of the Elders and blah blah blah. He's even doing a Sundance ceremony this summer."

"That's cool."

Nellie sighed. "Guess it's better than him drinking himself to death. I want another coffee, you want a coffee?"

Julie shook her head. Julie did not ram herself full of things every chance she had. *Try to be content*, Nellie told herself. *Try to be grateful for that meal that you ate and did not taste.*

Nellie held Julie at the table for an extra half hour after they finished. "I don't want to go back to work," she moaned over and over again.

Julie told her about a class she was thinking of taking in early childhood development. Nellie didn't have the heart to tell her that the pay was ridiculously low and the hours were early and long. Because Julie wanted to be around kids and didn't give a shit about things like that.

Nellie studied Julie. There were dark circles around her eyes and she looked bonier than usual.

"You feeling okay?"

Julie nodded.

"Any more doctors?"

"We're taking a break. With work and the re-election coming up Taz doesn't have time."

Nellie had sent him to Ottawa the day before to argue for more funding from INAC: "Don't come back without at least another ten percent." She knew how busy Taz was. Still she wished he had made the time. Then again she knew how sensitive men could be about their dicks.

Julie blew on her coffee. "It bothers him though: I know it does."

"There's always adoption."

"It's not the same though, is it?"

"All kids are weird to me. Short, always asking stupid questions—and those enormous freaky-doll heads. We got it made if you ask me."

Julie smiled and stayed for an extra coffee that she did not drink.

Nellie worked until nine and then dropped files on her assistant's chair. A nice passive-aggressive welcome-back message for the morning. She made an internal note to start looking for another assistant.

It was dark outside and she kept her keys in her fist as she walked outside. She was always ready for an attack. She saw a man standing too close to her car and pulled out her cell. But he got into the car next to hers. Nellie relaxed and thought about the last time someone had been in the parking lot waiting for her.

She had recognized the lanky body before she even got close. His head was tilted to the side in that way she hated so much.

Hold your head up straight for God's sake. You're a man, not a nervous teenage girl.

"Nellie." His voice was a chinook that had finally made its way to the prairies.

She'd always daydreamed about that moment when he would come back to her. She played out her reaction in different ways. Some days she threw her keys and hit him in the face, the sharp edge of the keys scratching that perfect skin. Other times she ran to him and he picked her up and they did that movie-style romantic spin. Other days they had sex on the hood of her car (although that entire parking area was covered with surveillance cameras so realistically that was never going to happen).

That day, however, she walked over to the car. They talked. They went for dinner. The next morning she lent him some money. That was months ago and she hadn't heard from him since.

Stop thinking about him. He doesn't deserve space in my brain. He can live without me. That was the refrain tattooed on her heart whenever she thought of calling him afterwards. She would hold the phone and have his number up and before pressing send she would stare at the inside of her wrist. She had pretty delicate wrists. They were her best feature by a long shot. In the twenty years that she'd known him he had never mentioned them.

Nellie had no idea what he loved about her, if he had ever loved her. Maybe he liked that she had always been there for him like the sun in the morning and the moon in the evening. And now that she wasn't, his love was withdrawn.

One part of her liked to put things under harsh lights to counter the romantic in her. She ruined things with her expectations. She needed to see them for what they were. This she had learned. After the hundreds of times Everett had taken her heart and snapped it like a hollow piece of firewood across his leg.

Besides she was dating now. Twice in one month a man had spoken to her and then somehow it transformed into a coffee date, a dinner date, and these dates were still sort of going. She had options other than the long-haired nomad. *And a modern-day nomad is a just a drifter*, she reminded herself.

And she had a trip to Italy coming up. It was one of those on the bus, off the bus things. She had already bought a hat.

Stuff was happening.

Then she had the Paris dream again. Once again she was in the City of Lights with her mom but this time her belly was big. They had to run to catch some bus that would take them out of Paris, back home, and Nellie couldn't make herself run. "Go, Mom," she kept saying. Because if her mom left then she could come back with help. But, of course, her mom would not leave her no matter how much Nellie yelled at her to go. Nellie woke up hungry.

She was eating a high-protein diet that a trainer recommended years before but she'd never followed. Then she read that being fit was eighty percent diet and twenty percent working out so she cancelled her gym membership and bought some protein powder.

She had a shake. It wasn't even close to satisfying. At her coffee place, she ordered a bagel to go with her coffee. She forgot to flirt with anyone.

Her assistant kept her eyes on her computer when Nellie walked in. When Nellie said good morning, her assistant replied in a cold voice. But her fingers were moving rapidly which was all Nellie cared about anyway.

There were three meetings that morning. Coffee. Danish (lemon). Coffee with cream. Date square (in the morning?). Coffee with cream and sugar (not fake sugar either). A shortbread cookie (it was dry).

She went to lunch with co-workers and had a salad. On the way back to the office, she picked up a bag of chips, the family size. Then ate and worked her way through the afternoon. Happy as a pig in shit.

Her mom called again about supper. Nellie picked the place. They served big portions.

At supper, her mom asked about her dates. Nellie made the men sound much hotter than they were, although she stumbled over their names. How had she forgotten about them already?

"I've been having weird dreams lately," Nellie told her mom. "You're in them."

"Mothers represent youth. Or nurturing." Her mother was always reading books about the occult and astrology and other things that Nellie scoffed at.

"Whatever it is, we're not doing well. We're in Paris."

"I've always wanted to go there."

"We'll go next year."

"Next year your sister is getting married."

"She'll find a way to screw it up."

Her mother sipped her coffee in silent agreement.

"I'll book the trip. Maybe Julie will be able to come. I'm a bit worried about her."

"Still nothing?"

"Nope. They probably can't. I don't know why they don't admit it to themselves and move on to other options. Adopt. Get a surrogate. God knows Taz can afford it."

"It takes time, Nellie."

"Well, whatever. They're wasting it. Do you want dessert?"

Her mother didn't but Nellie could talk her into anything.

That night they were in Paris again. Her mother was trying to dig something out of the ground. A weed that she figured they could eat. It would be bitter, Nellie knew, but she was so hungry she didn't care. Plus the baby was hungry. Nellie could feel the baby's hunger pains. *It's too much*, she told herself. *Babies are too hard.*

She woke up and sunlight filled the room which meant she'd slept in. She reached for her phone and made an appointment to see her doctor. She thought about her condo. She might have to buy a townhouse. Maybe something with a yard. Kids needed that right? She felt weak and shaky, like she'd drank too much the night before.

Her doctor snuck her in that day because she was a good patient. She was a few years younger than Nellie and her eyes drifted to Nellie's wedding hand as she asked questions. Her doctor wore a thick gold band with a sparkling diamond. *Lucky bitch*, Nellie thought for the hundred thousandth time.

In the parking lot outside the clinic, Nellie sat in her car. She always hated people who sat in their cars. It made them look suspicious. Or they looked like their lives were so utterly out of control that their car was the only place they could hide. She sat in her car for a long time figuring out where to go.

That night she did not dream.

ABOUT THE CONTRIBUTORS

Nathan Niigan Noodin Adler (Recipient, Published Prose in English 2021) is Two Spirit, Jewish, Anishinaabe, and member of Lac des Mille Lacs First Nation. He is author of *Ghost Lake* and *Wrist*, both published with Kegedonce Press, and co-editor of *Bawaajigan: Stories of Power* (Exile Editions).

Carleigh Baker is a nêhiyaw âpihtawikosisân / Icelandic writer whose work has appeared in *Best Canadian Essays*, *The Short Story Advent Calendar*, and *The Journey Prize Stories. Bad Endings* (Anvil Press) is her debut story collection.

Billy-Ray Belcourt (Recipient, Published Poetry in English 2018) is from the Driftpile Cree Nation. His award-winning publications include *This Wound is a World* (Frontenac House), *NDN Coping Mechanisms: Notes from the Field* (Anansi), *A History of My Brief Body* (Penguin), and *A Minor Chorus* (Hamish Hamilton).

Selina Boan (Recipient, Published Poetry in English 2022) is a white settler-nehiyaw (Cree) writer. Her debut poetry collection, *Undoing Hours* (Nightwood Editions), also won the 2022 Pat Lowther Memorial Award. Her work has been published widely, including *The Best Canadian Poetry 2018* and *2020*. She is a poetry editor for *Contemporary Verse 2*.

Lisa Boivin is a member of the Deninu Kųę́ First Nation, an interdisciplinary artist, and a doctoral candidate at the Rehabilitation Sciences Institute. She authored *I Will See You Again* and *We Dream Medicine Dreams* (Portage & Main Press / HighWater Press). Lisa created the artwork for the cover of *Carving Space.*

Leslie Butt (Recipient, Unpublished Prose in English 2022) is Innu and author of three self-published works: a poetry collection, *Bring on the Dark*, and two works of fiction, *Fifteen* and *Tanked.*

Cody Caetano (Recipient, Unpublished Prose in English 2020) is a writer of Anishinaabe (Pinaymootang First Nation) and Portuguese (Ponta Delgada) descent, and author of *Half-Bads in White Regalia* (Hamish Hamilton Canada). His writing has appeared in *The Walrus*, *The Globe and Mail*, and elsewhere.

Tenille K. Campbell is a Dene/Métis author from English River First Nation in Northern Saskatchewan. Her published books of poetry include *#IndianLovePoems* (Signature Editions) and *nedí nezų (Good Medicine)* (Arsenal Pulp Press).

Treena Chambers is Métis. She was born in what is currently called Rossland, in British Columbia, on the traditional territories of the Sinixt peoples. Her short story "Forest Fires and Falling Stars" has been published in *Fold Magazine.* Her essay "Unsettled Learning in Colonial Spaces" is included in *Unsettling Educational Modernism.*

Maya Cousineau Mollen (lauréate, poésie publiée en français 2020): Innue originaire d'Ekuanitshit (Mingan), et petite-fille du célèbre Jack Monoloy, Maya Cousineau Mollen écrit de la poésie depuis l'âge de quatorze ans. Son premier recueil, *Bréviaire du matricule 082*, paraît en 2019 (Éditions Hannenorak), suivi par *Enfants du lichen* en 2022 (Éditions Hannenorak).

Francine Cunningham (Recipient, Unpublished Prose in English 2019) is Cree and Métis, and the author of *On/Me* (Caitlin Press) and *God Isn't Here Today* (Invisible Publishing). Her writing has appeared in *The Malahat Review*, *Grain Magazine*, *The Puritan*, and more.

Dawn Dumont is from the Okanese Cree Nation. Her award-winning novels and short story collections, published by Thistledown Press, include *Nobody Cries at Bingo*, *Rose's Run*, *Glass Beads*, and *The Prairie Chicken Dance Tour.*

Bevann Fox (Recipient, Published Creative Nonfiction and Life Writing 2021) is a member of Pasqua First Nation, originally from Piapot First Nation. She is the author of *Genocidal Love: A Life after Residential School* (University of Regina Press).

Édouard Itual Germain (lauréat, œuvre publiée en français 2022) était l'aîné de onze enfants au sein d'une famille ilnue (Première nation des Pekuakamiulnuatsh). Son recueil posthume, *Ni kistisin / Je me souviens* (Éditions Hannenorak), est la seule œuvre publiée d'Édouard Itual Germain.

Marie-Andrée Gill (lauréate, poésie non publiée en français 2018 et poésie publiée en français 2020) (Ilnue) a publié trois recueils de poésie, *Béante*, *Frayer*, et *Chauffer le dehors* chez La peuplade.

Dallas Hunt is Cree and a member of Wapsewsipi (Swan River First Nation) in Treaty 8 territory. He's the author of a book of poetry, *Creeland* (Nightwood Editions), and a children's book, *Awâsis and the World-Famous Bannock* (High Water Press).

Michael Hutchinson is a member of the Misipawistik Cree Nation in the Treaty 5 territory. He's the author of a series for young readers, *Mighty Muskrats Mystery* (Second Story Press).

Brian Thomas Isaac (Recipient, Published Prose in English 2022) is a member of the Syilx Nation and was born on the Okanagan Indian Reserve. *All the Quiet Places* (Touchwood Editions) is his bestselling debut novel.

Aviaq Johnston (Recipient, Published Prose in English 2018) is an Inuk writer from Igloolik, Nunavut. She authored *Those Who Run in the Sky* and *Those Who Dwell Below*, as well as the picture books *What's My Superpower?* and *Grandfather Bowhead, Tell Me a Story*, all published with Inhabit Media.

Katłįà (Catherine Lafferty) is a member of the Yellowknives Dene First Nation. She is the author of *Northern Wildflower*, *Land-Water-Sky / Ndè-Tı-Yat'a*, and *This House is Not a Home*, all published with Fernwood.

Helen Knott is of Dane Zaa, Nehiyaw, Métis, and Euro descent from Prophet River First Nation. Her first book, *In My Own Moccasins: A Memoir of Resilience* (University of Regina Press), is a national best-seller.

J.D. Kurtness (lauréate, prose publiée en français 2018): née à Chicoutimi d'une mère québécoise et d'un père ilnu de Mashteuiatsh, J. D. Kurtness a publié chez L'instant même deux romans salués par la critique, *De vengeance* (2017) et *Aquariums* (2019).

Mika Lafond (Co-Recipient, Work in an Alternative Format 2018) is from the Muskeg Lake Cree Nation and author of the bilingual collection of poetry in nêhiyawêwin and English, *nipê wânîn* (Thistledown Press). Her play, *otâcimow*, was performed by the Saskatoon Indigenous Ensemble.

Elaine McArthur (Recipient, Unpublished Prose in English 2018 and Unpublished Poetry 2019) hails from the Ocean Man First Nation. She is currently self-publishing a children's book series.

Samantha Martin-Bird (Recipient, Unpublished Poetry in English 2021) is a member of Peguis First Nation. Her poetry has appeared in *ROOM* and *Contemporary Verse 2*.

Francine Merasty (Recipient, Work in an Indigenous Language 2019) is a member of the Peter Ballantyne Cree Nation and a fluent Cree speaker. She is the author of *Iskotew Iskwew: Poetry of a Northern Rez Girl* (Book Land Press).

Rene Andre Meshake (Co-Recipient, Published Work in an Indigenous Language 2020) is an Ojibwe Elder and visual and performing artist. He is the author (with Kim Anderson) of *Injichaag: My Soul in Story* (University of Manitoba Press).

Shayne Michael (lauréat, poésie publiée en français 2021): Originaire de la Première nation Malécite du Madawaska, au nord-ouest du Nouveau-Brunswick, Shayne Michael n'est pas à moitié Malécite ni à moitié Acadien. Il n'est la moitié de rien. *Fif et Sauvage* (Éditions Perce-Neige) est son premier recueil de poésie.

Émilie Monnet (lauréate, prose publiée en français, 2021), d'origine anishinaabe et française, est directrice artistique de la compagnie Onishka. Au croisement du théâtre, de la performance et des arts médiatiques, sa pratique explore l'identité, la mémoire, l'histoire et la transformation. *Okinum* (Les Herbes rouges, 2020) est son premier livre.

Jas M. Morgan is Cree-Métis-Saulteaux (Tootinaowaziibeeng) and the author of *nîtisânak* (Metonymy Press). They hold a Canada Research Chair in Digital Wahkohtowin & Cultural Governance and are an Assistant Professor at Toronto Metropolitan University.

Tyler Pennock is a two-spirit adoptee from a Cree and Métis family around the Lesser Slave Lake region of Alberta. Tyler is a member of Sturgeon Lake Cree Nation. *Bones* (Brick Books) is their first book.

Félix Perkins vient de Saint-Hilaire dans le Haut-Madawaska. Avec maladresse et amour de la nature, il se perd et se promène à travers ses héritages wendats, italiens, espagnols et québécois. Publié en 2020, *Boiteur des bois* (Éditions Perce-Neige) est son premier recueil de poésie.

Amanda Peters (Recipient, Unpublished Prose in English 2021) is a Mi'kmaq/Settler writer. Her work has been published in the *Antigonish Review* and *Grain Magazine. The Berry Pickers* (HarperCollins) is Amanda's first novel. She is a graduate of the MFA program at the Institute of American Indian Arts.

Michelle Porter is a member of the Manitoba Métis Federation. She is the author of *Approaching Fire* and *Inquiries*, both published with Breakwater Books, as well as *Scratching River* (Wilfrid Laurier University Press). Her novel *A Grandmother Begins the Story* is forthcoming in 2023 (with Penguin).

Kaitlyn Purcell is Denesuline-Irish and an urban member of Smith's Landing First Nation. Through her PhD she is creating her multimodal memoirs on dreamwork, personal archives, and intergenerational grief. Her writing can be found in *Artspeak, Contemporary Verse 2*, and *YYZ Artists Outlet. ʔbédayine* (Metatron Press) is her debut poetic novella.

Pierrot Ross-Tremblay (lauréat, poésie publiée en français 2019): Poète, intellectuel engagé et professeur à l'Université d'Ottawa, Pierrot Ross-Tremblay est un Innu de la communauté d'Essipit. Son premier recueil de poésie, *Nipimanitu / L'esprit de l'eau*, est paru aux Éditions Prise de parole.

Troy Sebastian\nupqu? ak·ɬam̓ is a Ktunaxa writer from the community of ?aq̓am. His writing has appeared in *The Malahat Review*, *The Walrus*, the *Toronto Star*, and *Ktuqckakyam.* He is a doctoral student in writing at the University of Victoria.

Keely Keysoos Shirt (Recipient, Unpublished Poetry in English 2019) is a creative and academic from Saddle Lake Cree Nation.

jaye simpson (Recipient, Published Poetry in English 2021) is an Indigiqueer Oji-Cree trans woman from Sapotaweyak Cree Nation. They authored the poetry and prose collection *it was never going to be okay* (Nightwood Editions).

Andrée Levesque Sioui est chanteuse et poète. Membre de la Nation Huronne-Wendat, elle y enseigne la langue wendat depuis 2010. Elle publie dans plusieurs collectifs dont *Nous sommes poésie* (2022, XYZ). *Chant(s)* est son premier recueil de poésie aux Éditions Hannenorak (2021).

Daniel Sioui a fondé en 2009 la Librairie Hannenorak, la seule librairie autochtone au Québec. En 2010, ce sont les Éditions Hannenorak qui furent créées. La même année, il met sur pied Kwahiatonhk! – Salon du livre des Premières Nations. Paru en 2021, *Indien stoïque* (Éditions Hannenorak) est son premier livre.

Jocelyn Sioui, l'un des très rares marionnettistes autochtones au Québec, est membre fondateur de Belzébrute, band de théâtre, et auteur-concepteur-interprète de *Shavirez, le tsigane des mers, Manga,* et de *Mr P. Mononk Jules* (Éditions Hannenorak) marque les premiers pas de l'artiste wendat dans le monde de la littérature.

Smokii Sumac (Recipient, Unpublished Poetry in English 2018 and Published Poetry in English 2019) is a member of the Ktunaxa Nation, and author of the poetry collection, *you are enough: love poems for the end of the world* (Kegedonce Press).

Tanya Tagaq (Recipient, Published Prose in English 2019) is an Inuk artist, improvisational singer, avant-garde composer, and best-selling author from Ikaluktutiak. *Split Tooth* (Viking Canada / Penguin Random House Canada) is her debut novel.

Diana Hope Tegenkamp is a queer Métis writer living on Treaty 6 territory, whose writing has appeared in *Contemporary Verse 2, Prairie Fire, Grain, Matrix, Queen Street Quarterly, Moosehead Anthology, Slingshot* and *Tessera. Girl running* (Thistledown Press) is Diana's first book of poetry.

Jesse Thistle (Recipient, Published Prose in English 2020) is Métis-Cree and author of the memoir *From the Ashes* (Simon & Schuster), and a collection of poems and stories, *Scars and Stars* (McClelland & Stewart).

Nazbah Tom (Diné) is a somatic practitioner and poet. They have been published in several anthologies including the Lambda Literary Award winner *Love after the End: An Anthology of Two-Spirit and Indigiqueer Speculative Fiction* (Arsenal Pulp Press).

Arielle Twist (Co-Recipient, Published Poetry in English 2020) is a Nehiyaw, Two-Spirit multidisciplinary artist originally from George Gordon First Nation. *Disintegrate/Dissociate* (Arsenal Pulp Press) is her debut collection of poetry.

Joshua Whitehead is a Two-Spirit, Oji-nêhiyaw member of Peguis First Nation (Treaty 1). He is the author of the book of poetry *Full-Metal Indigiqueer* (Talonbooks), the novel *Jonny Appleseed* (Arsenal Pulp Press), and the non-fiction work *Making Love with the Land* (Knopf).

Blair Palmer Yoxall is a citizen of the Métis Nation of Alberta. He is a published poet and emerging novelist.

CREDITS

Nathan Niigan Noodin Adler, "Coyote." From *Ghost Lake.* Kegedonce Press, 2020. Pages 81-93. Reprinted by permission of the publisher.

Carleigh Baker, "Moosehide." From *Bad Endings.* Anvil Press, 2017. Pages 157-162. Reprinted by permission of the publisher.

Billy-Ray Belcourt, "Notes from a Public Washroom," "Colonialism: A Love Story," and "The Oxford Journal." From *This Wound is a World.* Frontenac House, 2017. Pages 12, 27, 43-51. Reprinted by permission of the publisher.

Selina Boan, "the plot so far," "how to find your father," "in cree there is no word for half/brother," and "have you ever fallen in love with a day?" From *Undoing Hours.* Nightwood Editions, 2021. Pages 11, 26-27, 36-37, 74. Reprinted by permission of the publisher.

Cody Caetano, "Applied", "Announcement", and "Meu Velho Homem." From *Half-Bads in White Regalia.* Hamish Hamilton, 2022. Pages 210-215. Reprinted by permission of the publisher.

Tenille K. Campbell, #114, #64, #209. From *#IndianLovePoems.* Signature Editions, 2017. Pages 12, 13, 16. Reprinted by permission of the publisher.

Tenille K. Campbell, "the first time we fuck," "I wonder," and "sex sex sex." From *nedí nezų (Good Medicine).* Arsenal Pulp Press, 2021. Pages 76-77,78-79, 112-113. Reprinted by permission of the publisher.

Maya Cousineau Mollen, « Sept fois » and « Ishkuess du nord. » From *Bréviaire du matricule 082.* Éditions Hannenorak, 2019. Pages 13, 72. Reprinted with permission of the publisher.

Francine Cunningham, "On How to Keep on Living / *Passing,*" "On Identity / *Origin of a Designation,*" "On Mental Illness / *Lists,*" "On

Family / *Mother,*" "On Teasing / *Aunties,*" "On Identity / *Descriptions of Self from Outside of Self,*" and "On TV / *Pocahontas.*" From *On/Me.* Caitlin Press, 2020. Pages 11-12, 16, 20. Reprinted by permission of the publisher.

Dawn Dumont, "The City of Lights." From *Glass Beads.* Thistledown Press, 2017. Pages 207-215. Reprinted by permission of the publisher.

Bevann Fox, excerpt from *Genocidal Love: A Life after Residential School.* University of Regina Press, 2020. Pages 17-22. Reprinted by permission of the publisher.

Édouard Itual Germain. « Ni kistisin / Je me souviens, » / « Ni8ina8in / Mon present, » and « Ichk8te8 / Feu. » From *Ni kistisin / Je me souviens.* Éditions Hannenorak, 2021. Pages 19, 22, 73. Reprinted by permission of the publisher.

Marie-Andrée Gill, untitled excerpts from *Chauffer le dehors.* La Peuplade, 2019. Pages 12, 13, 58, 79. Reprinted by permission of the publisher.

Dallas Hunt, "Cree Dictionary" and "Nathan Apodaca." From *Creeland.* Nightwood Editions, 2021. Pages 10-11, 62-63. Reprinted by permission of the publisher.

Michael Hutchinson, Chapter 14: "Heading in One Direction." From *The Case of the Missing Auntie.* Second Story Press, 2020. Pages 84-89. Reprinted by permission of the publisher.

Brian Thomas Isaac, Chapter 10. From *All the Quiet Places.* TouchWood Editions, 2021. Pages 97-103. Reprinted with permission of the publisher.

Aviaq Johnston, "Giant." From *Those Who Run in the Sky.* Inhabit Media, 2017. Pages 101-108. Reprinted by permission of the publisher.

Katłı̨à (Catherine Lafferty), excerpt from *Land-Water-Sky/Ndè-Tı-Yat'a.* Fernwood Publishing, 2020. Pages 71-80. Reprinted by permission of the publisher.

Helen Knott, excerpt from *In My Own Moccasins.* University of Regina Press, 2019. Pages 243-251. Reprinted by permission of the publisher.

J.D. Kurtness, excerpt from *De vengeance.* L'instant même, 2017. Pages 44-46. Reprinted by permission of the publisher.

Mika Lafond, "*têpiya pîkiskwêwina*" and "just words." From *nipê wânîn: my way back.* Thistledown Press, 2017. Pages 68-69. Reprinted by permission of the publisher.

Rene Andre Meshake, "Quest for Words" and "Grandmother Pipe." From *Injichaag: My Soul in Story.* University of Manitoba Press, 2019. Pages 235-236, 240-241. Reprinted by permission of the publisher.

Shayne Michael, « Quotidien. » From *Fif et sauvage.* Éditions Perce-Neige, 2020. Pages 28-33. Reprinted by permission of the publisher.

Émilie Monnet, excerpt from *Okinum.* Éditions Les Herbes rouges, 2020. Pages 27-29. Reprinted by permission of the publisher.

Jas M. Morgan, "The story of nikâwiy and nindede...". From *nîtisânak.* Metonymy Press, 2018. Pages 12-18. Reprinted by permission of the publisher.

Tyler Pennock, excerpts from *Bones.* Brick Books, 2020. Pages p. 66, 76, 104-105. Reprinted by permission of the publisher.

Félix Perkins, untitled excerpts from *Boiteur des bois.* Éditions Perce-Neige, 2020. Pages 24, 49, 50, 53, 62, 68. Reprinted by permission of the publisher.

Amanda Peters, excerpt from *Waiting for the Long Night Moon.* Reprinted with permission from HarperCollins Publishers Ltd. and Amanda Peters.

Michelle Porter, excerpt from *Approaching Fire.* Breakwater Books, 2020. Pages 24-28. Reprinted by permission of the publisher.

Kaitlyn Purcell, "Farewell." From *ʔbédayine.* Metatron Press, 2019. Pages 10-17. Reprinted by permission of the publisher.

Pierrot Ross-Tremblay, « Les confluences I » and « Printemps du don. » From *Nipimanitu / L'esprit de l'eau.* Éditions Prise de parole, 2018. Pages 10-13. Reprinted by permission of the publisher.

jaye simpson, "00088614," "urban NDNs in the DTES," "decolonial pu$$y," and "about the ones i want to love." From *it was never going to be okay.* Nightwood Editions, 2020. Pages 26-27, 44-45, 68-69, 101-105. Reprinted by permission of the publisher.

Andrée Levesque Sioui. « Itual » and « Je veille mon enfant je veille. » From *Chant(s).* Éditions Hannenorak, 2021. Pages 28-29, 30-31. Reprinted by permission of the publisher.

Daniel Sioui, « Il faut régler le passé. » From *Indien Stoïque.* Éditions Hannenorak, 2021. Pages 17-24. Reprinted by permission of the publisher.

Jocelyn Sioui, excerpt from *Mononk Jules.* Éditions Hannenorak, 2020. Pages 140-153. Reprinted by permission of the publisher.

Smokii Sumac, "'do you want to take the Cadillac for a ride?'" and "ka paɫkiniṅ tik, or there are things our women have taught me." From *you are enough: love poems for the end of the world.* Kegedonce Press, 2018. Pages 36-38, 51. Reprinted by permission of the publisher.

Tanya Tagaq, excerpt from *Split Tooth.* Viking / Penguin Random House Canada, 2018. Pages 60-62, 91-93. Reprinted by permission of the publisher.

Diana Hope Tegenkamp, "If the measure of love is loss, why not live in it, this light?" and "Motherfield." From *Girl running.* Thistledown Press, 2021. Pages 107, 110-111. Reprinted by permission of the publisher.

Jesse Thistle, excerpt from *From the Ashes.* Simon & Schuster, 2019. Pages 121-124. Reprinted by permission of the publisher.

Arielle Twist, "Reckless," "The Girls," and "Silent." From *Disintegrate/ Dissociate.* Arsenal Pulp Press, 2019. Pages 21-22, 28-30, 56. Reprinted by permission of the publisher.

Joshua Whitehead. XXIV and XXV. From *Jonny Appleseed.* Arsenal Pulp Press, 2018. Pages 94-103. Reprinted by permission of the publisher.

Joshua Whitehead, "DO U WANT TO KNOW WHAT MAKES THE RED MEN RED [QUESTIONMARK]." From *Full-Metal Indigiqueer.* Talonbooks, 2017. Pages 86-88. Reprinted by permission of the publisher.